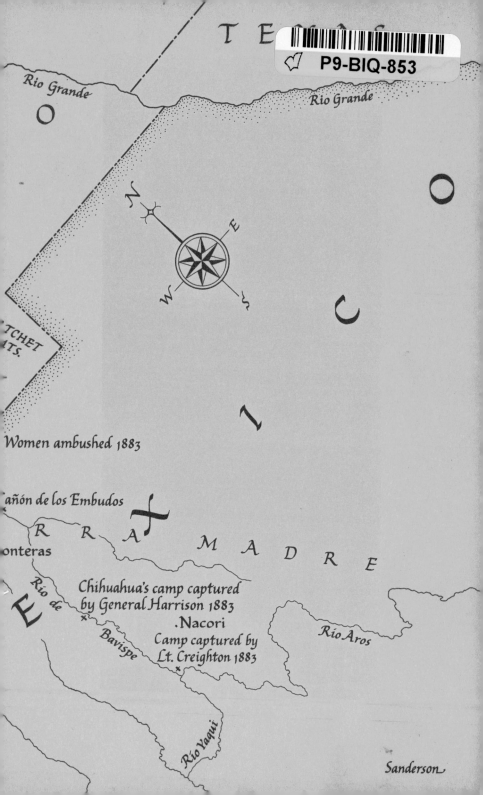

ulzana

James R. Olson

In *Ulzana* the author creates an American Indian hero. We follow Ulzana through all the stages of his life from infancy to boyhood, through his training as a warrior, his ritual life as son, husband and father, and through forty years of war against both the Mexicans and the "White Eyes." The Apaches were brave and ferocious. They were known as the cruelest of torturers, but their torture was a way of retaliating against exploitation by greedy Indian agents and frontier drifters.

In telling Ulzana's story James Olson has also told the story of the Chiricahua Apaches, their eventual surrender to the U.S. Army and their betrayal by the government. General Crook, who commanded much of the long fight against them, eventually winning their trust, devoted the entire remainder of his life to an unsuccessful attempt to redress the wrong done them. But Ulzana died a captive in an unfamiliar place.

Americans today yearn for the vanished beauty of their land and its primeval mystery. One way of discovering it anew is in the lost culture of the American Indian, so close to the Great Spirit

continued on back flap

0973

ulzana

ulzana

JAMES R. OLSON

HOUGHTON MIFFLIN COMPANY BOSTON

1973

FIRST PRINTING   V

PRINTED IN THE UNITED STATES OF AMERICA

Library of Congress Cataloging in Publication Data

Olson, James Robert, 1938–
  Ulzana.

  1. Apache Indians—Fiction.   I. Title.
PZ4.O519Ul   [PS3565.L83]   813'.5'4   73-7916
  ISBN 0-395-17123-7

I respectfully dedicate this novel
to the one person who made it possible,

MY MOTHER.

Foreword

THIS NARRATIVE is historical fiction, which means that an era has been re-created by erecting a fictitious framework around historical episodes. The characters are projected on a screen of events which occurred essentially as they are here related. Since this is primarily a story of the Chiricahua Apaches, all of the Americans mentioned in the narrative, with the exception of General Philip Sheridan, have been given fictitious names and personalities. In order to re-create the impression of a past time, it has been necessary to take some liberties in regard to the chronological order. The Apaches did not leave a written historical record. Therefore most of the friendships and relationships here presented are purely imaginary.

The Chiricahua Apaches were historically placed into three subdivisions: the *Chi-hen-ne* or Warm Springs People, the *Cho-ken-en* or Cochise Apaches, and the *Ned-ni* or southern Chiricahua. Since the fates of these three groups were virtually inseparable, no special attempt has been made to distinguish between them.

I have endeavored to portray the average Chiricahua Apache as a sympathetic individual, not so that the reader will approve or disapprove of his ideas and actions, but so that it may be possible to understand what he became in terms of what he experienced.

Many books and records have given pleasure and instruction during the research in preparation for this novel, especially Morris Edward Opler's *An Apache Life-Way*, without which this story could not have been written.

I would also use this opportunity to express my gratitude and indebtedness to the National Archives and Records Service, General Services Administration; the Arizona Pioneers' Historical Society; the Fort Sill Museum; the United States Department of the Interior, Bureau of Indian Affairs; Thomas B. Hinton, Associate Professor, the University of Arizona, Department of Anthropology; and many who have given of their time and knowledge.

JAMES R. OLSON

Contents

PART ONE

the BEGINNING

This is the miracle;
A child is born,
And that which was nothing
Shall become a man.

1

HE WAS A *Shis-Inday,* one of the People. Although he was shown exactly where he had been born in the high southern range of the Chiricahua Mountains, in later years only he remembered the precise location.

His birthplace was in a small canyon among the myriad of canyons and arroyos that lay like wrinkles on the ancient face of the mountain. A clear, cold stream, shaded by willows and cottonwoods, traced a bubbly course down its center. Near the head of the canyon stood a clump of pine trees. Here, on the soft carpet of fallen needles, he had drawn his first breath.

He was born during the late spring of 1845, the season called Many Leaves. The People had just returned from wintering in the lower, warmer regions, when his mother felt the labor pains and came to this place. Kneeling at the birthing pole, she had suffered the pain in silence and he was born, the second son of his father, Nah-kah-yen, and of his mother, Sons-ee-ah-ray.

When Nah-kah-yen saw the small, pink face, wrinkled like an old man's from the agony of the birth, he smiled at his wife. "We'll call him See-jah," he said. See-jah meant "our son," and was the only appellation he would be given immediately because a name was an intimate part of a person, influencing him all of his life. His true name could wait until he was older, when some outstanding event would suggest a suitable one.

Sons-ee-ah-ray first brought him to the canyon because it was a special world, a sacred place for him alone. Here the spirit which was him had first seen the world. At this spot, he would always be closest to the gods that directed the affairs of men. Here his prayers would be heard most clearly.

Sons-ee-ah-ray did not make a specific journey to the canyon, but when the band was again traveling near the site, she took him there. She made the special ceremony, rolling her baby on the ground in the four directions so that the spirits would know that his parents were pleased with their son. See-jah did not remember this first visit, but in later life he would return many times and feel the special importance that vibrated in the air for him. He could hear the laughter of the spirits in the voice of the bubbling stream. When he drank the icy water it surged through his body so that he could feel the strength which the mountain had imparted to the melted snow.

From a spot on the hillside, just above the canyon, he could look out over the land, rolling away to the south and west. In the far distance there were other mountains visible when the blowing dust did not hide them. It was a barren land, a vast expanse of sandy, treeless deserts and towering mountains, gray and melancholy, standing up against the sky like ghosts, their sides seamed and furrowed.

But in the spring, during the time of the rains, there was life. The deserts and mountains were covered with a carpet of wildly colored flowers. The air was clear and sweet, filling the lungs with life and strength. The sun was fresh, undiluted. At night the stars settled down to the earth, bright and clear.

He was glad that he had been born in the mountains because the *Shis-Inday* were a mountain people. In the high ranges they were safe among the cool pines and upland meadows. Game animals were always plentiful and fat. Everywhere edible nuts and berries abounded.

It was here that he was born and his spirit liked what it had seen. The mountains were a part of him now, just as he was a part of them. No matter what else might change in the world, it was in the mountains that he would always feel most at home.

2

THE PEOPLE, realizing that their lives and the life of the entire world was renewed in the young, had studied the legends from ancient times and the hard lessons of nature until a store of knowledge had been accumulated which taught them how to protect their children against the evils of the world, especially during the first two years of life, when so many died.

Even before See-jah was born, Nah-kah-yen began preparations for the first and most important ceremony of the *tsoch*, the cradle. This ritual was a prayer that the baby would be spared the evils and sicknesses so closely linked to birth. From this time until See-jah was old enough to begin his warrior training, he was handed into the care of his mother.

Sons-ee-ah-ray took special pains to make sure that he grew under the proper guidance.

When the baby was a month old she pierced the lobes of his ears with a sharp bone so that See-jah would learn to hear things sooner, and obey more quickly. She also gathered and boiled special herbs, bathing her son in the water to make his skin strong and protect him from cuts and bruises.

When the boy was one year old, the ceremony of putting on moccasins was held to set the boy on the correct path and to insure that he would always walk tall in the ways of the righteous and the just.

At two years of age See-jah was weaned and took solid food all of the time.

It was difficult for See-jah to separate his first memories. There were many things he knew, but did not remember how the knowledge had come to him. To feel and touch and do were the natural ways to learn, but as his experience broadened, his mind filled with many questions about things around him. It never seemed strange to him that question after question should come into his mind, sometimes so rapidly that he was hard pressed to ask them all. See-jah did not always understand the answers, or he had forgotten the details that would have solved the puzzle. But those things he could not understand could be imagined, and in that way he discovered and delighted in the expanse and depth of his own mind.

Spirits and ghosts and monsters were a vital part of life, guiding every activity. Almost from his first memories he could vividly recall the legends he was told around the winter fires, during the long, cold nights. In the flickering shadows dancing on the walls, he could see the figures of heroes and monsters struggling. Many of the epics were about Child of the Water and White Painted Woman and the beginning of all things.

When the land had been new there was a person called White Painted Woman, who was the Mother of all the People. One time, when it was raining, she lay in the open without clothes and Water entered in and conceived with her. Her son, called Child of the Water, grew quickly because of the ceremonies that White Painted Woman performed for him. It was Child of the Water who made all things as they were.

When he came into the world it was filled with monsters, but he was not afraid. After many great battles he conquered them. When he had made the earth safe and assured the survival of the People, he and White Painted Woman prepared to leave for their home in the sky. But first, White Painted Woman instructed the *Shis-Inday* in the rituals that they must practice to remain strong. There was a story about Child of the Water and White Painted Woman to explain everything that was good or bad in the whole world.

3

DURING THE LATE SUMMER of See-jah's fifth year there occurred an event which became his first complete memory. At the time of its happening he did not understand the significance of his father's tale about Mexicans murdering *Shis-Inday* for scalp bounties. He could not comprehend cruelty of this magnitude, and he accepted what he had heard as a legend.

Even the next day when Sons-ee-ah-ray told him that he could accompany her to a dance, he did not connect this with his father's story.

The chill of autumn was in the evening air. It was the season of Thick with Fruit and the dusty odor of dead leaves and frost-killed grass flooded his nostrils. The air carried the faint smell, brisk and cool, of snows that would soon be coming to the high places.

His mother wrapped a blanket around him to guard against the gathering cold, and would have carried him if he had not insisted on walking. Clutching tightly to Sons-ee-ah-ray's long skirts with one hand, he left the familiar confines of the village and followed her into the unknown hills. The sun was still visible when they started, but soon the long shadows spread and closed in about them. Small sounds that he would always associate with this memory chirped and cracked out of the darkness, stirring fears in See-jah's heart.

When mother and son came over a low ridge, a spectral conclave lay before them. In the center of the narrow valley, smoke ranged upward from a great bonfire, the sparks dancing high like wild stars. People were all around. Fingers of light lashed over them, heavy on those closest to the fire, and fading into the ghostly darkness on the further slopes. Over everything, like the washing of water, pulsed the slow, methodical rhythm of drums.

"Where did all of these people come from?" See-jah asked, awed by the size of the multitude.

His mother laughed. "Did you think that everyone in the world lived in our camp?" The firelight, reflected in her eyes, danced and sparkled, highlighting the excitement she felt. "There are many camps like ours, scattered everywhere."

Caught up by the awe-inspiring majesty of the fire and the drums, See-jah forgot his fear of the night. As his mother sat on the ground, he scrambled up into the branches of a scrub oak and settled on a limb where he was able to see over the heads of the adults.

See-jah's father was seated with the warriors in the first rank, nearest the fire. Behind Nah-kah-yen was See-jah's brother, Ish-kay-nay, who was fifteen, and although not yet a warrior was a war novice. Behind the warriors and novices were the women and the younger children, their mysterious figures almost lost in the deep shadows.

Ten paces to the west of the fire, Hosanto, See-jah's grandfather, sat cross-legged, with four other old men, each beating rhythmically on drums, their voices rising in a high-pitched chant. See-jah began to sway in time to the music.

Above the other sounds he heard his father's voice as Nah-kah-yen stepped into the cleared space around the fire.

"A terrible blow has fallen on our people," Nah-kah-yen shouted as the drums slowed, maintaining a subdued rhythm. "Many of our relatives have died because of treachery by the Mexicans. There is no way to atone for this evil except blood for blood."

Individually the warriors who wished to follow Nah-kah-yen in the raid stood and joined him at the bonfire.

"Remember the ways of war," Nah-kah-yen continued. "Some men return. Some men are killed. If any of these warriors die, I want no blame from their kin. They themselves have chosen to go and accept the chances of battle."

As the drums pulsated with their low, rhythmic throb, the warriors began to dance. They did not shout and scream, but made low grunting sounds that traveled up the hill over the louder and wilder yells of the women. The men danced faster and faster, approaching the drummers in a zig-zag line, firing their rifles into the air, just as they would do on the actual raid.

Then the names of the men who had not yet joined the dance were called. There was no law ordering the men to engage in the raid. Every adult male was allowed to decide this for himself. But there was power in the calling of a name. It was difficult to resist the summons and be thought a coward.

The drums stilled and Hosanto, the leader of the dance, called them individually. "You are a great warrior! Now you are being called! What are you going to do when we fight our enemy?"

One by one the warriors who had held back jumped up when their names were called. Firing their rifles into the air, they joined the dance.

The men were still dancing when Sons-ee-ah-ray lifted See-jah from the tree and bundled him in the blanket. In spite of his protests she carried him back to their camp, laid him on his bed of pine boughs, and tucked the blanket around him.

"Remember what you've seen tonight," she whispered.

"When you're a man like your father, the time will come for you to join the dance. Be brave and don't wait for your name to be called. The son of Nah-kah-yen must be courageous and strong. Some day you'll be a leader of your people." She leaned over and kissed him lightly on the cheek. "Sleep now so that you'll be awake when your father leaves in the morning."

See-jah lay quietly on the bed, but he could not sleep. His heart was still pounding from the excitement, and his mind was filled with thoughts of his own raids.

He must have fallen asleep, because the sky was becoming light outside the wickiup when he heard his mother and father talking softly. Ish-kay-nay was not beside him in bed, but he could still feel the warmth where his brother had lain.

He quietly turned on his side so that his parents would not know he was awake. The wickiup was dark, but he could hear whispered words, and he could distinguish their shapes standing in the heavy shadows.

"I'll pray to the gods for your safety," Sons-ee-ah-ray whispered.

"Don't worry," Nah-kah-yen answered, his deep voice softly reassuring her. "After all, this isn't my first raid. I'll be all right."

"Please be careful."

"What do you want me to do, cringe like a coward? Blood must pay for blood."

"I know. It's just that I'm frightened."

In the darkness See-jah saw the bodies of his parents come together and he knew that they were kissing. It was the first time he had seen a man and woman embrace and he knew it was a private thing. He turned his head away, ashamed that he had been watching.

"Wake the boy," Nah-kah-yen said after a moment of silence. "It's time to go."

See-jah feigned sleep when Sons-ee-ah-ray touched his shoulder, but he turned immediately and sat up rubbing his eyes. Nah-kah-yen had already left the dwelling.

"Your father is leaving," she said.

Although a thin band of yellow touched the lower peaks to the east, the rancheria was still buried in the heavy shadows of night. He could hear the soft sounds of the people in the neighboring lodges making their final preparations. Here and there he saw dark shapes leading horses across the open spaces.

Suddenly Nah-kah-yen loomed over him. "Well," he chuckled. "The sleepy one has finally gotten up. Here, this is for you." He handed See-jah a little hat made from rabbit fur with the ears still attached.

The boy slipped it on and shook his head, feeling the weight shift as the ears swayed back and forth.

His father laughed and picked him up. "You look just like a rabbit now. Maybe you'll grow up to be as quick and cunning as the little ones." He gave him a hard hug and set him down.

Ish-kay-nay brought the horses and stood silently under the discipline of a novice. Without another word Nah-kah-yen turned and swung onto his pony. With Ish-kay-nay following, he joined the other warriors, riding slowly south.

See-jah stood with his mother until the warriors were out of sight. Then he dashed off, anxious to show his friends the new rabbit-ear cap.

4

IT WAS EARLY morning and the sparkle of frost still lay in the places not yet sun touched. There was activity everywhere. Some of the women and young girls were stripping the hides and skins from the wickiups. Some were loading bundles onto the horses and mules and tying them into place. Others were busy arranging food caches.

The grazing for the pony herd was becoming scarce, and the wickiups were beginning to be filled with the stale odors of people and trapped smoke. Now that the nights were bitter cold in the mountains, it was time to move to a lower and warmer camp where the grass would be fresh and the winter delayed in coming.

Although his people never stayed long in one location, moving from place to place throughout the year, this time See-jah felt uneasy. Home life was a warm and pleasant thing and the ties that bound parents and children were very strong. Although See-jah had never bothered himself with these thoughts before, and he did not understand them now, it was a vague concern for Nah-kah-yen that made him seek out his mother and tug at her long skirt.

"How will father be able to find us if we move?" he asked.

Sons-ee-ah-ray was occupied with taking hides down from the frame of their old dwelling. "You ask more questions than an old woman," she said, pausing to push a strand of loose hair under her blue headband.

"But if we move while father's gone, he won't be able to find us," See-jah insisted.

"If you don't stop bothering me with questions, we won't be ready when the others are." There was a hint of irritation in her voice, but when she turned and saw the concern in his eyes, her face softened. "Don't worry. Your father's a good hunter. If he can find the deer hiding in the mountains, I'm sure he'll be able to find us." She carefully folded the hides and tied them into a bundle. "Maybe you wouldn't ask so many questions if you had something to do. Take the horse down to the creek and let it drink."

His uneasiness satisfied, See-jah grabbed the lead rope and tugged on it, urging the old mare to follow. "Be careful," his mother called. "Don't let her step on you. And don't take all day."

The trail to the stream turned and twisted around the rocky slopes until it was hidden from the camp. As soon as he was out of sight, See-jah pulled hard on the lead rope to halt the horse. It was not an easy task, because the wise old mare could scent water. But the pack animal had learned discipline under a firm hand, and she finally heeded the boy's commands.

See-jah reached up and patted the bony muzzle. "You be a good horse," he soothed, using the tone he fancied that the warriors assumed when they talked to their mounts.

He looked up at the towering beast and for a moment he was afraid of the idea that had suddenly popped into his head. However, it was only an instant's hesitation as the thought became a firm resolve.

Swallowing against a vague sense of uneasiness, he scrambled up on a tall rock and reached for the thongs securing the pack. The mare took a nervous step, suspicious of the unusual activity. "Whoa," See-jah soothed. "Stand still." She snorted, switched her tail at a fly, and turned her head to look back at the boy.

Taking a firm grip on the pack lashings, See-jah swung free of the rock. Frantically pulling with his arms and kicking with his feet, he managed to scramble aboard.

He had barely settled snugly in the space between the pack and the neck when the mare shuffled her feet, sending a jolt through See-jah's body. He leaned forward to firmly entwine his hands in the long hair of the mane, causing his eyes to turn downward toward the hard earth. Only the memory of the war dance and his mother's words about being brave enabled him to conquer the fright that twisted his stomach.

See-jah raised his head, determined not to look down, and kicked the mare with his naked heels. The first steps jolted, threatening to dislodge him, but he squeezed his legs snugly against the neck and hung on.

As the mare picked her way along the rocky path, See-jah's confidence increased, and he straightened up, releasing one hand from its grip on the mane. It was easy to imagine himself a great warrior, riding into battle. He felt proud and strong astride the steed, knowing that none of his friends had ever ridden by themselves.

The old mare ignored the extra weight on her withers, and slowly plodded down the narrow trail to the stream. When she reached the water, she waded halfway in, lowered her muzzle into the icy stream, and began to drink.

See-jah leaned over the lowered neck and watched, fascinated by the successive rings spreading from the long muzzle. Reflections were distorted, and the watery images danced and sparkled. Completely absorbed in watching the patterns in the water, he leaned forward further and further. When he felt himself slipping and tried to regain his balance, it was already too late. His desperate grab at the mane missed, and with a little cry, he fell.

The icy water closed over him, filling his mouth and nose. He came up sputtering and coughing. His pride and courage melted in the cold water. With tears of panic streaming down his cheeks, he struggled from the stream and ran all the way back to camp, the soggy ears of his rabbit cap slapping in his face.

Not hearing the laughter around him, he burrowed into his mother's arms. She wrapped him in a blanket and soothed his sobs while See-jah tried to blurt out the story.

"Maybe we should call you the swimmer," she said, laughing when he had finally explained. He stopped crying, beginning to enjoy his mother's sympathy. "But that can wait," she continued. "I sent you out with a horse and you came back alone. You go right back to the creek and get her. And this time don't try to ride. When you're old enough, your father will teach you."

See-jah walked slowly back toward the stream, his ears hot with embarrassment. But with each step his pace quickened, and his pride began to return. After all, he thought, I did ride all by myself.

5

THE WOMEN worked together constructing the rancheria's new wickiups in the fresh green valley. First they thrust long slender poles into the ground, every foot or so apart, in a rough circle. Then the tops of the poles were bent inward and bound together with yucca-leaf strands, leaving a small circular smoke hole at the junction. Brush was intertwined and woven between the bent poles, making a loose basketlike structure, an inverted beehive. Finally the entire lodge, except for the doorway and smoke hole, was covered with hides and brush. The women worked quickly, efficiently, maintaining a constant chatter.

Sons-ee-ah-ray worked with a sense of pride and accomplishment. She knew that the home she provided her family was one of the finest. The hide coverings were so snugly woven that even heavy winds and rains could not invade the interior. She took special pains to pack and smooth the earthen floor and keep it swept clear of litter. The blankets and robes were clean and kept in excellent repair. Nah-kah-yen had never complimented her on these things — they were expected of her — but she knew that her man saw and appreciated.

Today she worked with a sense of anticipation. From some source she did not understand, she knew the men would return soon. If not today, then tomorrow. She wanted everything to be in readiness for Nah-kah-yen.

While Sons-ee-ah-ray worked, See-jah played conceal and stalk in the creek bottom, where he had been sent so that he would not be underfoot. Pi-hon-se and Alchise, both older by nearly a year, were concealed somewhere in the heavy brush. Beneactiney and See-jah, along with Chino, who was the youngest, were trying to find them. See-jah was so occupied with the search that he did not notice the group of horsemen approaching. His first awareness was a murmur, almost like a rushing wind, as the women called to each other. Chino was the first to comprehend.

"The warriors are back!" he shouted.

Their game quickly forgotten, the boys scattered like quail. See-jah dashed inside his unfinished wickiup, seeking the rabbit-ear cap. He was bursting to tell his father about taking the mare to the stream and riding her and falling into the water and how the cap had been water soaked but how it had dried all right and was hardly damaged at all.

When he bolted recklessly out of the doorway and started to run toward the returning warriors, his mother grabbed him by the arm and held him back.

Then See-jah began to sense the emotion that tingled in the air. He looked around curiously. Everyone was holding back, waiting silently beside his dwelling. He was puzzled that no one seemed to share his excitement, and by the strange pressure of his mother's hand on his arm.

The warriors rode quietly. There was none of the laughter and joking associated with a returning hunting party. Even their appearance was different. They were covered with dust and streaked with sweat. Some wore strips of cloth, crusted over with dried blood. Their faces reflected a weariness that See-jah had never seen before.

He saw his uncle, San-dai-say, and his brother, Ish-kay-nay, but not his father. See-jah thought that it was strange his uncle should be with these men, because he did not live in this rancheria.

As the riders came on, some stopped at their dwellings and were greeted with shouts of joy and warm embraces. At other wickiups, wails of grief rose as the warriors passed and no one stopped.

San-dai-say and Ish-kay-nay halted in front of See-jah and his mother. For a moment they said nothing. Ish-kay-nay took the horses and led them away while San-dai-say stood nervously before them. His mother's hand tightened on See-jah's shoulder until the pressure hurt, and he became frightened.

When San-dai-say spoke, his voice cracked with emotion. "He was in the forefront of the charge. It was over quickly — there wasn't any pain." His mother began to sob and wail, and, still not understanding, See-jah felt her grief and also began to cry. His uncle touched him lightly on the shoulder. "I'll look after you and your mother."

"I don't want you," he sobbed, deeply frightened and confused. "I want my father. Where is he?"

"Hush," his mother scolded, her wails and sobs becoming more violent, increasing See-jah's fear.

"The boy doesn't understand," San-dai-say said, coming down on one knee. He pried See-jah loose from his mother's skirt and held him by his trembling shoulders. "You have to be brave now. You and Ish-kay-nay are the men of this house. Your father is dead."

It was like some weird nightmare when Sons-ee-ah-ray cut See-jah's hair at shoulder length and burned everything that had belonged to his father. Last, she took the hat with the rabbit ears and threw it on the fire. See-jah cried until his tears were used up and his little body was wracked with dry sobs. He cried for his father, but even more he cried for himself, because he vaguely realized that something important had happened that would change his life.

That night while his mother was still crying, and after she had tucked him into bed, he could no longer hold back the questions. "Where's my father?" he asked.

"He's gone to the House of the Spirits," she answered through her tears. There was a loneliness in her eyes that See-jah understood better than the concept of death. "You must never speak his name again, or he'll hear and it'll keep him from completing his journey."

For an instant See-jah brightened. "Then, if I call him, he'll come back."

"No! When a person goes to the place of the dead, he can never come back. If you call him he'll be confused and his spirit won't find rest."

See-jah began to cry again. It did not seem fair that his father should go away and never return. But he did not question his mother anymore. When she went to her bed, he waited a long time until her soft crying became the heavy breathing of sleep. Then he turned to Ish-kay-nay.

"Are you sleeping?" he asked.

"No."

"Why do people have to die?"

"People die because of Coyote," Ish-kay-nay answered as they lay together in the darkness. There was a long silence and See-jah was almost going to ask for an explanation when Ish-kay-nay continued. "In the beginning there was no death and all of the People lived forever. But Coyote had great power. One day when he was feeling mean, he went down to the river and threw a stone into the water. He said that if the stone sank, all living creatures must die someday. It's because of Coyote that people die. There's nothing you can do about it."

Ish-kay-nay's tone prevented See-jah from asking any more questions even though his confusion was immense. Far into the night he was plagued by thoughts and questions that his limited experience had not equipped him to handle.

During the following days the atmosphere around his wickiup was oppressive. Sons-ee-ah-ray cried frequently and was openly unhappy. Even Ish-kay-nay was morose and silent. See-jah was expected to be equally melancholy, but he could not. When he forgot and laughed, his mother would turn on him in anger.

"Hush! How can you laugh at a time like this? You should show respect."

But See-jah did not feel sad, and he could no longer pretend that he did. Already the idea that his father would never return had left him. Every day he half expected to see Nah-kah-yen riding into camp. After all, his father had often been away for longer periods of time when on hunting trips.

Rather than pretend grief, it was easier for See-jah to sneak away from his mother and seek the company of his friends.

"Look what I've got," Chino said as See-jah joined his companions at the creek.

"What is it?"

"A bird."

"Let me see."

"Be careful," Chino warned. "Don't let him get away."

See-jah took the cactus wren into his hands, pinioning the wings against the bird's struggles. "How'd you catch it?"

"It was just flopping around on the ground. It must have a broken wing."

"I saw it first," Pi-hon-se claimed, piqued at not being the center of attention. As the oldest, he considered himself a leader.

"Sure, but Chino caught it," Alchise said.

"It was probably injured by a hawk," Beneactiney suggested.

It was the first time that See-jah had seen a bird close enough to touch. He was captivated by the fragile beauty of the creature. The tiny heart pounded strongly, rapidly in his hand. The bright clear eyes intermittently clouded and cleared as the wren blinked. Sunlight glistened off delicate feathers as the bird turned its head with jerky motions.

Pi-hon-se was overcome with jealousy because the bird and the attention were not his. "A bird is a stupid thing," he said, taking the wren, and with a practiced twist, wringing its neck. He tossed the limp body back to See-jah.

"Hey," Chino protested. "Why'd you do that? It was my bird."

"It was only a bird," Pi-hon-se answered smugly. "Now we can do something more interesting."

See-jah held the lifeless, still-warm body in his hand, confronted at last by the full mystery of death. The wren had changed. Some indefinable thing had quit the creature, leaving it ugly. The feathers were now ruffled, no longer glistening in the sunlight. There was no thumping of life under the thin breast. A single, haze-clouded eye stared up from the head hanging limp and awkward on the broken neck.

Slowly the comprehension of death came to him. A pain began to throb in his breast as See-jah realized what death meant in terms of his father. Muscular arms no longer had the power to lift and hug him. The deep, strong voice was forever silent. A thick, black gloom descended and crushed him. Inconsolable grief squeezed the first real tears from his eyes. Face to face with the awful reality, suffering the pain of lost innocence, See-jah dropped the dead bird. His vision blurred by a flood of misery, he stumbled toward home and the sympathy of his mother's arms.

6

DURING THE DAYS following the realization of his father's death, See-jah never spoke of Nah-kah-yen, but he often thought of him. Sometimes he tried to remember his appearance, but could only see him as the shadow that dominated the great war dance and kissed his mother in the darkness of the wickiup. But he did remember the sound of his father's voice and the touch of his calloused hands when he had given See-jah the rabbit-ear cap. Even when he was older and should have known better, thoughts of rabbits or of his father always brought thoughts of death.

"It's time for you to have a new name," Sons-ee-ah-ray said one morning when the general grief had abated.

"Why?" See-jah questioned, railing against any impermanence. So many things had been altered in the world that he desperately wanted to cling to his own name, his identity. "I like my name. I don't want to change it."

"Now that your father is gone, it's no longer proper to call you See-jah, our son." Sons-ee-ah-ray saw the tears welling up in the boy's eyes, and she too felt a tightening in her throat. She knew that See-jah treasured the vague memories of his father. The matter of the name would be hard for the boy to accept, but children's names were frequently changed until a suitable one was found. She did not realize that the appellation she would give him now would be his for the remainder of his life. "You'll be called Ulzana."

"I don't like it," the boy sobbed.

"Don't cry." Sons-ee-ah-ray took her son into her arms and comforted him. "Ulzana is a good name," she whispered. "Speak it. There's the freedom of the wind in the sound, and yet there's also strength. It's a good name for a man."

"I hate it," Ulzana sobbed, unwilling to be reconciled. "I'll never like it."

But Ulzana did learn to enjoy the sound of his name. At first he only accepted it secretly in his heart, but little by little he grew proud of it. Then a thing happened which made the matter of his name seem unimportant.

The first indication Ulzana had of this event was when he overheard a conversation between Sons-ee-ah-ray and her father, Hosanto.

"I didn't accept," Hosanto said, paying no attention to Ulzana when the boy entered the wickiup. "But I didn't refuse either. It isn't good for you to be alone."

Sons-ee-ah-ray was silent for a time as she continued working on a buckskin shirt. "I hadn't thought of marriage again so soon," she finally said. "My heart is still heavy."

"Yes, I understand," Hosanto said. "But it's been six months since you were widowed. Sometimes the heart never heals. It was so with me when your mother died. But I was already old and didn't need a woman. Ish-kay-nay is nearly grown. It won't be long before he'll marry and live with his wife's people. I'm thinking of you and the little one. You aren't so old that you no longer need a man, and the boy certainly needs a father."

"Of course you're right," Sons-ee-ah-ray agreed softly.

"San-dai-say will be a good husband. He's a widower without children and I've noticed that he already loves Ulzana like a son. As your brother-in-law he has first call." Hosanto did not elaborate further on the custom, but he knew that Sons-ee-ah-ray was familiar with it. Her husband's brother had first right to marry her. Only if she refused him or if he relinquished the right, could she marry anyone else.

"I'll do whatever you think best for me and my son," she whispered, acknowledging the wisdom of his arguments.

Although Ulzana did not completely understand the concept of marriage, he realized that San-dai-say would in some way be taking the place of his father. It struck him that this was disloyal, that the memory of Nah-kah-yen was being betrayed.

"I don't want San-dai-say to live here," he protested when told of his mother's decision.

Sons-ee-ah-ray sighed. She did not know how to make the boy understand the necessity of her marriage. "We need San-dai-say. Without a man in our lodge we're dependent on the charity of others."

"Ish-kay-nay can take care of us. He's almost a warrior."

"That wouldn't be fair. Ish-kay-nay has his own life to lead."

"Then I'll take care of you."

"I know you would if it were possible, but you're too young."

"What if he beats you?"

"Ulzana, how can you say such a thing? You know San-dai-say has always been kind."

"Pi-hon-se's father beats his wife. I know because I've heard them fighting."

"You shouldn't listen to such things. But sometimes, if a wife is lazy, or crabby, or gossipy, a husband has a right to beat her. San-dai-say will have no reason to be stern."

"But what if he does?"

"He won't." Her tone made it obvious that the discussion was not going to be pursued any further.

Sons-ee-ah-ray spoke to her father about Ulzana's objections.

"The boy is young," Hosanto said. "He doesn't understand, and he's confused. With time it will be all right."

Thus it came about that San-dai-say became Ulzana's stepfather and moved into the wickiup, taking Nah-kah-yen's place.

Ulzana rebelled against these changes in his world. He felt that in some manner an injustice had been done to him, and he fought back in the only way he knew. Because his mother and stepfather seemed responsible, Ulzana began to disobey them.

San-dai-say tried not to notice the boy's disapproval. He strove diligently to be kind and understanding. He never mentioned the instances of bad behavior, because he could see the unhappiness and confusion stirring in his stepson.

But although Sons-ee-ah-ray was patient with him, when Ulzana disobeyed, she would warn him. "If you are bad, Clown will come and take you away. He'll put you in a big basket and carry you off. He does that to bad children who won't mind their parents."

At first the warnings about Clown frightened Ulzana and he obeyed, but when Clown never actually appeared, gradually the fear of the threats wore off, and he did not pay any attention to them.

One fall morning about a year after his father's death, Sons-ee-ah-ray took Ulzana out in search of berries. For a while he worked hard picking the ripe fruit, occasionally popping one into his mouth. But his interest soon began to be diverted by butterflies and birds and the small noises around him. In spite of his mother's warnings, he darted among the bushes, investigating curious sounds and fighting imaginary enemies.

While he was stalking a make-believe mountain lion, he heard a rustling in the bushes. He had taken one step toward the disturbance when a giant, painted white from head to toe, rose from the thicket. He did not have to see the hideous face to know that Clown had come for him.

As Clown started toward Ulzana, threatening him with a stick, the boy shouted a warning to his mother, turned and ran with all the speed his flashing legs could muster. He looked back once and saw Clown lumbering after him.

Ulzana dashed into his wickiup and hid under the blankets on his bed. When he heard someone enter, he tried to lie very still so that Clown would not find him.

"Don't worry," Sons-ee-ah-ray soothed. "I've chased Clown away."

Ulzana came out of his hiding place and let himself be wrapped in the security of his mother's arms. "Don't let Clown take me!"

"Don't cry. I told Clown that he must have been searching for a different little boy. I told him that you have always obeyed me. But unless you're good, next time he won't believe me. It's not easy to fool Clown."

From that time Ulzana obeyed his mother and stepfather. When he sometimes forgot and started to do a thing he was not supposed to, a simple warning was all he needed.

7

When Ulzana was eight years old, San-dai-say sat down with him on a little knoll near their camp.

"It's time for you to learn to use the hunting bow. There' ll come a time when someone's counting on you to get meat, and you'll have to be able to handle a bow capable of bringing down a deer. But first you'll have to prepare your body. It takes a strong hand to use a strong bow."

"I'm already strong." Ulzana made a fist and bent his arm, showing a hard little bicep muscle. "See."

"Yes, I know," San-dai-say said, lightly pinching the knotted muscle. "But you'll have to be even stronger. I'm going to give you a task to do every day. It's something you have to do and I want you to do it willingly, but if I must, I'll force you."

Ulzana nodded. "I'll do whatever you tell me."

"Good. Every morning I want you to run to the top of that hill and back before the sun comes up."

Even in the bright sunlight it was a long journey to the mountain peak, and in the early morning darkness, Ulzana knew that the path would be filled with terrors. For a moment he swallowed his pride. "What if Clown sees me?"

His stepfather laughed. "The time that Clown chased you, it was only me, painted white. You were a little boy then and wouldn't listen to your mother. Now that you're big enough to handle a bow, you can obey without being frightened."

Ulzana cast his eyes downward to avoid looking at his stepfather. He was ashamed that he had been too frightened to recognize San-dai-say in disguise.

"Remember, the harder you work at running, the sooner we'll be able to make the bow."

The skies were beginning to lighten with the false dawn when Ulzana woke the next morning. Slipping out of the wickiup quietly so as not to disturb anyone, he stood for a moment shivering in the chilly, pure air. The dark hulk of the mountain was barely visible against the black sky. It seemed a long way off, but not for an instant did he doubt his ability to run there and back.

He started off confidently, running at full speed, not having the slightest concept of pacing himself. From the time they could walk the boys had also run. But running for pleasure had not taught Ulzana to conserve energy. Before he had traveled a hundred yards he began to feel the strain and had to slow his pace.

The path grew steeper and each step became more difficult. His lungs seemed ready to burst from the strain of gulping for every breath and his legs lost their strength, becoming leaden weights. Every fiber of his body called out for him to stop, to rest, but Ulzana willed himself on.

Just when he began to believe that he could not go one more step, he reached the hilltop. His body cried out for rest, but he would not allow it. With a deep gulp of the cold air, he turned and started back down. Running downhill was easier, but he had little control over his exhausted legs. Twice he tripped over stones and fell, but both times he struggled to his feet and continued to run, not even aware of the pain in his scraped knees and hands.

The first edge of the sun was climbing over the mountain behind him when he collapsed in front of his dwelling. His chest heaved from the effort to suck in air. He tried to stand, but his legs were drained of all their strength and would not support his body.

Sons-ee-ah-ray helped him into the wickiup and gave him water and meat. In her eyes was the pain she felt for his suffering, but she did not speak of it. As her son ate, she rubbed animal fat into his aching muscles. "This will feed them and make them strong," she said.

San-dai-say did not comment.

Each morning Ulzana rose in the cold darkness and repeated the ordeal. The second day was worse than the first. Every muscle in his body ached, and his wind reserves were spent before he was halfway up the mountain. But the thought of slacking off, or cheating, or abandoning the task never occurred to him.

Slowly, day by day, the stiffness in his muscles eased. Miraculously, one morning, the agony was gone. The run was still not easy, but he found that his lungs no longer ached and his legs pumped without effort. He began to experience a great pride in the feel and power of his body. There was joy in tasting the huge drafts of air that expanded his lungs. He listened with love to the pounding pulse in his head and felt it in his breast when he threw himself down to rest. The vast open spaces, calm in the predawn stillness, expanded his heart with a love of the silence and solitude. His body alone was challenging this particular mountain at this particular moment. It was a contest he did not wish to share.

8

AFTER SEVERAL WEEKS of the daily runs, San-dai-say again took Ulzana aside. "You've worked hard," he said, smiling when the boy beamed with pride. "You'll still have to run every day, but now you're strong enough to use a real bow."

Under his stepfather's guidance, Ulzana learned the ancient skills of making the basic *Cho-ken-en* weapon. To construct a proper bow and the necessary arrows required approximately fifteen days—fifteen endless days for an impatient boy. But eventually the three-foot mulberry branch was split, shaped, smoothed, rubbed, and tempered in the hot ashes of the fire. Arrow shafts were straightened and smoothed and the split turkey feathers attached. Finally the bowstring, three strands of rolled deer sinew, was strung.

Then San-dai-say took Ulzana out behind the camp and waved an arm over the countryside. "Hunt here," he said. "Shoot birds or squirrels or any small things. But, before you try, I have to warn you that you can't just go up and shoot. They'll run away as soon as you come anywhere near them. If a bird is over there on a limb, you'll have to sneak around so that you can get within range of him."

Ulzana listened with impatience. "I'll practice hard."

"Good," his stepfather said, smiling. "And when you shoot your first animal, bring it to me."

Without waiting for further instructions, Ulzana rushed

off, his heart pounding with the excitement of his first hunt.

A short distance from camp he saw a small bird resting on the branch of a scrub oak. It was as if the mountain spirits were cooperating with him. His heart pounding like a ceremonial drum, he crept toward the bird, stepping ever so carefully among the rocks and twigs. Just when he was prepared to shoot, his foot snapped a twig and his quarry fled.

A loud laugh startled him and he spun around to confront Chihuahua, his brother. Now that he had completed his novitiate and was a warrior, Chihuahua was no longer called by his boyhood name, Ish-kay-nay.

"I see that your feet are clumsy," Chihuahua said, still smiling.

"It isn't so easy," Ulzana sputtered. "Birds have good ears."

Chihuahua stopped laughing. "I had the same problem when I first hunted with the big bow. But there are tricks I can show you."

Ulzana watched and marveled at Chihuahua's wisdom as he was shown how to place his feet so as not to disturb the sticks and stones.

Ulzana continued stalking small animals for several hours after Chihuahua left him alone. He was beginning to understand that it was not going to be an easy task to shoot an animal. Only once more was he able to approach close enough to fire an arrow, and then he discovered that his new bow was considerably stronger than he had anticipated, and his arrow passed a foot above his target.

For two weeks he continued to hunt without success. His heart grew heavy with the weight of failure. For an eight-year-old boy, two weeks was an eternity. But each day Chihuahua encouraged him, showing him more about stalking. Gradually Ulzana's feet became more nimble. He practiced with his new bow until its feel was familiar and comfortable, and he learned the idiosyncrasies of each arrow.

One morning, during the third week, he spied a pinyon jay preening its feathers on a branch only a few yards away. Quickly dropping to the ground, Ulzana crawled silently forward. Slowly he raised up and drew back his bowstring. The jay heard the soft twang and swish, but the arrow caught it before it could leave the limb. With a flutter of feathers, the bird fell to the earth.

For a moment Ulzana could not believe he had finally made a kill. He picked up the bird, feeling the warmth in his hand. With a yelp of sheer pleasure, he ran back to camp and handed the dead jay to his stepfather. "Here!" he shouted proudly. "I've killed a bird!"

San-dai-say deftly slit open the jay, removed the heart, and handed it to the happy boy. "Swallow this," he ordered. "It'll make you a good hunter and you'll always find a target for your arrows."

Ulzana quickly swallowed the tiny heart. Then he rushed off to find his friends and boast to them about his exploit.

As practice and success increased his confidence, Ulzana no longer hunted only small birds. He began to stalk rabbits, squirrels, grouse, and prairie chickens. Hardly a day passed when he did not contribute to the cooking pot.

Hunting was a solitary experience, and for the first time in his life Ulzana found himself dependent upon his own company. And in the solitude he discovered that life was good and fresh and full. Alone in the hills he gained a new appreciation of his environment. There were a thousand smells, each unique, softly giving a special significance to the very air he breathed. Away from the distracting sounds of people, there were the tiny noises of the land he had never before been aware of. And there was a beauty and imagery that expanded his mind.

When the sun turned the air syrupy, Ulzana frequently sought the shade of a gnarled tree, and lying on his back, he would send his imagination flying across the panorama of universe. Through half-closed eyes the contorted and twisted sierras became the slumbering legendary monsters. On those rare days when towering white clouds maneuvered across the expanses of opal skies, he saw those mythical creatures in motion, chasing, merging, conquering each other. Truly, wherever his eyes touched, the beauty of nature was exposed in all its nudity.

Ulzana was so absorbed in his own growing up that he barely marked a change in his household during this time. Chihuahua, his brother, married and, as was the custom, moved to the camp of his wife. Ulzana missed Chihuahua mostly at night, when the cold winds made him remember the warmth of his brother's body under the same blankets.

9

FROM THE TIME that they were six or seven years old, Ulzana noticed, boys and girls were separated. They no longer played and raced together. He began to notice that men and women hid themselves when they urinated or emptied their bowels, and he was taught to do this also.

It was difficult to be private in the *Cho-ken-en* camps, and what could not be concealed from Ulzana, he was taught to ignore. When he had to relieve himself, he was instructed to leave the dwelling without reference to his errand. If an explanation was necessary, he was simply to say, "I'm going out."

Since he was no longer a child he could not go naked, but had to wear his breechclout day and night. He was supposed to reserve himself from the company of girls, and even from thoughts about them. Under no circumstances was he allowed to be alone with any female, except his mother. Under these restrictions, he began to avoid girls, even to be ashamed and shy with them.

The physical activity of his training kept him occupied most of the time, but he could not totally suppress his curiosity. Changes in his own body filled his mind with questions. Hair began to grow in his private areas. At times, when he thought of girls, or dreamed of them, his penis became enlarged. One night, during his sleep, his body ejected its life fluid and he was ashamed and confused.

Sometimes he spoke of these things with his friends, and asked about the nature of females, because Ulzana could not speak of these matters with Sons-ee-ah-ray or San-dai-say. There was confusion among the boys, but as they talked about these concerns, they learned. Even Pi-hon-se, who had an older sister, had no more information than the others, although he pretended to know more than he told.

Coyote, the prankster, had done all the things that they were forbidden to do. Every evil, perverted, unkind thing that could be imagined had been done by Coyote at one time or another. Sometimes the boys overheard adults telling certain Coyote stories, and these tales were then repeated among themselves. There was a limited amount of knowledge in the stories, which answered some of the questions.

A young woman or girl sometimes took an older boy into the brush and gave him a boy's knowledge of these things. Then he would tell his friends and the knowledge was shared until it reached Ulzana and his companions. They knew that what they heard was improper, but in their curiosity they listened and learned.

San-dai-say was aware of the interest that Ulzana showed toward girls, and he attempted to frighten the boy away from females during this time of his life.

"You like to live and be healthy, don't you?" he said. "Then keep away from girls and women. They have sickness that steals away your health. Don't have anything to do with them. They have teeth in there and they'll bite off your penis. Then what sort of man would you be?"

Ulzana believed this until he found the courage to discuss it with his friends. They laughed and told him that the old people said those things to scare him. There was nothing to it. Then he was told the things that the older boys knew for certain to be otherwise.

Slowly, one by one, his questions were answered. He

thought about girls and discussed them, but he did not allow himself to dwell on these matters. Thus he grew and learned the things that a boy learns in becoming a man.

10

BENEACTINEY AND ULZANA squatted on their haunches in the bushes, concealed from the village by a patch of scrub oak. Beneactiney drew a small pouch from his belt.

"There isn't much, so be careful," he said.

Ulzana held a greenish oak leaf while his friend poured a small mound of tobacco onto it. Imitating the actions of the adults, Ulzana rolled the leaf into as tight a cylinder as possible, attempting to prevent the strands of tobacco from leaking out of both ends. When Beneactiney had constructed a similar cylinder, Ulzana held a glowing stick and both boys sucked vigorously to start their cigarettes burning.

Beneactiney coughed until tears streamed down his cheeks. "Cigarettes taste terrible."

Ulzana wasn't enjoying the experience any more than his friend. "You have to learn to like them."

"I don't think I want to learn."

"Maybe the oak leaves are what taste so bad."

Over their own coughing and wheezing, neither boy heard footsteps approaching. Suddenly the voice of doom lashed out at them.

"Hey! What are you young sneaks doing?"

Dropping the cigarettes, both boys turned guilty faces toward the old witch, Baychen. For an instant fear held them immobile. Then, not waiting upon the order of their going, they started to run. Unfortunately Ulzana was closest to Baychen and the smoke in his lungs had made him slow. He had taken a single step when Baychen clutched at his long hair and caught hold. He looked around in desperation for help from his friend, but Beneactiney had disappeared into the chaparral.

"Aha," Baychen chuckled. "You're Ulzana, San-dai-say's boy, aren't you? And you've been smoking. You know what happens to little boys who smoke, don't you?"

Ulzana's eyes were riveted on the witch. She was old, her emaciated body bent under the weight of her years. Her dirty gray hair was thin and scraggly. Her nose was an enormous hook over a puckered-in, toothless mouth.

"I'm sorry," Ulzana pleaded. "I'm really sorry. I won't ever smoke again."

"I could tell your stepfather."

"Please don't." Ulzana staggered, his head strangely clouded.

Baychen released her hold on his hair. "You look sick."

"I don't feel very well," Ulzana agreed.

"Here. Chew on this." She handed him some mint leaves from the basket on her arm.

Ulzana chewed the leaves, feeling the bitter taste of tobacco begin to lessen. He continued to eye Baychen suspiciously.

"Feeling better now?"

Ulzana nodded.

"Well, then, go ahead and get out of here." Baychen pushed him away. "I won't tell your stepfather. But don't ever let me catch you smoking again."

Ulzana did not have to be urged to leave. He ran back toward camp as fast as his legs could carry him.

"I never expected to see you again," Beneactiney said when Ulzana found him, Pi-hon-se, and Chino behind Chino's wickiup. "When Baychen caught you, I figured you'd end up in the cooking pot for sure."

"Ah, there wasn't anything to worry about," Ulzana said confidently, when he saw that his reappearance had impressed his friends. He could not resist the temptation to act the hero. "I wasn't afraid."

"But Baychen's a witch," Chino said, wide-eyed. "She could put a hex on you or make you sick."

"Why should she hex me? She likes me."

"You're just saying that. I'll bet you ran just as fast as I did," Beneactiney said, ashamed because he had been afraid and had deserted his companion.

"A witch doesn't like anyone," Pi-hon-se affirmed.

"They hate everyone," Chino agreed.

"Not Baychen. She likes me. And what's more, I like her."

Beneactiney shook his head. "Either she put a hex on you or you're crazy."

"There isn't anything wrong with me. I guess I can like Baychen if I want to."

"If you like her so much, why don't you go visit her right now?" Pi-hon-se challenged.

"I just talked with her." Ulzana felt the familiar squeezing of his stomach that came when his boasting had backed him into an uncomfortable corner. "There's no reason to see her again so soon."

"Because you're afraid of her," Beneactiney said.

"I'm not afraid of anything or anyone."

"Then why don't you go over there?"

Ulzana saw there was no honorable way to avoid the challenge of his friends, even though acceptance could mean his death. Baychen had released him once, but that didn't mean she would let him go a second time.

"What would I say?" he finally asked, attempting to find an excuse not to visit the witch. "I can't just walk in there."

"Here," Pi-hon-se said, holding up a plump rabbit. "Take this to her. Old people always need fresh meat."

When Ulzana hesitated, Chino taunted him. "What's the matter, are you afraid?"

"I'm not afraid of anything."

"Well, then prove it."

Ulzana grabbed Pi-hon-se's rabbit. "I'll show you all."

Making a valiant effort to hide his fears, Ulzana boldly stalked up to Baychen's wickiup. He stopped in front of the blanket-draped entrance and turned and smiled bravely at his companions, who had followed him at a safe distance.

Taking a deep breath, he shouted the required warning. "Baychen! I'm coming in." After a moment's hesitation he lifted the blanket and stepped into the cool, dark interior.

"So it's you again," Baychen cackled. "What do you want now?"

Ulzana's vocal chords were paralyzed. His legs trembled and he felt a great desire to urinate. Dumbly he held the rabbit toward the witch.

"Trying to bribe an old woman to keep her mouth shut, eh?" Baychen took the rabbit. "Well, don't just stand there like a lump, sit down."

Ulzana's legs collapsed and he sat cross-legged on the floor, reconciled to whatever fate awaited him. His eyes swept around the circular dwelling. Surprisingly it was not substantially different from his own home. Certainly he had not expected the familiar home smells of smoke and grease and sweat and dampness. Only the shadows in Baychen's lodge seemed to conceal spirits and monsters and terrors beyond imagining.

"It isn't often that I have any company," Baychen said, her voice softer. "Especially youngsters. I know you boys all think I'm a witch and run away from me. But I much prefer eating rabbits to little boys." She chuckled when Ulzana seemed to cringe. "Thank you for the rabbit. And because you were kind to me, this is for you." She pressed a sodden lump into Ulzana's hand. He stared dumbly at it. "Go ahead and eat it. It isn't poison."

Hesitantly Ulzana took a bite. The rich flavor of a sweet

potato filled his mouth. He smiled, finishing the treat in a
gulp. "Thank you," he murmured, remembering his man-
ners.

"Well, I'm glad to see that you've still got a tongue."
Baychen sighed deeply. "I haven't had any youngsters
around for a long time. After I was captured and before
my husband died, we always had children around here."

Ulzana's eyes went wide with surprise. "Who captured
you?"

"The *Cho-ken-en*."

"The *Cho-ken-en?*" Ulzana was obviously puzzled.

Baychen chuckled. "Have another sweet potato and I'll
explain. I was born a Mexican and grew up on my father's
rancho near Frontera." For a moment the old woman
was silent as her loneliness welled up inside her. But now
that the subject had been broached, she felt a need to talk.
"I was fourteen summers, and on the way to my wedding
when warriors swooped down on our caravan. They killed
everyone except me. I was given as a slave to Hosanto's
wife. I've lived with your people ever since." She smiled at
Ulzana. "That all happened a long time before you were
born."

"Why didn't you go back to Mexico?"

"*Quién sabe?* At first the women watched me too closely.
They made certain that there was no opportunity for me to
escape. And besides, I didn't know where to run. Those
first months as a slave were hard. I cried all the time, and
when I cried I was beaten. To be married was better than
being a slave, so I went to live with a warrior. My husband
was *muy hombre*, and I learned to love him. When he died
I was already as much a *Cho-ken-en* as you are. There was
nothing left for me in Mexico."

Ulzana spoke with his face down because he could sense
the loneliness and the bitter memories. "I'm sorry."

"Ah, no. I'm the one to be sorry. It all happened a long

time ago — before you were born — and I shouldn't bore you with it. You'd better go now. Your mother will be looking for you."

"Good-bye." Ulzana stood up, and for the first time realized that he was no longer afraid. "Thank you for the sweet potatoes."

"Please come and visit again." Baychen smiled. "I always have treats."

"I'll come again. I promise."

And Ulzana did return frequently. Although his visits to Baychen increased his stature among the other boys, Ulzana also derived other benefits. Not only did the old woman have sweets for him, but he sat for hours listening to her stories. She told him of Mexico and how the peons worked, scratching a living from the barren earth. Speaking of her childhood and of the stories she had been told as a young girl, she taught him Spanish words and phrases.

In return for this knowledge, he brought rabbits and squirrels and other bits of meat to Baychen. But mostly he supplied companionship and joy to a lonely old woman.

Thus it was that Ulzana began to realize the world was far larger than the horizons he had seen during his young life.

11

ULZANA HAD NOW REACHED an age where he was expected to prepare for manhood, and consequently his training increased in intensity. Besides the rigors of running up the steepest, slipperiest hills, and swimming and riding and wrestling, to develop his body, his entire life-style became directed toward survival. Knowledge and knowledge alone preserved life.

"Sometimes a man survives by luck," San-dai-say said. "But the ignorant are never lucky."

In this harsh land where enemies constantly threatened, alertness became his nature. His arrows and bow were always within easy reach, and his knife was constantly beside him. Every morning he was up before dawn, because that was the time enemies were most likely to attack the *Cho-ken-en* camps. He was taught to eat lightly, just enough to keep up his strength, so that if enemies should attack, he would be able to run. Only at night, at the evening meal, could he eat heartily. Then, if there were danger, he could hide himself in the darkness and escape.

With the learning of practical things there also came lessons in discipline. Frequently the boys were ordered to perform tasks just because they were difficult, or painful, or so foolish that obedience required strength of will.

In the fall, when a thin sheet of ice covered the calm

places in the stream, the boys were ordered to jump in. Sometimes they cheated, only throwing water on their heads. One morning Pi-hon-se was discovered at this deception, and his father, threatening him with a stick, made him jump into the creek. After Pi-hon-se had been caught, none of the others cheated. When they came shivering from the water, the boys would run back to their wickiups, where they were permitted to wrap a blanket around their trembling bodies but were not allowed to come up to the fire for warmth.

Sometimes San-dai-say ordered Ulzana to attack a tree, just because it was there. He had to hit and kick and scratch until his skin was scraped raw. Or perhaps Ulzana would be ordered to break off a thick limb, or pull up a young tree by the roots, even though a grown man could not have done so.

And he learned survival.

San-dai-say showed him how to live in the desert without water, holding a pebble in his mouth to keep the saliva flowing, or by chewing moisture from the grass. He learned how to find water in the barrel cactus, in the saberlike leaves of the mescal plant, and in the thickened stems of the prickly pear. He was shown which places held reservoirs of moisture during the dry seasons and how to follow the flight of desert birds to water in strange places. So that he could carry liquids across the arid wastes, he learned to make a water sack from the cleansed intestines of a horse or mule.

He was taught to recognize and read the signs left by all who crossed the land. A piece of grass, damaged by a passing foot, quickly browned as the moisture trapped in each broken and crushed blade oozed out. By snapping a fresh piece of grass and comparing the color and moisture content, he could determine how long ago the original had been disturbed. A man or animal could be tracked over the difficult places, like the rocky mountain passes, by searching for pebbles out of place. The degree of dryness on the underside of a disturbed stone told when it had been dislodged. The size and shape and attitude of a footprint told a great deal about who had passed.

The heat and texture of animal droppings were clues to the time interval since the animal had stopped. The sex of a horse could be determined by the attitude it assumed when urinating. A mare spread her rear legs and wet the earth behind her. A stallion did not spread his legs, and the stream of urine struck in front of the rear hoofs.

As Ulzana learned to find and distinguish the signs of other men, he learned to conceal his own presence. The bronze color of his body blended perfectly with the earth. If he burrowed into the sandy soil and arranged tufts of grass or pieces of stone to break his outline, he could virtually disappear. He was taught to build a fire without smoke in the day, or sheltered in a hidden spot at night. He learned how to travel at night, or to stay below crest lines or low to the land so he would not be seen in daylight. He also learned to muffle the sound of his pony's hoofs with pieces of buckskin or blanket so that he could pass within a hundred yards of an enemy without being heard and discovered.

He learned these and many other things the People had been taught by the land.

12

ULZANA THREW himself down on the soft grass beside the stream, delighting in the sensation of relaxing muscles. He had returned only moments ago from a hunting trip with San-dai-say, most of which had been spent in a series of tedious tracking lessons.

"Hey, Beneactiney," he called. "What're you doing?"

Beneactiney lifted his hand from the cold water and held it so that Ulzana could observe the swollen, scraped flesh. "My father set me against a tree," he said, thrusting his hand back into the stream. "The tree won."

"Was it a big tree?" Pi-hon-se asked as he, Chino, and Alchise joined them.

Beneactiney turned a serious face toward them, his brows slightly puckered. "It was the biggest tree I've ever seen," he answered. "The top was in the clouds, and a man would have to take ten big paces to walk around it."

The other four laughed. They knew there were no such trees in their mountains.

"The trees teach a good lesson," Alchise observed. "It takes courage to attack a tree when you know you can't defeat it."

"But it's children's play," Ulzana argued. "A time comes when a man grows above such things."

Pi-hon-se laughed. "Are you a man? You've only passed

thirteen summers and you talk as if the snow had already come to your hair."

"Laugh if you want to, but I'm beyond fighting trees," Ulzana boasted. "My body is already stronger than pain."

"You've got rocks in your head," Alchise said.

"You talk like a fool," Beneactiney agreed, laughing. He held up his hand again, and looking at it, he shook his head.

"I'll show you," Ulzana said. "Chino, get an ember."

When Chino returned with a glowing stick, Ulzana started a small fire. Then he placed a piece of dry sage on the back of his hand. "I can burn this to an ash without flinching." Taking a flame from the fire, he ignited the twig.

His friends watched in awe as the sage flared and burned hotly. Ulzana smiled in his triumph. At first there was no great discomfort, but as the skin on his hand was singed, waves of pain engulfed his body. He blinked hard to fight back the tears of agony, and keep his face calm with a forced smile. His hand ached to throw off the smoldering ember, but he held his arm steady, not allowing the tortured flesh to flinch.

When the sage was reduced to a white ash and the last glowing ember had died, the pain was a throbbing torment, but Ulzana would not admit it. In a gesture of nonchalance, he tried to brush away the ash, but the residue was welded to his seared flesh.

"See," he bragged when he regained control of his voice. "I told you. If you're brave you don't feel pain."

"Here, let me try!" Chino shouted, overcome with admiration. Chino was smaller than the others, his body thin, his complexion anemic. When he had been less than a year old a sickness had nearly killed him. Although he was now healthy, his size and strength seemed diminished. He had to struggle through every phase of his training, forcing himself to do a little more than any of the others in an effort to compensate for his weaker body.

He placed a piece of sage on the back of his hand and ignited it. Tears came to his eyes and he clamped his teeth against the pain. He endured the agony until the flames had died and the glowing ember pressed excruciatingly against his skin. With a sharp moan he brushed the sage away and held the injured hand against his mouth, sucking at the burned flesh. Tears of shame rolled down his cheeks.

"Maybe some day you'll be as strong as I am," Ulzana said, laughing at Chino's embarrassment. He turned to Pi-hon-se and Alchise. "Would either of you like to try it?"

"It's a foolish trick," Pi-hon-se said. But there was admiration in his eyes.

After the success of his self-inflicted test of bravery, Ulzana's conceit became unbearable. His friends were forced to submit to his intolerable arrogance, and he bullied the younger boys, forcing them to do his bidding. Overcome by his self-image of importance, Ulzana had become a tyrant.

"I hear you're as good as any man," San-dai-say said one morning.

Ulzana interpreted San-dai-say's remark as praise, and felt a strong pride that he had gained the attention of his teacher. "Yes. I'm already as strong as a warrior."

"We'll see about that. Come with me."

San-dai-say led Ulzana out of the camp to a small clearing hidden from casual observation by a clump of willow trees. Nah-kee, Chino's older brother, stood in the open space, the sun glistening off his broad chest and the knotted muscles of his arms and shoulders. Ulzana was as tall as Nah-kee, but Nah-kee was sixteen, and three extra years of experience was a formidable advantage.

"If you have the strength of a man, then you should be able to beat Nah-kee in a wrestling match," San-dai-say said.

For a moment Ulzana's confidence left him. Nah-kee had a reputation as a strong fighter. But if Ulzana were to retain any pride he had to accept the challenge.

Nah-kee smiled shyly, but did not speak, apparently embarrassed by the role he had been asked to play.

"You will fight until one of you surrenders." San-dai-say smiled at Ulzana. "This shouldn't be a problem for anyone as strong as a warrior. After all, Nah-kee is only a boy."

Ulzana and Nah-kee assumed spread-legged stances and clasped each other around the waist. "Don't be stubborn," Nah-kee whispered. Ulzana heard, but made no sign.

At a signal from San-dai-say, the fight began. Before Ulzana could react, Nah-kee hooked a leg behind him and threw him to the ground. Ulzana instantly bounced to his feet and threw his weight against Nah-kee. He was shocked to discover that pushing against Nah-kee was like fighting a rock.

For a moment or two Ulzana managed to hold his own, but Nah-kee's superior strength quickly asserted itself. Again and again Ulzana was thrown to the ground, and his face was rubbed into the dirt. His muscles ached from the strain of the fight, and every inch of his body was scraped and bruised. Tears of frustration blinded him as he grappled wildly. Only his pride enabled him to force his battered body to rise each time he was thrown.

Finally Ulzana was thrown to the earth and his body refused to obey his will. He was completely exhausted, unable to raise himself. Tears streamed down his bleeding cheeks as he panted out the words that almost choked him. "I give up."

Nah-kee helped Ulzana to his feet and gave him a brotherly hug. "It was a good fight," he whispered. "You've got plenty of courage."

"Let this be a lesson to you," San-dai-say said when Nah-kee had left and Ulzana was washing in the cold stream. "Remember that you have to be kind to those younger and smaller than you. No matter how strong or brave you believe you are, there's always someone who's stronger and braver. If you're a bully someone will make you eat your pride."

Ulzana had been taught humility. He stored this lesson among the other things he had learned. When he sometimes forgot and felt the pride in his muscular body overcoming this new respect for others, he had only to look at the scar on the back of his hand. Then he would remember.

13

DURING THE LATE SUMMER of Ulzana's fourteenth year, Cochise, the titular head of all the *Cho-ken-en* families, issued an invitation for the People to gather at Apache Pass, where an American had been allowed to build a stone house as a stopping place for the stage wagons that crossed the land to and from Tucson. Because the *Shis-Inday* were a widely dispersed people, a gathering of this magnitude was the cause of considerable speculation and anticipation, particularly among the youngsters.

"Why are we going to Apache Pass?" Ulzana asked San-dai-say.

"The American chief is sending fifteen wagons of presents for us."

"Why should he do that? He doesn't know us, does he? Is it a trick?"

"The American chief wants us to meet his agent."

"What's an agent?"

"A man who brings presents."

From this answer Ulzana realized that San-dai-say did not truly understand the nature of an agent, but he knew someone who would. Baychen had knowledge about people and ideas foreign to the *Cho-ken-en*.

"What is an agent?" he asked when he entered her lodge.

"Americans are a funny people," the old woman answered. "They don't believe anyone can live without their guidance. They send out a man, called an agent, who is supposed to teach us how to live."

"That's silly," Ulzana said, laughing.

Baychen shrugged. "There are many silly things in this world."

Ulzana was intrigued by the idea of seeing an American, one of the White Eyes he had heard of so frequently. "Have you ever seen an American?" he asked.

The old woman paused at the work of packing her household goods for the journey. "Only one. When I was a young girl, an American stopped at my father's rancho. He was buying cattle, and he came to us because we had the largest, finest herds in northern Mexico."

"What did he look like?"

"Ah, he was very handsome." She stopped work completely and closed her eyes as memory flew back across the gap of time. "That was many years ago, but I can still see him. He was tall and slim, and his hair and mustache were the color of winter grass."

Ulzana's eyes were narrowed in suspicion. "What's a mustache?"

"It's hair growing here." Baychen rubbed her upper lip.

"You mean the Americans let their face hair grow? Why don't they pluck it out?"

Baychen laughed. "The Americans aren't ashamed of it. Some of them even grow beards down to here." She held her cupped hand at her waist.

"Ugh." Ulzana shuddered as he imagined whiskered faces. "That's horrible. How could you believe a man handsome with all of that hair on his face?"

"I suppose if I saw him now, it would seem strange. But then I was used to seeing mustaches. Even my father had one." Baychen resumed taking down hides. "If I don't get busy, the camp will leave without me."

"I'll help," Ulzana offered. "Tell me more about the American."

Baychen sat down and allowed the boy to remove and fold the hides. "The night before the American left, we had a fiesta in his honor. There was music and dancing and laughter. All of the women were beautiful, and the men were especially handsome. But the American, with his blue eyes and golden hair, was the most handsome of all."

"Blue eyes?" Ulzana questioned. "Do all of the Americans have blue eyes?"

Baychen chuckled. "I asked him the same question. He told me that only the most handsome men have them."

"They must be a strange people," Ulzana decided. "With blue eyes and yellow hair, he sounds ugly."

"Oh, but he wasn't. He was very handsome. Once, when we were out of sight of my mother, he kissed me. For that night my heart was his."

"Were you going to marry him when you were captured?"

"Oh, no. My marriage had been arranged when I was still a baby. I was to wed a Mexican man I had never seen before." Baychen paused a moment. "But that night I loved the American."

"You miss the life in Mexico, don't you?"

Baychen sighed. "Yes, I miss the old life. But mostly because I was young and beautiful then. When you're as old as I am, you too will look back and dream of your youth."

Just as no fourteen-year-old can imagine the aging process affecting him, Ulzana dismissed Baychen's last comment as the harmless ramblings of an old woman. "I can hardly wait to see an American," he said.

The *Cho-ken-en* camp moved north like a rolling current of dust. The air tingled with excitement. The women and old people would have an opportunity to see friends and relatives from whom they had been separated for many years. The boys would have their first opportunity to see the nearly legendary leaders of the *Shis-Inday*, Cochise and Mangas Colorado.

Ulzana had promised to ride with Baychen in order to help her during the long march, but the adventure of the journey kept him constantly riding off in all directions. Consequently it was Sons-ee-ah-ray who stayed beside the older woman, allowing her son the freedom of exploration.

With Beneactiney, Chino, Alchise, and Pi-hon-se, Ulzana rode miles in every direction, exploring each mountain canyon and desert valley. None of the boys had ever been this far north, and each mountain slope hid a mystery that demanded investigation. At night when the main party settled for the evening, the boys moved off, camping together beside their own fire, and talked late into the night about the multitude of things they had seen during the day and those they expected to see at Apache Pass. Especially they talked of the Americans, a strange breed of people as remote to their concept of life as the moon was remote from the earth.

After nearly five days on the trail, the small band reached their destination. Many other rancherias had already arrived, and dust trails on every horizon marked the approach of still more. It was like nothing Ulzana had ever seen. Everywhere were the brush lodges of the People, in various stages of construction. A murmur of voices, talking, laughing, shouting, rose like a cloud over the mountains. Everyone was happy, excited, and noisy.

Even before their camp was settled, the five boys scrambled through the rocks to a point where they could observe the adobe stage station, which stood isolated at the crest of the pass. Boys from the other rancherias had the same idea. The hills around the pass were literally moving with a tide of youngsters. None of them had ever seen one of the Americans' stone houses. The *Shis-Inday* had no permanent dwellings, and the idea of a stone house, where odors and stale air were trapped forever, was repulsive to them.

Apache Pass was a twisting valley between the Dos Cabezas Mountains on the north, and the Chiricahua Mountains on the south. In some places the hills were close in on the pass, with high, rock-strewn slopes, but in other spots the gap widened and gave way to little meadows. The American house was in one such open place not quite halfway through the pass. From east to west, the ugly, brown slash of the road cut through the high grass of the valley like an unhealed scar.

The station, glistening white in the reflected light, consisted of a red-tile-roofed building and a large corral. The sun stood a bit down in the western sky, and there was an occasional movement in the shade of the adobe walls when a mule flicked its tail at a fly. There was no other sign of life.

"Where are the Americans?" Chino asked.

"They must be inside the house," Beneactiney guessed.

"I'm going to wait right here until one comes out," Ulzana vowed.

"Let's go up closer," Pi-hon-se suggested. "Maybe we can get close enough to look through one of those holes." He pointed at a narrow window.

In the still air the boys heard a door open and close. In an instant all the *Shis-Inday* youngsters disappeared behind the protection of the rocks. To an unpracticed eye, the hillside would have appeared deserted.

A man came around the corner of the station house and walked slowly up the hill toward the spring, seemingly unaware of the hundred pairs of eyes that followed his every movement.

"Look," Alchise whispered. "He *has* got hair growing all over his face. I can't even see his mouth."

The American was totally different from what any of the

boys had imagined. Even in the heat of midday he was completely covered with clothing. A large pistol hung in a holster on his hip, and his eyes were hidden beneath the wide brim of a hat. He did not seem tall or especially strong. His step was heavy and clumsy in hard-soled boots. The four boys watched in silence while the American filled a water bucket, walked back down the hill, and disappeared inside the station office. Then they left the pass, each disappointed in his own way that the White Eye had not been as impressive as they had imagined.

Scouts ranging to the north and east reported that the American agent and his wagons were approaching, and by sunrise the following morning, the hills around the stage station were bristling with people. The warriors gathered in the valley near the adobe building itself while the women and children stayed on the hillsides toward the rear, but in positons where they could see and hear. The leaders of each separate rancheria stood slightly apart with Cochise and Mangas Colorado.

The sun was nearly straight up in a cloudless sky when the agent arrived. He stepped down from the lead wagon, conspicuous in black coat and tall hat. A murmur went up from the multitude of *Shis-Inday* when it became obvious that there were only three wagons instead of the fifteen that had been promised.

The agent did not appear to notice the murmur, or if he did, he must have considered it an expression of approval. He cordially greeted Cochise and the other leaders, personally presenting a red coat, a single blanket, and a knife to each of them.

Then, with an exaggerated display of generosity, he directed his drivers to unload the wagons and distribute the goods to the multitude of *Shis-Inday* who were pressing closer to the tiny caravan. It was immediately obvious that there were not enough presents to go around. Ulzana managed to grab a small string of brightly colored glass beads, which he hung around his neck. He noticed that Alchise received a small mirror, but many of the People obtained nothing.

The angry murmur increased with the sound of blood lust in it. Cochise prevented the violence from erupting. He grabbed a bag of corn and emptied it into two piles on the ground. He spoke to the agent in a deep voice, loud enough to silence the murmur and enable even the farthest people to hear his words.

"These represent the many gifts the chiefs in Washington gave you for my people," he said, pointing to both of the piles. "The first pile represents what the agent kept for himself, and the second is what he saved for the Chiricahua." Cochise took several handfuls of corn from the pile he had designated for the *Shis-Inday* and threw them to one side. "This is some of our goods given away to others while the agent camped on his way to this place." Then he threw away several more handfuls of corn until the pile was greatly reduced. "These are the presents he sold to the trading posts." Cochise pointed with disgust at the remaining corn. "This little bit is the three wagons he brought here."

The assembled people murmured their approval as the agent turned to the station keeper. "Tell him it isn't true. Tell him he's wrong."

"I don't reckon I can do that," the station keeper said, his beard split by a broad grin.

"For God's sake, man, why not?"

" 'Cause the way I see it, Cochise has it figured out just about right."

Cochise had stood silently during this exchange, but when he saw that the agent was not going to offer a better explanation, he threw the presents into his face. "I will give

you one hour to leave these mountains," he said, his features
hard and threatening. "If you are not gone by then, I will
thank you for your presents in the manner they deserve."

Ulzana broke the string of beads around his neck and let
them fall to the earth. The excitement had evaporated, and
the disappointed *Cho-ken-en* began to leave the pass.

As Ulzana walked away, San-dai-say clasped him on the
shoulder. "Let this be a lesson to you. Mexicans and Americans think the *Shis-Inday* are only animals to be fooled and
tricked. Never trust them. They'll act like your friends
until you're fooled. Then they'll cheat you or kill you."

Ulzana nodded. He stored this in his heart so that he
would never forget what he had seen this day.

14

"MY MOTHER made this broth for you," Ulzana said, kneeling beside Baychen's litter. It was the summer after the American agent had come to Apache Pass, and Baychen was ill.

Illnesses had visited the People from time immemorial, but for the most part they were a mystery. The aged and the young appeared to be more susceptible to attacks, yet there did not seem to be any pattern to indicate why some were afflicted and others were continually healthy. Bad air, evil spirits, witches, ghosts, and some animals could afflict one man and leave his brother healthy. Practical experience, remedies learned by the ancients and handed down from generation to generation, and certain religious rites enabled some illnesses to be conquered. However, it was not always possible to ascertain the exact cause of the affliction, and each illness required the knowledge of a special shaman.

Several shamans had been consulted to treat Baychen and they had used their acquired powers in an attempt to diagnose the affliction and drive away the evil spirits. But the old woman's sickness defied all efforts, perhaps because she was too old and lacked the strength to fight.

"I'm not hungry," Baychen said, her voice barely a whisper.

"You should eat to get better."

Ulzana felt a genuine concern for his friend. The sickness had wasted the flesh from her bones. Baychen had always been thin, but now her skin hung like an empty bag so colorless that it seemed translucent. Her sunken eyes made her prominent nose dominate her face.

"I'm too old. I won't ever recover from this sickness," she said. But she allowed Ulzana to hold her head and tilt the bowl to her lips. She took a small sip and began coughing violently.

"Maybe we should let the broth cool a little more," Ulzana suggested, standing up to set the bowl aside.

"Don't leave!" Baychen pleaded, panic evident in her voice. "I don't want to be alone."

"Don't worry. I'll stay as long as you want me."

The old woman seemed to relax. "You're a good boy." Baychen's filmy eyes stared lovingly at Ulzana. The boy looked quite handsome with the light behind him. Jet black, straight hair framed his full face and large, strongly curved nose. His mouth was full and firm, the chin well formed. He was stocky and broad-shouldered — a perfect specimen of a *Cho-ken-en* boy.

As Ulzana watched, Baychen fumbled with a thin gold chain that hung around her neck. She slipped it over her head and handed it to him.

"This is for you," she said. "It's the only thing I have left from long ago."

Ulzana placed the chain around his neck, fingering the tiny gold cross, and smiled warmly. "Thank you. I'll keep it until you're better."

"Keep it to remember me after I'm gone."

Baychen smiled at the confusion she saw in Ulzana's eyes. It was the *Shis-Inday* custom that everything belonging to a person was destroyed when he died. If any memento remained, it had the power to draw back ghosts to haunt.

"Don't throw it away when I die. The cross is strong

magic from the Mexicans. It won't call back my ghost. If you wear it my spirit will find happiness."

"I'll keep it," Ulzana promised, afraid, but confident that Baychen would not do anything to endanger him.

"I'm afraid," Baychen suddenly said, her voice changing and tears welling up in her eyes. "I'm afraid to die."

"Don't be afraid." Ulzana took her hand. "You aren't going to die."

Baychen slowly shook her head. "You don't understand. I'm afraid for my soul. I'll die without seeing a priest — without confessing. I was baptized in the Church, and all of these years I've been living in sin. My marriage was never blessed. My soul will die with me. I'll go to hell because of my evil."

Ulzana did not know what a soul was, nor had he ever heard of hell. Baychen had told him many stories wherein she had spoken of this thing called the Church. He had even come to learn some of her strange notions about gods. Baychen seemed to believe that there were three gods, all of one family, with the one called the Father being the ruling deity. One god, the Son, had been born after men came into the world, and evil men murdered that god — which was a contradiction, since gods could not die. He knew that in some way all of this was related to souls and churches and Baychen's fears.

"You won't die," he said, not knowing how else to comfort her. "I won't let you die."

"Pray for me," she whispered.

"The shaman will pray for you. I don't have the power."

"No. A shaman can't pray for me, but you can. I want you to say a special prayer for my soul after I'm dead. You don't need power to say it. The power is in the words. I'll teach you. Repeat after me. *Hail Mary.*"

"I don't understand," Ulzana protested, confused by the unfamiliar words.

"Please. You don't have to understand. Just repeat it

now and remember the words for later. *Hail Mary.*"

"Hail Mary." Ulzana tried to fix his mind on the words he did not comprehend.

Baychen sighed heavily when she had finished the prayer. "Good. Will you remember it?"

"Yes." If Baychen had not considered it so important, Ulzana would have thought the entire prayer absurb and meaningless. "I'll remember it."

She pointed at the cross around Ulzana's neck. "When I'm dead make a sign like that from sticks and put it over my grave. Then say the prayer for me."

"You aren't going to die." Tears were beginning to form in Ulzana's eyes.

"Promise you'll do it," she pleaded. "Please!"

"I promise."

The next morning Baychen died, alone during her last moments. Ulzana had left her side to obtain some broth while the old woman slept peacefully. When he returned, he did not realize for a long time that she was dead. He sat at her side, waiting for her to awaken. When he finally tried to stir her, there was no response, and her flesh was cold and dry to his touch.

Sons-ee-ah-ray prepared the body, clothing Baychen in her finest buckskin dress, and carefully brushing her thin gray hair. Ulzana and Sons-ee-ah-ray, with help from San-dai-say, buried her blanket-wrapped body in a gully up the slope from the camp, and piled stones on the grave to protect it from wild animals.

When Sons-ee-ah-ray and San-dai-say left Ulzana alone at the grave, he lashed two sticks together with rawhide and laid the makeshift cross on the mound. Then he spread his arms and raised his face toward the sky.

"Baychen asked me to pray for her," he said into the wind. "She was a good woman and did no evil. You are her god and I do not know you. The prayer I say is her prayer.

Hear it now. 'Greetings Maria, overflowing with honor, the master is with you. Blessed are you compared with other women, and filled with merit is the child born of you. Holy Maria, mother of the god-child, pray for us who have done evil, at this, our time of death.'"

For a long while after the prayer was finished, Ulzana stayed beside the grave. He had seen Baychen warm and vibrant one day, and the next she had been cold and stiff. The thing that had been her was gone. It was this thing, this personal spirit, different from all other spirits, about which he thought.

Baychen had lived most of her life among the People, but she had died a stranger. At the very end she had turned her mind to the customs of her birth. Ulzana hoped with his entire being that her gods had welcomed Baychen among them.

15

NIGHTS GREW CRISP as the season called Earth Is Reddish-Brown touched the land. Leaves whispered their way from limb to earth, weaving a golden shawl to warm and cover the rock-bound soil. Preparations were well under way for the rancheria to move to fresh grazing lands when Chihuahua rode into camp and stopped at the lodge of San-dai-say.

Ulzana ran out to greet him, pleased to see his brother after so many months. But Chihuahua had other things on his mind. A fever of excitement burned in his eyes.

"Come in and listen, little brother," he said. "I bring very important news."

Chihuahua was barely able to contain himself until the formalities had been observed. "The war with the Americans has begun," he finally announced. "Cochise has taken up the lance against them."

Ulzana felt his pulse quicken and he leaned forward, eagerly awaiting details.

For a moment San-dai-say remained silent. "How can this be?" he finally questioned. "Cochise allowed the bluecoats to build clay houses and live on the land. His clan supplies firewood and fresh meat for the stage station in Apache Pass. He's offered his hand in friendship. I don't understand why he would raise the lance."

"But it's the truth." Then Chihuahua told the story of how this had happened.

Sixty soldiers, commanded by the boy-nantan, Gerald Baker, had camped at the stage station and raised a white flag, calling for a council. Nantan Baker ordered Cochise to immediately surrender an American child who had been taken in a raid, or the soldiers would punish the *Shis-Inday*. Cochise rightly denied knowing anything about the raid. In spite of the fact that the *Cho-ken-en* had come into Baker's camp under a flag of truce, he ordered their arrest. Naturally the warriors bolted. Although Cochise made good his escape, five men were seized and held as hostages.

Cochise still desired to avoid a fight, attributing Baker's actions to the foolishness of youth. The next morning, when tempers had cooled, he approached the station house under a white flag and attempted to explain that his band did not have the American boy. Baker called Cochise a liar, and refused to return any hostages until the child was safely in his hands.

Suddenly a shot rang out. Baker and his soldiers quickly retreated, but the *Cho-ken-en* grabbed the station keeper and his two helpers as hostages. In the confusion the captives held by the soldiers tried to escape. Two were felled by a volley from the Americans before the others were overpowered and bound.

Cochise stood on the high ground above the station house and called to the Americans, offering to exchange his prisoners for the captive *Cho-ken-en*. Baker again refused.

During the night the soldiers left the canyon. In the morning buzzards were circling the western end of the gorge. When Cochise investigated, he found the *Cho-ken-en* hostages dead, hanging from a tree.

In retaliation he killed his six prisoners, vowing that the grass in Apacheria would be stained with American blood.

When Chihuahua finished his story, there was a long,

thoughtful silence. At last San-dai-say spoke. "This fight is an evil thing. It won't be good for the *Shis-Inday*."

"All of this belongs to us," Chihuahua said. "The land, the water, the wood, and the grass are all ours. The White Eyes come, taking, always taking, and giving nothing in return. We are treated like animals."

San-dai-say nodded. "Yes, but we have many other enemies. We don't need another foe as strong as the Americans."

"This was forced on us. The White Eyes are our enemies."

San-dai-say stood and took a deep breath. "Send word to Cochise that I will fight beside him."

16

WHEN ULZANA was sixteen, he knew by the bulk and power of his body that it was time to present himself as a novice. There was no compulsion that he should do this, but it was expected of him when he felt ready.

San-dai-say had been expecting this for some time, seeing the request growing in the boy's eyes. He sat a long time observing Ulzana fidget under his scrutiny.

The boy was not tall, but compact and strongly built, like a puma. His chest was broad, deep, and full. He stood straight and proud, the sunlight glistening off the cords of muscle that rippled under his lean flesh. His long black hair was brushed apart and fell beside his cheeks, held away from his face by a broad, flat band of scarlet cloth. His face was wide at the cheekbones, tapering slightly to a firm chin. His eyes were bright, clear, and bold; black coals almost lost under his furrowed brow. There was an intelligence in them, showing his restlessness, his determination.

San-dai-say knew that Ulzana would one day walk among his peers as a powerful and perhaps even influential figure. But there was no spark of greatness in the boy. He did not consider this a flaw. Very few men were chosen for the burdens and trials of greatness.

Finally San-dai-say nodded his satisfaction. "You're certainly old enough to begin the novitiate. And we'll need warriors in the days to come. Since you have requested it, I'll take you on the next raid."

Thus Ulzana was accepted for training and was taught the special regulations of the novitiate.

"During this period of training you'll be called Child of the Water, and the warriors will treat you with respect because you'll be under certain restrictions," San-dai-say told him. "Also, because this is the most special time for you, whatever you do will have a profound influence on the rest of your life."

On the four raids of his novitiate he would carry a hollow reed to use as a drinking tube so that no water would touch his lips. A warrior had to learn to control his thirst so that the desire for water would not drive him to rash actions. He would also carry a stick from a fruit-bearing tree, to be used whenever he had to scratch himself so he would learn to think before relieving bodily discomfort. He was taught the ceremonial words that were used only by the novice, and only when he was on the raid. The heart was "that by means of which I live"; pollen was "that which is becoming life"; the owl was referred to as "he who wanders about at night"; and many more. If he did not use these ceremonial words, he would become unlucky.

While he was an apprentice he would be allowed to eat only cold food, and at no time, either during the raid or in camp between raids, could he be gluttonous, or that would become his nature. He must be careful of his morals, not talking freely or obscenely about women. If he were loose, and had sexual intercourse, that would be his nature throughout life — slobbering after women, an object of ridicule among the other men.

Many duties would be expected of him when on the raid. He would stand guard. He would have to get the water and wood and do the heavy work around the night camps. He must get up early in the morning and build the fire and care for the horses. He must stay awake until permission to lie down was given. The warriors would order him around, and he would have to obey them quickly.

There were no raids planned especially for the novice. Sometimes a young man had to wait months before completing his training. But Ulzana suspected that because of the war against the White Eyes, his novitiate would be over quickly. Yet, with the hot blood of youth pounding through his veins, he was anxious to begin.

17

ON THE FIRST RAID of Ulzana's novitiate the war party led by San-dai-say did not go against the Americans. Instead they ranged deep into Sonora to replenish stocks of ammunition and horses.

Ulzana would not be allowed to engage in any fighting during this training period. As Child of the Water he was sacred. Therefore he would be left far to the rear in times of danger. For a novice to be killed or injured would bring disgrace to a war party and its leaders.

But even so, there was danger for him. Sometimes in a battle a novice might be separated from the rest of the party, and would have to manage for himself. It was known that occasionally, youths thus cut off from the main party were lost forever to the great deserts. Ulzana thought about this and pondered until what might happen was almost as real as what did happen.

Several days after they began the trek into Mexico, the raiding party came upon two wagons moving south through Sonora. For three days San-dai-say kept his band hidden, but watching. Their keen eyes missed nothing, scanning every movement, observing every act by the Mexicans. San-dai-say would strike only when, and if, he was certain the risks equaled the gains. It was Ulzana's first lesson in the art of war. Kill without being killed. Conquer and live to enjoy the fruits of victory.

There were five sleepy men, two women, and four children with the wagons. Each man carried a single-shot, muzzle-loading rifle, two cap and ball pistols, and a knife. The Mexican leader rode a great yellow horse in front of the train and carried a knife as long as a man's leg. The women drove the wagons, while a man rode on the seat beside each. The other men rode behind the last cart. The trail the wagons followed crossed a vast stretch of open desert before entering a range of low hills. It was in these hills that San-dai-say chose to set his ambush.

The Mexicans rode into the ambuscade without suspicion. The *Cho-ken-en* erupted from the earth and struck with a savage fury while Ulzana waited with the horses and watched. It was over in the space of a few heartbeats. All of the Mexican men died. One of the captured children was merely a baby, too young to travel on the desert. San-dai-say smashed the baby's head against a large boulder. Then the wagons were burned.

With the captives and the plunder it was a slow journey back to the stronghold. On the second day after the ambush a patrol of Mexican soldiers stumbled onto the raiding party's camp. In the first moments of confusion, Ulzana and a warrior herded the captives into the hills while the others stayed behind to delay the Mexicans. The warriors melted into the desert as Ulzana watched and learned how to sting the enemy and fade and come back to sting again. Four soldiers died before San-dai-say faded into the desert for the last time and headed for the home mountains. None of the *Cho-ken-en* had been injured.

The war against the White Eyes went well for the *Shis-Inday*. In the early season of Large Leaves the soldiers burned the buildings at Fort Buchanan and Camp Grant, and moved away to the east, leaving the territory. Not having yet learned of the American war in the East, the *Cho-ken-en* believed that they had defeated the soldiers and driven them off.

In celebration of their victory, the warriors rode through the valleys, sweeping the territory clean of settlers. Those Americans who survived the raids of the first weeks crowded behind the walls of Tucson, which had become an island in the sea of terror. Some of the refugees stayed there, but others had given up hope and traveled in large groups toward the west. Every trail from Tucson was cluttered with the bones of dead men and the hulks of burned wagons.

Thus, on the second raid of his novitiate, Ulzana went against the White Eyes.

It should have been an easy coup. There were only four Americans, all too busy digging into the earth for yellow iron to be watchful. But one of the warriors carelessly slipped on a loose stone, making a loud noise. The White Eyes grabbed their rifles and fought like demons. Not until two were dead and the others were wounded did San-dai-say carry the battle.

The two wounded Americans were tied to a saguaro cactus and the warriors shot arrows into them as they twisted and writhed in agony. Each time a clear space was exposed, another barb was shot. Both White Eyes spat defiance until they died. Ulzana learned to respect the Americans that day. They were brave and fought well. But more important, they knew how to die.

On the last raids of Ulzana's novitiate the *Cho-ken-en* again went into Mexico searching for horses and easy plunder. They assaulted several small ranchos, killed a few Mexicans when it could not be avoided, and captured a dozen or so horses. But the pickings were not easy. Many of the Mexicans had deserted their homes and moved far to the south, out of the normal range of the *Cho-ken-en.*

The day burned hot on the land, the sun changing from a fiery red ball to a white, glaring spot in the sky. The early morning breeze died in the heat and the hard-baked earth became warm, reflecting the sun like an oven, driving the coolness of the night from the land.

It was a hard, barren country they traveled, crawling north out of Sonora after the fourth raid of Ulzana's noviatiate. The land rolled over sandy hills sculptured by the ceaseless winds and cut in jagged patterns by the erosion of rushing torrents from the distant mountains. The desert was covered with a thick layer of dust that swirled around the horses, got under clothing, into every pore, and crunched between teeth.

The long hours on horseback had made Ulzana crotchsore and neck-stiff; his back ached and the skin on the inside of his thighs was rubbed raw from sweat and his coarse blanket and the motion of his pony. His eyes were red from the sun and the sting of salt streaming down his face.

It was with a fatigued pleasure that he felt the coolness of the mountain breezes when the raiding party crested a rise and saw the huddled wickiups of their home camp.

San-dai-say laid his hand on Ulzana's horse and stopped him at the top of the rise. He was pleased by the eagerness with which Ulzana had absorbed his lessons. When he had shown his stepson a sign on the trail, or had told him a secret of the land, the boy had studied it and turned it in his mind until there was nothing left in it to be learned.

"You're no longer Child of the Water," he said. "Give me the drinking tube and scratching stick. You won't need them anymore. The next time we go on a raid, you'll be an equal."

Ulzana handed the implements to his stepfather. He tried

to feel an exultation. For as long as he could remember, he had worked for this moment, but now his mind was clouded with fatigue. He did not feel different from the way he had felt a moment before. Being a warrior did not ease the bone-numbing ache.

PART TWO
the seeds of fate

Our deeds are seeds of fate,
Sown here on earth
But bringing forth their harvest in eternity.

—G. D. BOARDMAN

1

THE SUNLIGHT streaming into the wickiup touched his cheek and woke him. For a moment he was ashamed for having slept so late, and wondered why Sons-ee-ah-ray had not awakened him. Then he remembered that he was now master of his own life, and that his mother would no longer treat him as a baby.

It was a good time, a warm time, and Ulzana's mind was suddenly filled with thoughts of the future. He could imagine a long life full of honors as a raider and full of wealth as owner of an immense horse herd.

Even San-dai-say's words of caution did not dampen his new enthusiasm. "Your time of learning isn't over just because you're a warrior," his stepfather had said. "What I've been able to teach you is just the beginning. Some things are learned only by experience. Foolish young men don't live long enough to become wise old men."

After eating some cold venison, he stepped out of the wickiup into the strong sunlight. The camp was quiet except for the low talk and laughter of the men, the women speaking softly among themselves, the distant squealing of young children playing in the grass under the trees. For a moment he stood, letting his glance sweep the rancheria, seeing everything with new eyes.

He walked slowly toward the stream, conscious of eyes

upon him. He nodded to the men who sat in the shade talking, repairing equipment, cleaning weapons. They smiled and nodded in return.

Alchise and Beneactiney, who had also completed their novitiates, were already at the stream. *"Juenie,"* Ulzana said in greeting.

He stepped into the creek and splashed himself clean. By the time he had finished washing, Chino and Pi-hon-se had joined them. Chino, having completed only two raids of his novitiate, was not yet a warrior, but he was still a close companion to his boyhood friends. Ulzana sat on the bank letting the sun and wind dry him.

"Well, what do we do now?" Alchise asked.

It was a question on all of their minds. As children and novices, they had been under rigid disciplines. As warriors they were suddenly their own masters, with no one to tell them what to do or how to do it.

"I think I'll get married," Pi-hon-se said. "You aren't really a man until you have children."

Chino laughed. "Who would have you — or any of us — as a son-in-law? None of us owns more than one horse, and we certainly haven't proven ourselves to be good providers."

"That's only half of the problem," Beneactiney said. "Where do you find a wife? All the girls I've met were some sort of cousin."

"I don't have any relatives in Eskina's camp," Pi-hon-se said. "Maybe there'll be a girl there."

"I suppose I'll have to look in my brother's camp," Ulzana said.

Alchise laughed. "Coyote must have been talking to all of you. I'm in no hurry to get married. First I want to have some fun and collect some horses."

"I agree with Alchise," Chino said. "It'd be just my luck to find a woman with poor relatives and I'd have to work my head off supporting them. I'm going to enjoy life for a while."

"You aren't even a warrior yet," Pi-hon-se sneered.

"Well, it won't be long. Just two more raids."

"Don't tease him," Ulzana said. "When he's accepted he'll be the youngest warrior in camp."

"And the bravest," Chino boasted.

Pi-hon-se laughed.

"It's sad, though," Ulzana said after a moment's reflection. "When we get married, we'll live in our wives' camps and maybe never see each other again."

"Men often meet on hunting trips," Alchise observed.

"But that won't be the same," Beneactiney said. "We've been together so long we're almost like brothers."

Chino stood up. "Let's swear to it."

"Swear to what?"

"Let's swear that we'll always be brothers. That way, no matter what, we'll be kin, just as if our blood were the same."

"We could be blood brothers," Pi-hon-se agreed.

"I say we do it," Ulzana decided.

All heads nodded except Pi-hon-se's. "What about Chino?" he asked. "Four of us are men — Chino's still a novice."

"I think Chino should be our brother," Ulzana argued. "Brothers don't have to be warriors."

"I agree," Alchise said.

Beneactiney nodded. "Me, too."

Each cut a gash in the tip of his index finger. As the blood flowed they held their cut fingers to each other, allowing the crimson fluid to mingle.

"As our blood mixes, we are brothers as surely as if our seed had come from the same loins and our nourishment from the same breast," Ulzana vowed. "That which we owe to our kin we now owe to each other."

"So be it," the others chimed.

The five young men were still standing with joined hands, their spirits sworn into eternal brotherhood, when the sound of a galloping horse interrupted their moment of fraternity.

Nah-kee, Chino's brother, thundered into the center of the camp, sliding his lathered horse to a stop.

"The soldiers have returned!" he shouted. "I saw them with my own eyes."

"How many?" Ulzana asked. The return of the soldiers would mean more White Eyes coming into the land and he would have an opportunity to fight them.

"About two hundred. But these soldiers don't wear the sky blue coats. Theirs are the color of dust."

"I've heard of these gray-coated soldiers," San-dai-say said. "The *Chi-hen-ne* say that they came into their land when the blue-coats left."

Hosanto, the oldest and wisest warrior in the village, spoke. "I've heard that the gray-coats fight the blue-coats. The White Eyes are hungry for land as we are hungry for meat. Now they fight among themselves to see who will keep the land."

"It's true." Nah-kee nodded. "That's why Cochise didn't stop the gray-coats. If they fight the blue-coats, then they're our friends."

Hosanto grunted. "Cochise is a fool. When the Americans fought the Mexicans we thought we could be their allies. Soon both the Americans and the Mexicans were against us. It will be the same this time. Inside all White Eyes are the same. Before the season of Many Leaves, we'll have to fight the gray-coats."

Hosanto's words had the wisdom of prophecy. If anything, the gray-coats were worse than the blue-coats had ever been. They hunted the *Shis-Inday* relentlessly in an attempt to exterminate the entire nation. They even offered a bounty on every *Shis-Inday* scalp: man's, woman's, or child's. There was nothing that the People could do except strike back to revenge the dead.

2

THE VALLEY TWISTED like a restless snake between the bluffs of a sharply ending plain on the east and the more gently sloping foothills to the west. An insignificant stream was all that remained of the raging prehistoric river that had cut this wide channel through the desert. Even though the river was high now, swollen by the melting winter snows, gravel islands thrust above the surface like bald patches on its shimmering skin. On both sides of the river bed, lush green sacaton grass, tall as a horse's belly, bowed under a light breeze, a sea of undulating green and silver.

The Dragoon Springs Stage Station had been a large rectangle completely surrounded by a ten-foot-high, three-foot-thick wall of rock slabs. A single gate on the northern side faced the ugly brown scar of the road. In the year that had passed since the stage line had been abandoned, the relentless desert had already begun to claim her own. The walls were crumbling, and weeds were covering the rutted roadway.

Ulzana lay concealed in the grass beside the path east of the station, his stomach tightened with fear. It was a day of white skies and heat. High, thin clouds filtered the sunlight until colors paled and sounds carried flat, echoless. The air was hot and dry, and when Ulzana inhaled he could feel the burning deep inside. His heart beat rapidly, and he was not sure whether it was from the heat, or the fear. He was about to have his first action, kill his first man, or perhaps die himself. He wasn't afraid of fighting. At least he did not think he was. What he feared was the thought that he might prove to be a coward. Making his acts of inner readiness, he waited as patiently as his youth would allow.

One hundred gray-coats, preceded by a small scouting force, were marching toward Apache Pass. San-dai-say, with twenty warriors strategically located, was waiting for the advance party of soldiers to ride into the abandoned stage station.

Since this was to be Ulzana's first fight, he was expected to be in the forefront of battle. He squeezed his musket and looked for Chino and Pi-hon-se. The younger boy had finished his novitiate only two days before, and Ulzana had promised to stay close to him.

He could see neither Chino hidden in the grass only a few feet away, nor Pi-hon-se concealed across the road, but he took comfort from the nearness of his friends. These three were stationed to prevent the gray-coats from galloping through the ambush. They were to block off escape down the eastern road.

The twelve Americans rode cautiously up to the stage station, their eyes searching for signs of danger. They suspected nothing until the first shot catapulted a man from his saddle. Two of the gray-coats wheeled their mounts and tried to ride back the way they had come. They did not make it. One of the soldiers spurred his mount and bolted east, directly toward Ulzana.

The American loomed so large in Ulzana's sight that at the instant his rifle roared and bucked, he could see the expression of fear and panic in the soldier's eyes. For an instant Ulzana was blinded by the smoke of burnt powder and his nostrils were filled with the acid smell. A riderless horse galloped past him and the twisted body of the American lay crumpled in the road.

The firing became general, the shots so close together that they sounded like a continuation of one another as the gray-coats took refuge in the ruined stage station.

A bullet kicked up dust in front of Ulzana, spraying dirt into his face, but he did not notice. Chino had jumped up and was running into the road toward the dead American. Ulzana tried to call out, but his words were lost in the crackling sounds of the battle.

Chino had not gone more than ten paces when he was suddenly thrown backward by an invisible blow. He tried to rise from the ground when he was struck once more and slammed back to the earth. He did not move again.

Above the sound of firing Ulzana became aware of thundering hoofbeats and the yells of the rest of the gray-coats coming to help their comrades.

San-dai-say gave the prearranged signal and the *Cho-ken-en* began to draw back, firing as they retreated. Ulzana knew that he should also retreat, but he could not leave his friend lying on the earth.

Pi-hon-se rose from the grass and dashed across the road past Chino's body. Ulzana grabbed his arm. "Wait. We have to get Chino."

There was a look of pure terror in Pi-hon-se's eyes. "He's dead."

"He's our brother," Ulzana insisted. "We can't leave him."

Pi-hon-se shook off the hand on his arm. "He's dead. Leave him alone." He ran through the grass and disappeared.

For the flicker of an eyelash Ulzana looked at the spot where Pi-hon-se had vanished. In his heart was the bewilderment that was the beginning of hatred. Then he turned back toward Chino. Ulzana must do alone that which had to be done.

He dashed forward, ignoring the danger. A bullet buzzed past his ear like an angry bee, and he felt its hot breath on his cheek. He grabbed Chino by the arms and legs and lifted him over his back, momentarily surprised that the body was so light. Then he stumbled into the cover of the thick growth.

He ran with his burden until his legs would not carry him any further. Ulzana gently laid the body on the soft bed of grass under a twisted mesquite. His hands and arms were covered with the sticky blood that leaked life from two gaping holes in his friend's chest, but Chino still lived.

"Don't worry," Ulzana said, trying to stop the flow of blood with a sprinkling of hoddentin. "I'll carry you back to our camp. The shamans will be able to fix your wounds."

Chino coughed, spraying Ulzana with a bloody froth. "It's already too late," he said.

Ulzana shook his head in a senseless attempt to prevent the inevitable.

A dullness was growing in Chino's eyes. "It doesn't hurt. I'm not afraid to die."

"Don't talk that way. You won't die." Ulzana felt tears flooding his eyes. Chino, always small, looked like a boy at this moment. "Why did you do it?"

Chino tried to smile. "The rifle. I wanted the American's rifle."

"Don't talk."

Chino shook his head slowly. "Do you remember the time when we were boys?" He coughed again and struggled for breath.

"You can rest here," Ulzana said, not hearing his friend. "I'll go for help."

"No," Chino said, desperation in his voice. He clamped a hand on Ulzana's arm. There was no strength in the grip. "Don't leave me." He closed his eyes and was silent for a moment. Only the heaving of his chest showed that he was still alive. Finally he opened his eyes again. "Do you remember the time you burned sage on your hand? I tried, but the pain was too much and I had to brush the fire away."

"That didn't mean anything," Ulzana said, regretting that he had ever attempted the silly stunt. "We were only boys."

"This time I won't flinch. You were right. If the body is strong enough, the pain isn't bad." He coughed again and went limp in Ulzana's arms. His chest heaved once and was still.

"Chino," Ulzana pleaded. "You can't die. Speak to me."

When there was no response Ulzana held his friend's body tightly to his own breast and tried vainly to hold the life in him. Finally, without shame, he wept.

3

"WHY DID YOU RUN?" Ulzana asked. He stood face to face with Pi-hon-se. Their eyes met like knives, the hatred burning deep.

"The signal had been given. We were all supposed to leave." Pi-hon-se did not have the grace to be ashamed of his deed.

"What about our friend?"

"He was dead. Why should I die to save a dead man?"

"Because he was your brother. We all swore it."

Pi-hon-se was barely able to speak, the hatred of Ulzana was so strong in him. He could never forgive the man who had been witness to his cowardice. "It was a stupid thing — this swearing. A man is brother by blood only."

Ulzana spat at Pi-hon-se's feet. "Then you aren't my brother. His death will be between us." Ulzana slashed his finger, allowing the blood to drip to the earth. "This is your blood that mingled with mine when we swore brotherhood. No longer will it flow in my body. The day will come when my knife will rest in your heart."

"I'm not afraid of you. I don't need you," Pi-hon-se sneered. "I don't need anyone."

But the *Cho-ken-en* society was too closely bound for Pi-hon-se to ignore the general criticism. Even though Ulzana did not speak of the incident to anyone, there were no se-

crets in such a small camp. The story of Pi-hon-se's cowardice at Dragoon Springs was soon common knowledge and he
was avoided by all. It was as if cowardice were a contagious
disease that would contaminate everyone who came near.
Then one morning Pi-hon-se was not seen around the
rancheria. Much later it was learned that a marriage had
been arranged for him with a girl from Eskina's camp. He
had gone to live with his wife's people, freeing this camp
from the shame of his presence.

"It isn't good to think too much of these things," San-dai-
say counseled, because he saw that Ulzana was brooding.
"Chino died bravely. A man who has ʰlearned how to die
has learned much."

But for Ulzana, his friend, dead in battle, was a sick thing
in his mind. He mentally re-enacted the events at Dragoon
Springs, trying to determine what had gone wrong. Again
and again he saw Chino dash into the road to be slammed
to the earth by the invisible punch of leaden bullets.
Perhaps if Ulzana had been quicker, more alert, he could
have done something to stop his friend. But there were no
answers. It all seemed pointless.

Then his mind fixed generally on the end of things.
Perhaps death itself was pointless. And if death had no
meaning, then surely he must question the purpose of life.
A man was born, walked under the sun, slept beneath the
cover of countless living stars, breathed, ate, talked, joked,
and then was no more. All that remained of the clay that
had lived was forgotten. Nothing remained of him.

In his grieving Ulzana wandered alone through the
mountains, not going in any particular direction, with no
special purpose. Yet he was not surprised when he found
himself in the canyon where he had entered life. Perhaps
the spirits had brought him here to know the mystery of
why death must be, and how life served a purpose.

Before he rested he rolled on the cushion of pine needles
to the four directions and whispered a silent prayer to the
spirits. Then he slept on the needles where he had been
born.

As he slept he dreamed of a great stone house of the
Americans, surrounded by trees and plants which were
alien to anything he had ever seen. Yet all of the people in
the dream were *Shis-Inday*. Everyone was filled with a sadness, and in his fantasty Ulzana saw himself, much older
and without his weapons, forlornly pacing the wide stone
walls that surrounded the American camp. Whatever made
the People sad was not a fear of death. It was as though
this place was a refuge from death.

Ulzana woke. Although none of his questions had been
answered, he had come to a realization. The end of youth
cried out in fear of death, as the young ever fear the end of
life. Yet he sensed that there were things worse than dying,
such as Pi-hon-se's cowardice. He came to know that as he
grew in knowledge and experience he would discover the
meaning of life. A thing as pleasant as living must have
merit.

He returned to his camp and put all thoughts of Chino
and death to the back of his mind. He occupied himself
with life and prepared to plunge himself into the war that
swirled around his people.

4

FOR ULZANA it was an opportunity to avenge Chino. For the *Shis-Inday* it was an opportunity to inflict such punishment upon the Americans that they would never again return to this land.

During the day smoke rose from the high places, and at night torchbearers hurried through the mountains, calling together the warriors from the scattered camps. Mangas Colorado, Victorio, Nana, Loco, and all of the *Chi-hen-ne* warriors gathered. Cochise, Chihuahua, Zele, Ponce, and the men of the *Cho-ken-en* bands came. Never before had so many fighting men come together to challenge a common enemy. The bitterness, the jealousies, the feuds among themselves were, for the moment, put aside.

Ulzana huddled with Alchise and Beneactiney behind a barricade of stones, about halfway between the western end of Apache Pass and the abandoned stage station. Toward the west, out on the flat desert, Ulzana could see the column of soldiers approaching.

This was the advance party of the blue-coats who had driven the gray-coats from the land. They approached Apache Pass as if they did not expect trouble, three hundred foot soldiers, strung out in marching formation. Not seeing the *Shis-Inday* in the hills around them, their

thoughts were of the water waiting in the cool spring behind the stage station.

Ulzana clutched his musket tightly and waited impatiently as the White Eyes came on. They were about two
thirds of the way up the ascent to the pass when Cochise
gave the order. With a blood-curdling war whoop, Ulzana
fired. The sound of his musket mixed with the roar of others as a torrent of bullets and arrows poured upon the
Americans.

Desperate from the lack of water, the soldiers ignored
their heavy losses as they advanced as far as the stage station before they were stopped by a heavy fire from the surrounding heights where Mangas Colorado had positioned
his warriors. Still six hundred yards from water, the White
Eyes were trapped. The bodies of their dead were already
bloating under the sun, and not a single *Shis-Inday* had
been injured.

Secure behind his barricade, Ulzana leisurely loaded and
fired his musket. It would only be a matter of time until the
Americans were all dead. They could not return down the
canyon through the gauntlet of fire, and to go forward toward the springs was certain death.

A half dozen soldiers suddenly dashed from the safety of
the station walls and sprinted west down the pass. Caught
by surprise, Ulzana did not fire, and realized that for a moment all firing in the canyon ceased.

The soldiers stopped in the center of the pass and struggled to control large iron tubes mounted on wheels. A spo-
radic firing from the *Shis-Inday* resumed, but Ulzana did
not participate. He was fascinated as to why the White
Eyes considered the iron tubes worth more than water or
their lives.

Braving the fusillade of bullets and arrows, the soldiers
wrestled the iron tubes and their wheeled carts up the slope
to the adobe buildings. For many long moments there was

no firing from the soldiers as they exposed themselves to work over the strange tubes.

Suddenly the lull was shattered by a great explosion, louder than anything Ulzana had ever heard. One of the metal tubes jumped, spitting out flames and billows of smoke. For a terrible instant there was complete silence as even the wind held its breath. Then the hillside across from Ulzana erupted in another immense explosion as earth and rocks were thrown high into the air.

The other iron tube spoke and the hillside above Ulzana erupted. The earth quaked and he crouched behind his barricade, terrified, shielding his head from a shower of earth and rock. Again and again the iron tubes belched, and each time the *Shis-Inday* breastworks disappeared in smoke and flame as warriors were torn to pieces by deadly missiles that smashed through rocks and trees, seeking out warriors wherever they hid.

As Ulzana watched, an iron ball struck the earth to his left, bounced once, and rolled lazily up the hill. Zele stepped from behind his protective rock and put out his foot to stop the rolling ball. The shot continued unimpeded. Zele's foot and leg were suddenly gone, the shattered stump spurting jets of blood as the shocked warrior stood a moment, balanced on one leg.

Not ten feet from Ulzana, San-dai-say was suddenly lifted from his position by one of the explosions and his broken body slammed to the earth like a buckskin doll.

The next explosion buried Hosanto, his grandfather, under an avalanche of debris.

The Americans had a weapon that the bravest warriors could not stand up against. Even if they groveled in the dirt like worms, the iron balls smashed them.

In a panic, Ulzana, Alchise, and Beneactiney fled beyond the ridges of the pass with the rest of the frightened and stunned warriors.

Even as he shivered with fear, Ulzana knew that something momentous had occurred. The *Shis-Inday* had never before been defeated in battle by the Americans. The ambush had been perfect. By all the laws of war the White Eyes should have died. Instead, the *Shis-Inday* had been smashed. It was the beginning of the end for the People. With the tubes of fire, the soldiers could come into the land by the hundreds, and they would become the masters of the earth.

When the victorious soldiers left the pass, he recovered San-dai-say's and Hosanto's bodies and buried them as was proper, because they were his kin. But the pain in his heart was beyond grief.

Sons-ee-ah-ray mourned her husband and her father with tears and wailing. Ulzana had no tears to spend. The wells of his heart were dry. He could mourn the deaths of San-dai-say and Hosanto because they had been his kin and his teachers, but not in the same manner as he had mourned Nah-kah-yen and Chino. There was no time for such a luxury. He must prepare himself to mourn the living and learn the new lessons of blood and tears and defeat. The *Cho-ken-en* had been the rulers of the earth, unequaled in battle. The world had changed and nothing could make it right again.

From this day forward the *Shis-Inday* would hit and run, strike swiftly, killing as many as they could, and then fade into the deserts and mountains. But the outcome was already decided. The Americans were too many, too strong.

5

A SPECKLED roadrunner moved through the brush in jerky stops and starts. It paused, snapped up a tiny green lizard, and moved away, unaware of the man lying hidden in the sand and sage.

Ulzana had been watching the American rancho since sunrise. The house, nestled between two low hills, was an ugly, squat rectangle of adobe with grass growing on the sod roof. There were seven people living here: an older man, his wife, two nearly grown boys, a girl of ten or twelve, and two children, still hardly more than babies.

The man came out and drew a bucket of water from the well. His shapeless trousers were stuffed into worn black boots. Loose suspenders hung about his waist, and a dirty red undershirt covered his thin chest. His forehead was divided horizontally, sunburned red below, and stark white above, where his hat normally rested. He splashed water on his face and dried it off with his shirt. The smell of Americans came across the desert to Ulzana, a dead, flat, stale odor of tobacco and sweat.

The first shot splattered into the wood of the well. The American reacted immediately, dropping his shirt and turning toward his rifle, which leaned against the house, only a few steps away. He never reached it. Ulzana's bullet caught him and he fell without a sound. The warriors broke from cover, screaming their individual war whoops, and rushed the cabin.

One of the older boys suddenly appeared at the door. His rifle cracked once. Ulzana was stopped in midstride and flung backward, as though he had slammed into a tree at a full run.

He struggled to his feet, took one step, and fell again. He was puzzled at the failure of his legs to support him. Then he began to feel the burning in his side. Not a terrible pain like the fire had felt on his hand, but a dull, throbbing ache. Ulzana put his hand to the wound and felt the warm, wet blood flowing through his fingers. He fought against the blackness that threatened to close over him. The world became unreal, as if he were standing to one side, watching, but not personally involved.

Rough hands lifted him from the ground, and he looked up into Alchise's face. He tried to say something, but his voice caught in his throat, and he was not sure that any sound came out. He heard Alchise speak, but the words were garbled and came from such a far distance that he could not understand them.

Vaguely he felt someone stopping the flow of blood by plastering the wound with hoddentin and mud. Then he was lifted onto a horse. With Beneactiney walking alongside, supporting him, his pony moved slowly with a swaying rhythm that sent spasms of pain through his body.

But these impressions came to Ulzana as if in a dream. They were unreal images separated by periods of total darkness as he fainted and woke and fainted again. He was not aware of when they reached camp. He teetered on the borderline between life and death. Sometimes he thought that he woke from the delirium, or perhaps it was merely a manifestation of the ethereal world that made him think he felt his mother's cool hands working on the wound in his side, or applying refreshing cloths to his head to fight the fever.

He was never certain whether he saw the terrible painted masks of the shamans as they danced and chanted, imploring the spirits to take the sickness away, or whether he was confronted by the demons of the place Baychen had called hell.

Then he woke, the clouding fever gone from his head, and there was no doubt that he still lived in the world of men. Ulzana tried to move, but his body was heavy and his head spun from the effort. Sons-ee-ah-ray was at his side immediately, her cool hands caressing his brow, her tears washing her smile.

For the first time in his life Ulzana saw his mother as a person. She had always been only his mother — someone who was there when he needed her, but unchanging, unfeeling, like the mountains. Now in her eyes he saw an aging woman with fears and hopes and loves. Twice she had been widowed, spending her youth and her dreams on two husbands. Ulzana was all that remained to her in a lonely, hard life. She was no longer young and pretty, but behind the graying hair and wrinkles there was the residue of a great beauty. In her voice and cool hands there was the culmination of the beauty born of love and service.

"The fever is gone," she said, a weariness in her voice that told Ulzana she had not slept for a long time. "You must eat now to bring your strength back."

The first drops of warm liquid that touched his stomach awakened a ravenous hunger. "How long have I been sick?" he asked.

"Many days. There was a time when we didn't know if you'd live." Sons-ee-ah-ray shuffled away to refill the bowl. "I prayed and the spirits allowed you to stay with me."

He ate the nourishing broths that his mother prepared, and under her tender care, his strength began to return more rapidly each day. When he was able to rise from his pallet, he would walk about a few moments and then sit in the sun, letting the warmth enter into his body and feed his muscles.

He discovered that his mind was now freed from the thoughts of death that had troubled him. That part of his life had died in the fever. He had almost found death, and had looked it in the face and found that there was nothing to fear. Death was but a sleep, and in sleep there was no pain or suffering.

Ulzana put aside his musket and stared absently across the valley, which lay green and lush under the warm sun. A soaring, red-tailed hawk caught his eye and he watched it gliding on invisible columns of air, searching the earth for prey. The hawk drifted north, and when it became a black speck over the mountains, he focused his attention on cleaning his rifle. Every few moments he flexed his shoulders, delighting in the stiff tingle of healing muscles.

It was a lazy time for him. Sometimes he would watch a hoop and pole game and grow excited with the betting. Sometimes he played with the rawhide cards against Alchise and Beneactiney. But mostly he sat in the sun in front of his wickiup, watching the children at play. It was on such a day that Beneactiney brought him the news of Mangas Colorado and the *Chi-hen-ne*.

"He's dead," Beneactiney said simply, without emotion. He took a sack of tobacco and thin brown papers from his belt and handed the makings to Ulzana, who rolled a clumsy cigarette before returning the tobacco.

"How did it happen?" Ulzana asked, not terribly shocked. Death was now a part of life, like eating or sleeping, a thing that every man must do.

It was a short story. Mangas Colorado had gone to an American camp under a white flag. He did not return. When the *Chi-hen-ne* warriors went looking for Mangas Colorado, they found the body of their chief where it had been hidden in a dry wash. His legs were scarred where heated knives had been pressed against them. His body was torn from many leaden bullets. The corpse had been decapitated, and the head was never found.

Ulzana listened to this story of Mangas Colorado with a sadness. Not a sadness for his death because he had been foolish to trust the white flag, but rather, a sadness for all of the *Shis-Inday*. It was Mangas Colorado who had been able to make peace with the many families of the People and hold them together. He had been a diplomat, a wise judge. But he had been too free with his trust. Because he had been an honorable man, he expected this of others. Now that he was gone, only Cochise remained as a great leader.

However, if Mangas Colorado had been diplomatic, Cochise was too outspoken. Where the *Chi-hen-ne* chief had been trusting, Cochise was suspicious. He would not be able to hold the various bands together. Without Mangas Colorado to unite them, the *Shis-Inday* would henceforth fight as separate peoples.

6

ULZANA'S STRENGTH grew daily. Although he was still too weak to join in raids, he could hunt and he took advantage of the opportunity to be out alone in the hills.

He knew the mountains as he knew no person, because he had lived with them and on them until they had gotten inside of him and taken hold. The sunset, or a cool breeze coming down from the high places, or just a stone lying a certain way could make him feel good and big and free. The land was fresh and new, and coming over a ridge, he could feel that he was the first man ever to see into the green valleys. It was as if it had all just been made, clean and good and waiting for him to come along and find it. Sometimes the vastness and the beauty would well up inside him until Ulzana felt he would explode from the sheer joy of seeing and smelling and hearing.

Hunting was good, especially on this day. He shot a young buck, his arrow taking him just behind the shoulder. The buck traveled less than a mile before lying down in a brush-choked gully. Ulzana came up cautiously, keeping out of range of the hoofs, but the animal was dead. He bled and gutted the deer, and hoisted the carcass onto his pony. The horse shied away from the smell of blood, but Ulzana secured the burden and mounted.

He was still at least a mile from camp when he heard

echoing rifle shots. The sharp cracks bounced from canyon to canyon, and at first it was impossible to pinpoint their direction.

He cut loose the buck, letting it fall to the ground. Then, fixing the spot in his mind so that he could find the meat when he returned, he kicked his pony into a trot.

As the sharp reports became louder, he was also able to distinguish the shouts of men and the screams of women and children. There could no longer be any doubt that the sounds came from his camp. With a sinking heart, he left his horse and advanced on foot.

The cacophony of sound stopped and an ominous silence lay over everything as Ulzana eased himself to the top of the ridge overlooking the village. The fight was over, but the signs of the battle were obvious. Soldiers had come into the little canyon from the open end and had ridden through the camp, firing as they came. Bodies of women and old men lay scattered among the burning wickiups and on the encircling slopes where they had died attempting to escape from the troops.

Above the sounds of crackling flames and shouting men came the piercing wail of a child. Even as he tried to locate the source of the crying, Ulzana saw a soldier approach the body of a squaw. The baby was strapped in the cradle on her back, crying in fear and confusion. The trooper drew his pistol and carefully sighted. The report echoed above the other sounds, momentarily silencing them. The baby cried no more.

Ulzana remained hidden, watching until the soldiers finished their destruction of the camp. When they had ridden from the valley, he stumbled down the mountain slope into the ruins of the village. From their hiding places among the rocks and canyons, the squaws and children who had been quick enough to escape the troops slowly came back.

The wickiups had burned quickly, leaving a haze of

smoke almost obscuring the scene. It lay close to the land, a gray cloud rising from the burned embers and climbing to the treetops before flattening out in a layer of cold air and spreading like a blanket, dulling the fierce rays of the sun. Over everything was the odor of burnt blankets, blood, fear, and death.

Ulzana found Sons-ee-ah-ray lying near the smoldering ruins of her wickiup. Her dead fingers held a hunting bow and an arrow that she had never been able to fire. A faint suggestion of surprised disbelief distorted her features.

Ulzana squeezed his hands into fists at his side until the knuckles became white and a cry of anguish was ripped from his throat. Dry sobs racked him, his massive shoulders heaving in agony. Sons-ee-ah-ray lay as though asleep. Only the bright red stains on her chest and shoulder belied the fact that she was a woman in stone, beyond the recall of his lamenting sobs.

Ignoring the wails of the women around him, he straightened her body, smoothing her hair and dress and gently closing her blind eyes. For a long time he knelt beside her, feeling nothing, thinking of nothing. At last he wrapped her in a partially burned blanket, picked up all that remained of the woman known as Sons-ee-ah-ray, and carried her a short distance from the camp. He buried her in a shallow gully, covering her with dirt and stones.

When he finally turned away from the burial place, he took no notice of the things around him, but they became etched in his mind. The thin wisp of smoke wrapping itself among the rocks that protected Sons-ee-ah-ray's grave, the chirping of a single cricket, and a green lizard darting under a gray rock. When he thought of the tomb, these were the things he would remember.

He left then, never looking back, never returning.

7

"She was my mother too," Chihuahua said. "Don't you think I feel the same pain you do? But you're suffering too much."

"You weren't there. You didn't see it."

Ulzana was empty, drained. He had believed that the stunning impact of death was behind him. He knew that he could never become callous to the dying.

"I didn't have to see in order to grieve. But many will die in these difficult times," Chihuahua said. "You carry too heavy a burden from the past to be able to walk in the future. Clear your heart before the bitterness becomes a part of you."

Ulzana laughed cynically. "Perhaps bitterness is what we need to fight the White Eyes."

The long lines for the fire horses had been laid across the territory, bringing more and more White Eyes. Soldiers came until they crossed the earth by the thousands. The impregnable mountain villages of the *Cho-ken-en* were raided and burned. The women and children were taken to be sold into captivity and prostitution. No longer were the People allowed the luxury of fighting for their lands. Now they were like the cornered puma, fighting for survival, for just the spark of life.

Scattered rancherias were forced to move closer together

for mutual protection. Sentinels watched from the high places, day and night. A snapping twig or rolling stone caused the stomach to squeeze and the heart to leap. War parties ranged the territory over which the *Shis-Inday* had been lords since time immemorial, but ruled no more.

The suffering had reached inside Ulzana and twisted his heart. He was a lost soul bound in the frustration of impotence. If he could have given his life so that the old ways would come back, he would gladly have done so. But it was futile. Even as he plunged into his personal vendetta against the Americans, he had known that it was hopeless.

Chihuahua shook his head. "You fight as if this were your personal war. Remember that no man is alone."

Ulzana sneered. "All men are alone."

"You don't really believe that," Chihuahua said, shocked.

"No one can see into another's heart. Whatever is locked inside must be borne alone. No one — not even blood kin — can understand another's burden."

"If that were true you wouldn't be sitting beside me now. Yes, we are each locked within our own souls, but it is for that reason that men are not alone. Because we each carry our hidden burden we need friends so that we may know they also have burdens. Whatever you feel now someone else has also felt. I tell you that no one can experience pain, or joy, or love, or hate, without every other man being affected in some manner."

Chihuahua knew that he had to reach through his brother's hatred before it destroyed him. Already Ulzana fought too savagely, delighting too much in the suffering of his enemies. His cruelty knew no bounds as the sickness growing in his mind drove him. Even his best friends had begun to avoid looking into his tormented eyes.

"The bitterness in your heart has already stolen your sleep," Chihuahua said. "Last night I heard you mumbling most of the night."

Ulzana nodded.

During the restless nights, the ghosts of his victims visited his dreams. He killed them again and again, the nameless procession of twisted faces. Last night he had dreamed of the American with the yellow beard. In his dreams, Ulzana was privy to the agony of the White Eye's last moments.

The American lay naked, spread-eagled on the sand, tied hand and foot to stakes. His face, neck, and hands were burned red from the sun, but the rest of his body was dead white, almost luminous in the heavy light. He became the shell of a man, trembling with fear. Ulzana could sense the American's head throbbing with each beat of his heart. He could feel the tongue thick in his mouth as the sun burned on the naked body and pushed against the tightly shut eyes like a physical force. The White Eye's throat parched in the heat and his screams became croaking noises. His tongue stuck to the roof of his dry mouth as it began to swell until it almost choked him. The light grew brighter until it exploded in an unending flash through his blurred eyes. His mind strained at the bounds of sanity. He screamed a long, sharp animal cry of desperation.

Then Ulzana had awakened, covered with perspiration, his own heart racing. He was afraid that Chihuahua or Oskis-say had heard. But when no sound came from them he relaxed. After a time he slept again, but there was no end to the dreams. More, many more ghosts came to visit him.

"Even revenge can fill a man," Ulzana acknowledged. He had suddenly discovered that there was no satisfaction in his revenge. He had thought that the blood of his enemies would wash the bitter taste from his mouth — that the death of so many men would ease the ache, but it did not. He sighed. "I have the ghost sickness."

Chihuahua nodded. "I suspected as much. Hatred can bring on the ghosts of enemies you've killed. Zuahte is an owl shaman. Go to him and he'll cure you."

Ulzana nodded. "You're right."

Zuahte sat smoking in front of his small wickiup when Ulzana approached.

"I need you," Ulzana said.

Zuahte looked up and nodded. "My power is against the ghosts of enemies," he said. "If you suffer from the ghosts of relatives, I can't help you."

"It's the ghost of enemies."

Zuahte carefully pinched the end of his cigarette, crushing the life from the glowing tip. He opened the paper and let the tobacco fall back into his pouch. "Come in." He stood and led Ulzana into the lodge.

"You're young," Ulzana said.

Zuahte shrugged. "I learned the ceremonies from my grandmother. It's the knowledge that gives the power, not age." He indicated a couch of fir branches and hides. "Lie down."

Ulzana lay on the skins and tried to relax. "Can you cure me?"

"It'll be expensive. If my power drives away the ghosts, you must pay a pouch of tobacco, a rifle, and twenty cartridges. Agreed?"

"Agreed."

"It'll take two days and you'll have to stay here during that time," Zuahte said as he marked his body with the symbols of yellow clay. "You must relax. Drive all hatred and fear from your heart. Let your mind relax."

With a bowl of ashes, Zuahte marked Ulzana's forehead, the top of his head, and his chest. Then the shaman rolled and lit a cigarette. He took a puff and blew the smoke to the east. He handed the cigarette to Ulzana and had him do the same thing.

Zuahte's voice rose in a chant to the four directions, each in its turn. For two days and nights Zuahte prayed. He gave Ulzana food and drink that caused him to sleep and not dream. Then on the second night Zuahte prayed, "By tomorrow morning may all evil disappear and go to the east. May all the sickness that was above the heart in Ulzana go to the west. From now on let him eat again."

On the morning of the third day the sickness, the lust for blood, the parade of ghosts, left him. There was only a dreariness and loneliness and the knowledge that he had flung his youth into an empty void.

With the sickness cured, he abandoned his personal vendetta, and became a man again. He did not forget. But the dreams came no more, and his weary mind found rest. Now he raided only for supplies, and fought only for the survival of his people. Like revenge, war had lost its sweetness, and he became filled with a repugnance toward the blood and death.

8

In answer to Chihuahua's summons, Ulzana found his brother standing on a rocky shelf staring across the valley toward the western mountains. Although Chihuahua was only in his thirties, he had been elected leader of this camp. With the increased responsibility, he had become withdrawn and frequently wandered off, dwelling upon his own thoughts.

Chihuahua did not turn when he heard Ulzana approach. His eyes were fixed on the valley. "It's a beautiful view, isn't it? Our fathers left us a land worth fighting for."

"We fight every day. This will always be our home," Ulzana answered, staring toward the west, impressed as always with the majesty of the mountains — sometimes snow white, sometimes hazed by blowing dust, sometimes shiny with the evening light.

"Have you heard that Eskiminzin has gone to live at Fort Grant?" Chihuahua asked.

"Has he fought the soldiers?"

"No. He's gone to the Americans with the white flag."

Ulzana shook his head. "Mangas Colorado also went to the Americans with the white flag. He's dead."

There was a sadness in Chihuahua's eyes. Like most of the other *Cho-ken-en*, he had grown tired of the war. The invasion of their homes, the destruction of their property, the constant apprehension of death had brought him to the realization that peace was the best way of life. "But this time it may be different. Eskiminzin has gone on the caged earth, but it's a place of his own choosing."

"Can the Americans be trusted? Their promises are always broken."

"This time there is hope. The Americans have given him back the Aravapai lands. They give food and clothing and help the sick."

"What do you want of me?" Ulzana asked.

For a time Chihuahua squatted on his haunches and traced idle finger patterns in the dust. "I want you to go to Eskiminzin," he finally said. "Be my messenger. Speak to him. See what is to be seen."

"What am I to seek?"

"Peace!" Chihuahua almost shouted as the fire came to his eyes. "This is a war without end. More and more Americans come. We kill one and ten more come. We can't win this fight."

"I don't believe in this thing," Ulzana said. "I don't trust the Americans, but I'll go."

"This could be a good opportunity for us," Chihuahua answered. "We're not too proud to learn from the Aravapai. Take whichever men you'll need and go."

"I'll only need Alchise and Beneactiney. Will you be here when we return?"

"No. It's time to move. We'll be at the place of the red rocks."

"I'll be there in ten days."

For an entire day the three young *Cho-ken-en* remained hidden in the desert hills around Fort Grant. When they were satisfied that there was no immediate danger, Ulzana led Alchise and Beneactiney into the Aravapai camp, riding boldly, their rifles carelessly held across their ponies' necks.

Eskiminzin stepped from his wickiup and greeted them cordially. He was short and stocky. Good humor and happiness sparkled from his eyes. He looked more like a fat Mexican rancher than an Aravapai war chief.

"How did this happen?" Ulzana asked.

"We're not a mountain people," Eskiminzin answered. They sat in the shade of an old cottonwood. "When the soldiers drove us to the high places, we didn't adjust. The little ones cried from hunger. I sent two women to Fort Grant to beg food." For a moment Eskiminzin hung his head. "It isn't easy to beg. But I couldn't let the children die."

The three *Cho-ken-en* did not speak, but in their eyes was an understanding of the thing Eskiminzin had done.

"Nantan Wilson has a good heart," the Aravapai chief continued. "He sent food and blankets. When I saw his generosity, I came here and asked permission to live on our old lands. The soliders have chiefs like a pile of rocks. Wilson is like a rock on the bottom. He must ask of every rock above him until finally the uppermost rock, the chief in Washington, says what to do.

"At first Wilson told me that the Aravapai should go to San Carlos, where land had been set aside. I told him that San Carlos wasn't our home and that the White Mountain People who live there are not our people. I said that our fathers and their fathers before them had lived here and raised corn in this valley. Wilson allowed us to stay while he talked to his chiefs. Now we have permission to build our village and live in this valley.

"We hunt when we please." Eskiminzin waved his hand over the corn fields. "We plant and laugh. The soldiers play with our children and help us work. They guard us against the White Eyes who hate the Aravapai. It's a good life."

Ulzana and Beneactiney and Alchise could see this miracle all around them. Everywhere they could see smiles in

the faces of the Aravapai. Soldiers moved through the
camp, playing with the naked children, laughing with the
men and helping them with their work. It was a miracle.
White Eyes and Apaches walking like brothers, trusting
each other as men should.

This was what Ulzana told Chihuahua when he returned
from Fort Grant. "If I hadn't seen it with my own eyes I
wouldn't have believed it. The Americans can be trusted."

As knowledge of the Aravapai success spread, all of the
Cho-ken-en began to dream of peace. In the season of
Thick with Fruit, Cochise went to Fort Apache and talked
with the Americans, but nothing was decided. The older
men, the wiser chiefs, still remembered the fate of Mangas
Colorado and the treachery of the soldier Baker. They said
to wait. The Americans were friendly now, when peace was
new to them, but what of the future?

Ghost Face came and went. The time of Little Eagles
was almost over and still they waited. Then the pact was
broken. It was not the soldiers.

The mob of drunken Mexicans and Americans from Tucson came at night. There was no warning. With clubs and
guns and knives, the mob beat and shot and hacked to
death the Aravapai while they slept in their blankets, secure
in the knowledge that they were at peace. There was no
time to fight. They could only run. Some — only a few —
managed to escape. When the soldiers finally arrived, the
drunken mob was gone. The soldiers grieved with the Aravapai, and helped Eskiminzin bury his dead, but the experi-
ment was done.

The hope for an honorable peace had died at Camp
Grant, at least for the present. The hatreds were too deep
and the blood flowed too freely. The People were sick of
fear and hiding, but the fighting could not end. Men must
have dignity.

9

THE STARVED, withered grass was hidden by a deep carpet of shadow, but the stunted brush and the tall cacti were becoming distinct shapes. Eerie shadows that had teased his eyes in the darkness lost their strangeness as the jagged peaks to the east were outlined by a swiftly growing band of pale green.

Ulzana watched at the stream until the women came down to fill their clay water jars. He felt the now familiar twisting of his stomach and the tightening in his throat when he saw Sy-e-konne. She walked with a smooth, fluid motion, tall and slim, holding herself straight and proud. A laugh played around the corners of her mouth and even from his place of concealment, Ulzana could see a sparkle dance in her dark brown, slightly slanted eyes. Her deep black hair flashed almost blue in the first rays of the morning sun.

Above all things Ulzana wanted to touch Sy-e-konne and feel the warmth of her skin; to breathe the fragrance of her hair; to enfold her in his arms until he felt her heart beating against his. But his desire was pure, innocent of any evil intentions.

Sy-e-konne waded part way into the stream, where the current was swift and the water was not muddied by the children playing along the banks. She submerged the clay jar, waited until the huge bubbles stopped, then carried the full vessel to the bank where her mother, Zha-ah-zhe, handed her another.

As Sy-e-konne was doing this, Ulzana circled around and approached the stream from the direction of the camp. He tried to appear nonchalant, as though it were entirely by accident that he had come for a drink at this time. He swaggered slightly, walking proudly, for he was a well-known warrior, wealthy and worthy of esteem.

"There was frost this morning in the high places," he said to Zha-ah-zhe. His heart was beating wildly and his throat was dry, making it difficult to speak. He kept his eyes away from Sy-e-konne, seeing her only as a shadow from the corner of his eyes. It was not proper that he take too much notice of an unmarried girl.

Zha-ah-zhe was not fooled by Ulzana, but she pretended ignorance. "Yes. It'll be a long winter this year."

Ulzana knelt beside the stream to take a drink.

"The water is muddy there," Sy-e-konne said, her soft voice sending a thrill through him. "Please drink from my water jug."

She handed the jar to Ulzana and their fingers touched. Sy-e-konne blushed and dropped her eyes. Ulzana took a long drink of the cold water and wiped his mouth on the back of his hand. "Thank you," he said. Then he turned and strode away.

He was a lonely man lost in the reverie of love. His thoughts were full of Sy-e-konne and the future. They filled him with a vague longing that was like a dream. He wanted to speak with her and discover if she felt the same way toward him, but it was not allowed. It would be shameful to go openly with a girl, and since Sy-e-konne was not yet married, her parents kept a close watch on her.

He was confused and at a loss about the thoughts and feelings that filled him. Yet there was a joy in his infatuation. When he closed his eyes, he saw Sy-e-konne's full, oval face smiling at him, and the songs of the birds were filled with the murmur of her voice.

Ulzana woke in the middle of the night and stirred the embers of his small fire. He added a few twigs and lay back on his pallet. It had been good to be alone on the nights during a hunt, with an early moon washing the spurs and boulders white, and a fire at his feet turning the air sweet with its smoke. But looking back on the beauty of those desert camps, he could remember the nagging ache even during the good times. Then there was a great loneliness brooding over the land, a presence that he could feel in the earth and all around. Always there seemed to have been the same silent hills, the same desolate blackness about him. Then he was a small thing in the vast emptiness with only his fire for company.

Ulzana could wait no longer. With the first streaks of dawn changing the earth from sleep to life, he went to Chihuahua.

Chihuahua licked his fingers clean of grease and wiped them on the front of his shirt. Os-kis-say and his seven-year-old daughter, Ah-nit-za, were cutting a deerskin into the pattern for moccasins. Atelueitze, his oldest son, aged twelve, had left the dwelling with the first light. Osceola, his four-year-old son, stuffed a piece of boiled meat into his mouth. "I'm going out," he mumbled as he bolted through the entrance, nearly running over Ulzana.

"Whoosh! He goes like the wind," Ulzana said, stooping to enter.

Chihuahua laughed. "Little boys are always in a hurry. Especially that one."

Os-kis-say looked up from her work and smiled. Ah-nit-za giggled and squirmed close to her mother, trying to hide behind the generous folds of her skirt.

"You're visiting early," Chihuahua said, yawning and stretching. "Sit. Share my food."

"I'm not hungry," Ulzana answered, sitting cross-legged on the robe across the fire from his brother.

Chihuahua looked at him and smiled. "If a man has no appetite, he's either sick or in love — or maybe both."

"You're my only relative," Ulzana said seriously, apparently not noticing Chihuahua's attempt at humor. "I have no one else to speak for me. Since you're my brother I've come to you."

"So, the sickness is love." Chihuahua was pleased. He had been worried about Ulzana. There had not been enough joy in his life. Perhaps he had been born at a bad time. The years of war against the Americans had left their marks. "Who's the girl?"

"Sy-e-konne, daughter of Bes-he. I wish you to speak with him for me."

Chihuahua did not answer immediately. To be a go-between was a serious and delicate matter. Success was a measure of his persuasiveness and rejection was considered a personal affront to the agent. Only a close relative would even consider doing it. However, because he was a leader, an influential man, it would be difficult for Bes-he and Zha-ah-zhe to turn him down.

"I'll give you my pinto mare if you'll be my agent," Ulzana ventured when Chihuahua did not speak.

He did not appear to notice the offer of the pony. "You've chosen well. Bes-he has a fine family and Sy-e-konne is an industrious worker." Chihuahua stirred the ashes of the fire and smiled at his wife, who was pretending to take no interest in the conversation.

"She's pretty," Ulzana added.

Chihuahua laughed. "Even better, she has a sweet disposition. Nothing is worse than living with a woman who's cranky."

"She's strong," Os-kis-say ventured. "She'll bear many fine children."

"It seems that my mean and cranky wife approves." Chihuahua gave her a mock scowl. "You've been alone long enough. I'll speak to Bes-he. If he agrees to the marriage, I'll accept the pinto mare." Chihuahua did not need or particularly want the horse, but it was necessary for Ulzana to pay for this service.

Together they walked to Bes-he's dwelling.

"Wait here," Chihuahua said. From this spot he knew that Ulzana would be able to hear the conversation, but would not be seen by the women of the household. A married man must show respect for the female relatives of his wife by avoiding them. If Sy-e-konne's family accepted Ulzana as their son-in-law, the avoidance would begin at that moment. If Ulzana were inside, Bes-he could not accept the proposal because Zha-ah-zhe was there and the custom would be broken.

"We're always pleased to have you honor our home," Bes-he said when Chihuahua entered. "Sit and eat."

"I've already eaten," he answered, accepting a place on the robe.

"Then have a smoke with me."

Chihuahua was too nervous to enjoy a smoke, but he realized that the formalities must be observed.

"You're always welcome in my home," Bes-he said after rolling and lighting a cigarette. "But there must be a reason for your visit."

"I want your daughter to marry my brother," Chihuahua answered. "He has seen Sy-e-konne and he likes her."

"I know your brother," Bes-he said. "He's a good provider and a brave warrior."

"He has no equal in battle," Chihuahua boasted. "Horses come to him like the chicks follow the hen. He'll provide well for your family. If he marries your daughter, then I, too, will be your relative."

"What presents does he offer to show that he'll be able to provide as a good husband should?"

"He'll give five horses with saddles."

"That's a large gift for one wife." Bes-he's eyes were wide in amazement.

"I know." Chihuahua was pleased with the reaction. Two horses were all that a father could expect. "My brother gives this because he can afford it."

"Sy-e-konne has seen your brother and is pleased with him," Bes-he said after a short pause.

Zha-ah-zhe stood and walked to the entrance. She stepped into the open with a blanket over her head. Turning her back to Ulzana, she walked to the far side of the wickiup. "I am going to hide from this man," she said, expressing the custom of avoidance.

Without a word, Ulzana rose and walked away, his feet scarcely touching the ground. He had been accepted. Sy-e-konne would be his wife.

10

I COME TO YOU," Sy-e-konne had said, with no emotion in her words, only a simple statement of fact.

Ulzana had turned his gift of five horses into Bes-he's herd. Sy-e-konne and Zha-ah-zhe had finished building and equipping a new dwelling. When all was prepared, she came to him. There had been no ceremony. They were married by mutual consent and the approval of her parents.

Now Ulzana could not sleep. It was difficult to realize that he was a married man with the obligations and duties of marriage. The first fear, the shyness, was gone, but now he felt the apprehension of responsibility. Never before had he been personally accountable for anyone else. His life had been his own. Now it belonged to Sy-e-konne and her family.

He lay quietly and stared up through the smoke hole in the roof of the wickiup. Beneath the star-salted sky, wrapped in a breeze smelling of new grass and a fresh beginning, there was a beauty that made his heart ache. He reached out until he touched Sy-e-konne's slim hand and took it in his own. She moved to his side then, not waking, but snuggling her warm body against him. He could feel the softness of her naked flesh and it delighted him, once more stirring latent passions. Her head rested against his chest. He breathed the fragrance of her hair and lightly kissed her forehead. Without speaking, he tried to convey with the pressure of his hand the feeling of beauty and love and gratitude that filled his being.

The moon began to rise, silver in the ashy blue of the night. It bathed the land with a soft glow that filtered down through the openings in the wickiup. A small beam touched in her hair, lingering there as though caught in the soft, silken tresses. Ulzana touched the spot reverently and felt a depth to his soul that he had never known before.

Sy-e-konne stirred at his touch and looked up. Their glances locked, their eyes drawing them together until their lips met. A desire and softness grew in Ulzana and he held Sy-e-konne close, his hands caressing her back. The sweet perfume of her moist, warm breath stirred his very soul. Her lips, near his ear, murmured over and over again, "I love you."

Sy-e-konne had been out with the women gathering berries and wild potatoes. The fire was out when she returned, so she borrowed a glowing ember from Zha-ah-zhe and restarted it. The water in the kettle was beginning to boil when Ulzana came in.

"Did you have any luck?" she asked, suppressing her joy. He had been gone for two days on a hunting trip.

He took some of the raspberries she had just gathered and popped them into his mouth. "Two bucks. I kept one hind quarter and a hide."

"Good. I'll take care of them after you've eaten." She knew that he had given some of the meat to Nah-kee's widow. It was the custom to provide for those who had no one to hunt for them.

She did not eat until Ulzana had finished. She watched, her chin on her hand, and after a time lost interest in what he did, studying his face. It was a good face with fine, strong features. Although she had not been consulted in the choice of her husband, Sy-e-konne was happy. In the days and weeks since she had come to live with Ulzana, she had learned to love him.

She knew that he was of the deserts and mountains, where even the beautiful is deadly and life is a cruelly won prize. The land had taught him survival, and he was gruff and hard on the surface, but she had felt a softness deep inside him at the times when they lay silently together under the blankets of winter.

When he was not with her, she came to find her mind filled with him. Not specific thoughts. Just an awareness of him, a feeling that in some way he was a part of her and she was a part of him.

Thus Sy-e-konne grew to love the husband chosen for her, delighting in the touch of his calloused hands and the occasional smile when she told a story or joked with him. Life was full and good as man and woman found joy in each other.

From the time of her earliest memories, Sy-e-konne had been trained for her life role. She worked with her mother and other female relatives until she attained adult standards in the quality of her labors.

When she had been very small, she had played with a shapeless buckskin doll and had learned to run and shoot the small bow. But as she grew older and began to wear long buckskin dresses, she did more and more of the things that only a woman must do. She helped to bring in wood and water, and she was instructed in the use of the tumpline, a strap passing across the forehead and supporting a back pack.

When she was older, during the time that boys were learning to hunt and to master the secrets of the land, she was taught by her mother the things a woman must know. She learned to sit with her legs close together, flexed and to one side, not cross-legged as the men sat. She learned to be reserved, not to show overt friendliness to boys. When the time for her first menses approached, she was told that she must dispose of her pads carefully because menstrual blood was dangerous to men, causing their joints to swell and ache. She had to be brave and endure any accompanying pain, because as long as she acted like a child, she would have a hard time at menstruation.

She was taught the proper way of gathering mescal because it was the principal food of her people. She also learned to build a wickiup and sew moccasins. She was taught what plants and flowers could be used for food and how to tan hides. She became proficient at weaving baskets, making clothing, and cooking.

At the time of her first menstruation, Sy-e-konne had been given the ceremony of the puberty rite. It was an expensive ceremony but it insured long life and helped her through this phase of her life-journey. Before the puberty rite a female was only a girl. Afterward she was a woman and eligible for marriage.

The ceremony and feasting had lasted for four days and nights. The drums beat their strange rhythms, and Sy-e-konne had taken the lead in the dancing. Prayers and gifts were offered.

When the ritual was completed Sy-e-konne was a woman with the duties of a woman. She must marry and bear children. This was all done as White Painted Woman had instructed the People.

11

FRESH NEW LIFE sprang from the meadows and the river banks and the animals. It swelled in the women as the husbands seeded their wives with their own flesh so that life might go on forever, just as the rivers and mountains went on, always new, yet possessing the land from a source lost in time and memory.

Ulzana selected a piece of boiled meat from the pot simmering over the fire, popped it into his mouth, and licked his fingers. He chewed the venison slowly, watching Sy-e-konne as she stitched a pair of moccasins. He was content as a man at war could be. Sy-e-konne was a good wife, taking care of his needs and not asking for things which he could not provide. They had not yet exchanged a cross word, and he had not been obliged to beat her as some men beat their wives. He worked hard for his family, going on many raids and stealing horses and blankets. Even after giving Bes-he and Zha-ah-zhe the choice spoils, his personal wealth was great.

He had also killed men. He no longer found any pleasure in the killing, or the mutilating of men, but he knew it was a thing that could not be separated from war. In peace men could prosper and grow fat, but in war they had to suffer and die or there would never be peace.

Sy-e-konne finished with the moccasins and sat across the fire from Ulzana. "I have something to tell you."

Her words brought him back from his reverie and he smiled at her. "What do you want to tell me now? Did you find a bird's nest under your blankets?"

"Even more important than that," Sy-e-konne said, blushing at the intimacy of her information, "I carry your child."

For a moment Ulzana sat in stunned silence. Then he looked up at Sy-e-konne and she at him. For a brief instant they were each conscious only of the other.

Ulzana stepped across the fire and took Sy-e-konne's shoulders in his hands. He tried to make her lie down. "You should rest. Take things easy."

"Don't be foolish," she said, laughing. "It'll be a long time before the baby comes, and I have to work. Do you want cold food and worn moccasins? Besides, the child gets in the right position for coming out if I move around. If you make me lazy now, it'll be hard when the time comes."

In the following days Ulzana took special notice of Sy-e-konne when she walked around the camp. Even though he respected her wishes and did not interfere with her normal chores, he felt a deep concern for mother and child. He no longer lay with her because he knew that intimate relations would harm the fetus.

He made sure that she did not walk too much, and took sufficient rest periods, and did not sit up for long periods, or lift heavy burdens. She had to eat sparingly of fat meat lest the child grow too large and delivery become difficult. Animal intestines could not be eaten, or the child would be stillborn, strangled by the umbilical cord. Ceremonies where the masked dancers appeared were avoided because the sight of the hooded figures might hurt both Sy-e-konne and the unborn child. The baby might not come out and thereby kill Sy-e-konne. Or the baby could be born with a caul over its face.

"It'll be a boy," Sy-e-konne told him one night, snuggling against Ulzana for warmth.

"How can you tell?"

"Here." She took his hand and placed it on her swollen belly.

At first he felt only the hardness of the taut flesh, but then he felt a kick. The unborn life was struggling inside his wife.

"I felt it move," he said, his voice filled with wonder. "It's alive."

"He's alive," she corrected him. "It's the boys who fight and kick. I'll give you a son."

12

THEY SAT in a rough circle under the shade by the bank of the stream: Cochise, a war leader of all of the *Shis-Inday;* Chihuahua, already considered a wise leader; Tah-za, oldest son of Cochise; Victorio, the heir apparent to Mangas Colorado; Nana, the wise old man of the *Chi-hen-ne;* Loco, leader of those *Chi-hen-ne* who did not choose to follow Victorio; Mangas, son of Mangas Colorado; Juh, leader of the *Ned-ni,* the southern people who made their homes in the Sierra Madre; Goylaki, a most prominent medicine man.

They did not talk all at once, these leaders of the People. Words were careful things, to be chewed over until the meaning was clear. When words were turned and twisted and all nuances and meanings were exhausted, then it was time to speak again. This way the mind keeps quieter to do its thinking, and slowly a pattern of understanding is woven, without the shadow of meaningless chatter.

Chihuahua used the long pauses to study the faces of the others. In a man's face there was often a hint to the meaning of his words.

Cochise looked old and tired. His deep black hair was laced with threads of silver, and his scarred body no longer moved with youthful grace, even though the muscles were lithe and wiry. The weariness, the burden of a leader fighting a war he cannot win, showed in his eyes. The vitality of youth was gone, replaced by a deep sadness.

Goylaki, whom the Mexicans called Geronimo, was young, but already a shaman who had power in war. Because of this, he was privy to the council of chiefs. His body was short, running to heaviness. His nose was broad and heavy, the forehead wrinkled, his chin full and strong. But his eyes were deep, without a single softening curve around them. It was a face that Chihuahua did not like.

"I'm no longer leader of all the People," Cochise began. "The *Shis-Inday* are men. They aren't bound to any other man, so that they must do as they are told. They can decide in their own hearts whether to make war or live in peace."

"That has always been the way of our people," Chihuahua agreed.

"Yes," Cochise nodded. "But the Americans do not understand these things. They are bound to their chiefs. If they're told to make war, they make war. If they're told to make peace, they make peace. Their minds are not their own. And they believe it's that way with everyone else."

Victorio gestured impatiently. As the successor to Mangas Colorado, he was most aware of the treachery of the Americans. "We aren't children. We've seen all these things with our own eyes. This can't be the reason that Cochise has asked us to come here — to speak of the way the White Eyes follow each other."

"No. You're here because I can't speak for the People unless they tell me what to say. The big American chief has asked for a peace conference. He doesn't know that the word of Cochise belongs only to Cochise."

"The Americans can't be trusted," Victorio shouted. "As soon as we stop fighting they think we are women."

Nana, the oldest warrior, signaled that he wished to speak. Nearly seventy, he was stout, fat, and wrinkled. But for a man to survive to his age required wisdom. For that reason his words were always heeded. "I'm an old man. Sometimes my mind is not as good as when I was young, but I remember how the Americans have treated us. Have you so quickly forgotten your relatives hung by Baker? Do you forget what happened to Mangas Colorado when he honored the white flag? Has age made you forget the Aravapai?"

"No, I haven't forgotten," Cochise said. "How can I forget when the wails of mourning come from every dwelling in our camps? Each of us has lost someone to the Americans. But our people grow weak. Now it's time to think of peace so that our wounds may heal."

"It wasn't the soldiers who killed the Aravapai," Loco said. "It was the White Eyes and Mexicans from Tucson. Eskiminzin had grown fat. If his eyes had remained open, this would not have happened. Could a drunken man sneak up on a *Chi-hen-ne* or *Cho-ken-en* camp?" He shook his head. "I think not."

Chihuahua stood. "When the soldiers left our land, we thought that we could win. We drove the other White Eyes away, but they came back. In the direction where the sun rises, the Americans are as plentiful as the blades of grass on the hillsides. Even if we killed all of those who now live on the land, in six months, they would come again in such numbers as to drive us off of the earth. This is a war we cannot win."

"Since when has my brother feared the White Eye soldiers?" Victorio asked.

"Since I've been old enough to know a strong enemy," Chihuahua answered.

Victorio shook his head angrily. "Is life so sweet tasting that you would have it at any price? Do you hate war so much that you'll go to the caged earth where the Americans can kill you when they wish? Where you must beg food from them?"

Cochise held up his hand. "This hand has killed before, and it will kill again if necessary. I'm too old to love life, but I must think of my people. We are not many. In the mountains, sometimes the puma and the bear cross trails. The puma is quicker, smarter, and a better fighter, but he cannot win. The bear is bigger and stronger. In a fight, the puma can only delay the inevitable end. We are like the cougar. The Americans are like the bear. While we're still strong and quick, we should listen to them and see what sort of peace they offer."

Victorio stood. "I say that we should treat the Americans as they treat us. When they put up the white flag, we should kill them as they would kill us if we went into their camp."

"No!" There was a firmness in Cochise's voice that silenced even Victorio. "Anyone who raises his hand against the white flag also strikes at Cochise."

Victorio sat down sullenly. "I'll listen to the words of peace. But if the Americans don't keep their promise, I'll never listen again."

Cochise nodded. "That is all that I ask of any man."

13

THE SUN WAS nearly straight up when Johnson, Cochise's American friend, led the White Eye general and his escort of soldiers into the stronghold. They planted the white flag in an open spot below the village and sat before the leaders of the *Shis-Inday*. The hillsides around them were covered with the women and children who gathered to watch and listen.

Cochise stood in the center of the group, naked except for his headband, long loincloth, and tall moccasins. "My people are tired," he said. "We have suffered greatly and there are only a few of us left. I have talked with the Americans before, and their words have been like the sand. Each time they say a thing, the winds shift and the words are blown in a new direction. We want peace, but we must have words that are like the stones, unchanging when the wind comes."

An air of expectancy hung over the conference as the general spoke slowly so that Johnson could translate. "The Great Father in Washington wants to live in peace with his red children. He is anxious to do what is right, but peace he must have. If he does not get it in one way, he will have it in another. He would give these mountains and valleys as a reservation to Cochise, and they should be a home for him and his children for all time. You will be fed until your people learn to work for themselves. This reservation affords sufficient farming land to support your people. If Cochise makes peace he must live on the reservation and never permit his warriors to raid on the settlers. If stolen stock is found it must be delivered up to its rightful owners. No Apache will be allowed to leave the reservation without a written pass from the agent, and permission will never be given to go on any kind of excursion across the line into Old Mexico."

"The Mexicans are our enemies," Victorio argued. "No man alive can remember a time when we were not at war with them. The Mexicans are no concern of yours. If we fight them it is our business."

The general shook his head. "The Americans are not at war with the Mexicans. If you raid them, you will be punished."

"We are not farmers," Chihuahua protested. "We are hunters."

"You will be permitted to hunt, but you must also learn to plant so that you become independent."

"You say that we must do this, or we must do that, but always it is us who must give up our way of life." Victorio was furious. "What do the Americans give up? This is our land. Why don't you live on the caged earth and let us remain on the open earth?"

"We will feed you and give you blankets. It is better for you to live on the caged earth so that there won't be any trouble and we can protect you."

"If the Americans go away, we will protect ourselves and not trouble you."

"The Great Father in Washington can send soldiers into these mountains until they are like the drops of rain, without end. He can fight Cochise and his warriors until all the lodges of his people are empty. But he does not want this. He loves the Chiricahua. All of the people on this land are his children, and he wants to be at peace with his children."

"I have not seen this white chief in Washington, and he has not seen the Chiricahua," Cochise said. "He sends agents to watch over us. The great chief may think of the Chiricahua as his children, but the agents do not. They think that the Chiricahua are animals to be put into cages and to beg for enough food to feed their children."

"These things do not have to be. The great chief wants his children to be happy."

"Then these are the conditions the Chiricahua demand. We will accept only our friend Johnson as agent over us. He knows that we are men and he will treat us as such. My people want the lands of our home mountains, from the line the Americans call the border of Old Mexico, to the Peloncillo Mountains. Victorio's people want their old lands at Ojo Caliente. Soldiers and Americans can pass over the roads and trails of these lands, but they must not live upon them."

Johnson translated Cochise's remarks and then spoke for himself. "If I'm to be agent, then I insist on two more conditions. No one, not even the soliders, can come on the reservation without permission. The Chiricahua must listen when I speak, and I must have absolute authority and control over them."

Cochise nodded. "I have no objection to these terms."

"I do not see any reason why these conditions can not be met," the general said. He stood and shook hands with Cochise. "It will be as you wish. You can have your home mountains and Victorio can live at Warm Springs. Johnson will have authority over all of you. There is just one other thing. Some Mexicans and Americans have been taken captive by your warriors. They must be returned to their families."

"When the Mexicans and Americans steal Chiricahua women and children they are never returned."

"It is never good to take people from their homes. If I

can locate any Apaches held as prisoners, they will be returned to you."

"Some of the Mexicans and Americans living with us have come to love our people. Some are married to our men. They may not wish to leave us."

The general looked toward Johnson. The interpreter nodded. "Cochise is right. Some of them probably won't want to leave. Either their people are dead, or they realize they won't be accepted among their former friends. You know what hell some of them would go through among our good citizens."

"I ask only that you allow the captives a choice," the general acknowledged. "They must be able to return to their own people or remain here, whichever they decide."

"So be it," Cochise agreed.

The general smiled. "The Great Father has promised you this land. It will be yours and your children's forever."

Even Victorio bowed to Cochise's authority. The People had relinquished much, but perhaps peace was worth the cost. Where once the *Shis-Inday* had been masters of the earth, they were now limited to a land a man could cross in less than a day. But there was peace.

For the first time since Ulzana had entered manhood and become a warrior, he could relax. His soul was scarred with the memories of his friends and relatives who had not survived the war, but now he could regain his perspective on life. He could learn to love again without the fear that those he loved would be consumed by the fires of war. Not only were the People at peace with the White Eyes, but Ulzana was at peace with himself.

14

THE WIND DANCING across the rolling desert had lost its bite and there was a touch of warmth to it. The night's penetrating chill gradually softened as the land gave back the sun's heat. Clouds that gathered in the western sky still laid a white shawl on the high western mountains, but the snow quickly melted, rushing down rocky slopes and swelling the streams and rivers. Rain came in torrents and soaked into the porous earth until the barren desert plants brought forth many-hued blooms and green grass grew where sand had been king. There was a stirring, a movement of life. Newly born animals opened their eyes to a bright, colorful world. Everything was soft and warm, fresh and clean. Spring brought life to the land. The winter death was gone and the survivors sang their joy into the dancing wind.

With the spring there was peace, and with the peace a change came into Ulzana's life.

The oak birthing pole had been erected when Sy-e-konne felt the pains that announced the baby was ready. Accompanied by her relatives she went to the birthing place where she knelt with her legs apart, steadying herself against the pole.

Alchise and Beneactiney led Ulzana away into the hills. Ulzana was not permitted to be at the birth except in the event of an emergency, because Zha-ah-zhe, his mother-in-law, from whom he had to hide, would be present.

He reluctantly went with his friends, already strongly
aware of the obligations he would assume as a father. After
the birth, he would have to practice continence with his
wife until the child was weaned at the age of two. The ab-
stinence from the body of his wife would be a difficult
thing, but it was necessary. If Sy-e-konne became pregnant
before the baby was weaned, her flow of milk would stop
and the child would not grow strong. Also, the more virtue
that Ulzana could hold within himself, the more he would
have to give into his sons with his very seed when he begot
them on their mother.

"Look at Ulzana," Beneactiney said, laughing. "He looks
like a novice on his first raid."

"I remember my first child," Alchise said. "I walked
around in a daze. The second was born while I was away
hunting and I didn't even know about it until it was all
over. I came home and had a son waiting for me." He
looked at Ulzana's worried face. "I think it's better that
way."

"It's the same with all fathers," Beneactiney said. "But it
doesn't do any good to worry."

"I'm not worried," Ulzana lied. "Sy-e-konne's strong. It's
the waiting for my son that's so hard."

"For your son," Alchise chided. "How do you know it'll
be a boy?"

"Sy-e-konne said so. She said the baby struggled much in
her belly and that's the sign of a boy."

Alchise laughed. "My wife told me the same thing before
my daughter was born."

It seemed to Ulzana that it had been an eternity before
Os-kis-say came up the path, smiling broadly. "It's over,"
she announced. "Sy-e-konne has given you a man-child."

Alchise and Beneactiney slapped him on the back and
loudly congratulated him, but Ulzana had one more question before he could fully realize the impact of the moment.
"My wife," he stammered. "How is Sy-e-konne?"

"Fine. She was very brave."

Ulzana returned to his wickiup, his thoughts a mixture of joy at having a son and fear because of the great responsibility that was now his.

Sy-e-konne lay on the freshly gathered bed of pine boughs, clutching her baby. He had never seen her looking so tired, her face almost white from the strain of giving birth. But there was a happiness in her eyes that belied the pain she had felt.

"Look at your son," she whispered, her voice weak and tired.

Ulzana stepped forward and looked at the tiny, wrinkled bundle of reddish-pink flesh that had sprung from his seed. He watched in awe as the child sucked on its fist.

"He didn't cry," Sy-e-konne proudly announced. "He'll be as strong and brave as his father."

"He looks like a newly born rabbit," Ulzana said. "That's what we'll call him. Kah, the rabbit."

Sy-e-konne smiled. "A rabbit for now, but someday he'll be an eagle."

Peace reigned over the earth. The *Cho-ken-en* rested and became strong again. Ulzana's son grew chubby and laughed and brought a lightness to the hearts of his parents. The baby, the new life, was a profound mystery to him. The season of Little Eagles turned into the time of Many Leaves and food was plentiful. Game came near the camps. Johnson was a good agent for the People and they were happy on the reservation in their home mountains.

One huge sadness came into their lives during the late season of Many Leaves, for a time overshadowing the happiness. Cochise, the great leader of their bands, died.

The sickness that had been in him, growing each day and sapping his strength, had finally triumphed. The power of the shamans had not been enough. All of the *Shis-Inday* mourned his passing because they had loved him. With tears and wailing, they carried him deep into the mountains and placed his blanket-wrapped body in a crevice and covered it with sand and stones.

Cochise had done all that a leader could do. His bands were secure on their own lands. He had left them with honor and dignity. In his own way, Cochise had won his war with the Americans.

Tah-za, his oldest son, was elected leader of Cochise's camp. This was not a hereditary position, but because of the love of the People for his father, Tah-za was selected. There would never again be a Cochise, a leader of all the People. If the Americans should break their promises and war should come, then who would lead the People?

PART THREE
destiny

No man of woman born,
Coward or brave,
Can shun his destiny.

—HOMER

1

SHELTERED in a slight depression on the western bluff, Pi-hon-se and Azul quietly sat on their horses. Neither man moved, but a light breeze sweeping up from the plain ruffled the fur of the ponies and rippled the bright calico shirts, giving a sense of motion to the scene. Through bloodshot eyes, Pi-hon-se watched the Sulphur Springs Stage Station. His head throbbed and his stomach felt queasy, as though the morning's breakfast did not rest easily on last night's whiskey. After a long interval, he nodded to Azul and both men guided their mounts down the steep hill.

The food supply on the reservation was exhausted, and Agent Johnson had given permission for the *Cho-ken-en* to hunt in the Dragoon Mountains. During the hunting excursion, Pi-hon-se had stopped at the stage station to buy some ammunition. It had not taken him long to learn that the station keeper, Henry, and his assistant, Spivak, would sell whiskey to him even though it was forbidden.

In the beginning Pi-hon-se had been willing to settle for a few drinks, but gradually his thirst had increased. Yesterday he had purchased several bottles and carried them back to the encampment. In the midst of a colossal drunk there had been a fight, and two warriors had been killed.

Most of the *Cho-ken-en*, nursing hangovers and mourning

the deaths, broke camp and headed back to the reservation. But Pi-hon-se, Azul, their leader Eskina, and a dozen others had not yet had enough whiskey. It was for the purpose of replenishing the supply that Pi-hon-se and Azul rode up to the station, tied their ponies outside, and swaggered into the building.

The room smelled of stale, sour sweat, and spilled whiskey. The thick, choking odor of the smoking lamp curled back from the log and sod ceiling. Everywhere was the special aroma of White Eyes, flat, acidy.

"Whiskey," Pi-hon-se shouted through the empty room. The smells were making his stomach grumble.

Henry came through the blanket-draped doorway to the back room, scratching himself under the ribs. His scowling face reflected his unhappiness at seeing the Apaches. He had heard about the drunken fight in their camp, and was afraid the authorities would investigate to discover where they had obtained the liquor.

"Look," he said. "Why don't you fellas go back home? Ain't you had enough?"

"Whiskey," Azul insisted.

"All right. All right." Henry rummaged behind the bar for two dirty glasses. "I'll sell you a coupla shots, but no more bottles. You 'Paches've had enough."

The whiskey burned its way down Pi-hon-se's throat, but did little to settle his churning stomach. "More," he demanded, slamming the empty glass down on the bar. "Give bottle. Need much whiskey."

"Nothin' doin'. You ain't gettin' no more whiskey here. I ain't gonna get in trouble 'cause of a coupla drunken 'Paches."

"More whiskey."

"I said you couldn't have no more." Henry turned toward the rear of the station. "Spivak, get on out here. We're gonna have trouble with these here Injuns."

"Whiskey." Azul made a threatening gesture with his rifle.
"You ain't gettin' no more whiskey, so's you'd better get
outta here while the gettin's good." Henry turned half away
from Pi-hon-se and reached for the shotgun he kept under
the bar.

Pi-hon-se's first bullet caught him in the shoulder, spin-
ning him against the wall. His fingers closed on the shotgun. The second bullet caught him in the face. He jerked
from the impact and slowly crumpled to the floor. Spivak
fired from the doorway. The blanket spoiled his aim, the
bullet smashing harmlessly into the wall next to the station's
open door. Azul was more accurate. His shot ripped
through the blanket, catching Spivak in the chest. He fell
backward into the sleeping quarters, ripping down the blanket when he grabbed at it for support. Azul stepped into the
doorway and pumped three more bullets into Spivak's
twitching body.

Pulling the blanket from Spivak's clutching fingers, Azul
held it while Pi-hon-se filled it with all of the whiskey bottles he could find. As Azul took the whiskey to their ponies,
Pi-hon-se smashed the oil lamp against the bar. It exploded
in a flash of orange flames and thick smoke.

Pi-hon-se took a long drag at the whiskey bottle and
wiped his mouth with the back of his hand. His stomach
was feeling better now. He looked back at the station from
the top of the hills. Black smoke rolled from the windows,
and tiny red flames were already licking at the roof. He
laughed loudly before turning to follow Azul toward Eskina's camp.

2

WHEN THE DEAD MEN were discovered at Sulphur Springs, Eskina's band eluded the pursuing soldiers and sought refuge in Mexico. All the other *Cho-ken-en* studiously observed the terms of the treaty and resisted all enticements to leave the restrictions of the reservation and join the renegades.

But the Americans considered the crime of two men a sign that all *Cho-ken-en* were criminals. Cochise had not yet been dead for two years when the promises made to him were broken. Agent Johnson was removed from authority and the chief in Washington sent a new man to supervise the *Shis-Inday*. He came with orders to move the People to San Carlos.

"I'm too old to change," Loco said, the old questions crowding into his mind. Was it better to die a free man, or to go on to the caged earth at San Carlos where his people would be unhappy? "All my life I've lived as a free man, walking where I wished to walk, doing what I wished to do. I came here to live even though the White Eyes laid down an invisible line which they said I could not cross. They told me that I could not go past this mountain or that stream. I'm not an animal to be put in a cage. My spirit chafed at the restrictions, but I came so that my people would be able to live in safety."

"Why?" Chihuahua asked, not able to understand why the White Eyes had decided this. He gestured toward the others, seeking an answer where there was none. "Why are the Americans going to send us away? Our warriors haven't raided against the settlers. We haven't gone into Old Mexico. We've kept our word. Why have they broken theirs?"

"The Americans don't need an excuse to break their promises," Geronimo said, his eyes wild, angry. "This land was to be ours forever. How quickly eternity has passed. The White Eyes believe that if we are told to crawl on our bellies, we'll do it. Not me. I won't go to San Carlos. A man must walk with his head high. I'd rather die in battle than watch my children starve in that desolate place."

"The water at San Carlos is not fit to drink and the flies eat the eyes out of the horses," Juh added.

"I don't know," Loco said, confused and undecided. "Perhaps it won't be too bad. The Americans will give us food and blankets. The Sierra Blanca People survive at San Carlos." Loco lowered his eyes and sighed deeply. "There's no profit in fighting. If we run the soldiers will come after us. We'll run and hide and starve. Our women and children will die. The Americans have treated us well here. I'll take my people to San Carlos and see what sort of life we'll have there."

Geronimo looked at Loco with scorn. "I thought you were a warrior. I was wrong. You fear death so much that you'd crawl on your belly if the Americans told you to. They'll make a woman of you. You'll dig in the ground and haul wood and hoe the fields. They'll give you prayer books instead of food. When your people are too weak to fight, you'll come to us and ask for help."

"Yes," Loco said, nodding slowly. "If I need help I'll ask for it. But I believe the Americans will be kind. It's better to see my children alive than to grieve over their bodies."

"Loco is right," Tah-za said. "It is best to go to San Carlos."

"I don't love war," Chihuahua said. "I don't wish to hear the death wails in my camp. But there are some things more important than life or death. I couldn't look my wife and children in the eye if I didn't act as a man. The Americans have broken their pledge and punish us because of what a few have done. We are no longer bound by our word. It's better to die in battle, clean and free, than to crawl in the dirt. Victorio still lives at Ojo Caliente. The Americans don't blame him for what Pi-hon-se and Eskina have done. I'll take my people and go there where we can live at peace."

Despair showed in Tah-za's eyes. "It isn't so simple. If you run the soldiers will hunt you down. Your women and children will die like animals."

"I won't go to San Carlos," Juh said. "And I won't hide with Victorio at Ojo Caliente. I'm not a criminal. My people, the *Ned-ni*, are the southern people. I'll go back into Mexico."

Geronimo stood. "I'll go with Juh. There's no profit in peace with the White Eyes."

Tah-za hung his head. "So be it. We will all go our separate ways. No more will we be one family. The future will show who has chosen wisely."

3

"WHEN?" Sy-e-konne asked. The apprehension was strong in her since she had heard that they were leaving the home mountains.

"Tomorrow. Before the agent comes with the soldiers." Ulzana lifted the hot awl from the fire and held it against the wet hide. The smell of burning leather hissed at him.

For a long time Sy-e-konne said nothing. She was afraid of her thoughts and it was not her place to question the decision of her man.

"Do you think it's wise — I mean running to Ojo Caliente? Loco is going to San Carlos."

"Loco is a fool."

"But if the soldiers follow us, there'll be fighting."

He looked up, trying to read her face. But she busied herself, avoiding his eyes. "I've learned to enjoy the peace," he said. "It's a good feeling not to be afraid. I chose to go to Ojo Caliente with Chihuahua to avoid a fight. But either way, a man must have respect for himself — dignity."

"Isn't there any dignity at San Carlos? Do you have to run to be a man?"

He set aside the hide and walked over to her, taking her shoulders in his hands and turning her to face him. "I'm doing this for our unborn children. Do you think they could have any respect for a father who didn't believe enough in freedom to fight for it? Would they love me if I let the Americans train me to work like a mule?"

"No," Sy-e-konne whispered.

"San Carlos is a dead place. The land is flat, without cool breezes or green things. The water tastes of alkaline. Sickness lives there. I want our children to taste the beauty of the mountains — to know the old ways."

Tears welled up in Sy-e-konne's eyes. "I'm afraid."

He pulled her close and wrapped his arms around her, soothing her as he would a child. "I know. I'm afraid too. But if I don't do this thing, I won't be a man. If a thing's worth living for, it's worth dying for."

"I don't want you to die."

Ulzana pushed her away and laughed. "Only the good die young." He slapped her playfully on the buttocks. "Now get busy. We've talked long enough. There are many things that must be done before tomorrow. And if we're lucky there won't be any fighting."

Under the cover of the predawn darkness, the *Cho-ken-en* left the old strongholds and fled, Juh and Geronimo south toward Mexico, Chihuahua northeast toward Ojo Caliente. Tah-za and Loco remained behind awaiting the soldiers who would escort them to San Carlos.

Chihuahua's band traveled quickly through the darkness. The column moved out into the eastern plain — mounted men heavily armed, women with pack horses, children, old people, mules, more men flank and rear. There was no talking or laughter. Even the animals seemed to be conscious of their clomping feet and walked with a muffled gait. The whole mass was like a shadow flowing across the land.

With dawn they reached the safety of the Burro Mountains in New Mexico. Looking back from the first ridge, Ulzana sat his pony in silence, his eyes sweeping the desert behind them.

Sy-e-konne stopped her horse beside him. "What will happen to us now?" she asked. Kah, wrapped in blankets, was cradled in her arms, asleep.

The march slowed, not stopping, but cutting the gait of the ponies to a walk. The column flowed on around them.

"We'll be safe at Ojo Caliente," Ulzana said. He was not as confident as he wanted his words to sound. There was no reason to believe that the Americans would let Victorio remain on his lands. Deep in his heart Ulzana knew that he would someday have to decide whether to go to San Carlos or follow Juh and Geronimo into Mexico. But for now he did not want to burden Sy-e-konne with this knowledge. Instead he smiled.

"Ojo Caliente is much like our home mountains. Kah will be happy there."

4

ALTHOUGH THE BANDS at Ojo Caliente remained undisturbed in the Mimbres Mountains, they were not isolated from their friends and relatives. Frequently Juh and Geronimo came up out of Mexico to visit the rancherias and spread whatever news they had gathered. They were the first to tell those at Warm Springs about Tah-za.

The son of Cochise had gone on the iron horse to visit with the White Father in Washington. The great leader of the Americans had listened to Tah-za and smiled and given him a large medal to wear around his neck, but did nothing to help the *Cho-ken-en*. The cold, damp air of Washington entered into Tah-za's lungs; he sickened and died.

Nachite became leader of the band at San Carlos. Nachite — the tall, the handsome, the weak. He was a brave warrior, a man of courage, but he was not a leader. His ear was easily taken, and he followed the advice of braggarts and cowards and fools. He followed Geronimo.

"Leave the caged earth," Geronimo urged. "There's freedom in Mexico."

"I was born in these hills," Victorio replied. "As long as the Americans don't bother me here, I don't feel as though I'm on the caged earth."

"The Americans never bother us in Mexico," Juh said. "They won't cross the invisible line."

There were times when it was difficult to ignore the renegades. The *Cho-ken-en* could still live by hunting and gathering mescal, but always there were borders that they must not cross. Sometimes when they were hunting they would flush out a deer and then watch helplessly while it bounded away across the line no man could see, but which held the *Shis-Inday* as effectively as a fence. At such moments the frustrations, the desire to run, were great. There was a two-way pull on them. In one direction was the road of the Americans — narrow, hazardous, but promising peace. In the other direction was the road of the old ways — free, open, independent, but clouded by the stigma of war.

For nearly a year the bands at Ojo Caliente resisted the entreaties of the renegades. Perhaps they would always have remained if the Americans had acted differently.

Geronimo and Juh had been on the reservation for several days when the agent came to Ojo Caliente with a hundred White Mountain Apaches who were his agency police. He called all the warriors together for a council.

"This land is no longer yours," the agent told the assembled people. "It has been decided that all Apaches should live at San Carlos. Land has been set aside there for you."

Victorio was livid with rage. "How is it that this land is no longer ours? When the world was young and the animals walked on two legs like men, we were here. We have not sold this land. We have not given it away. Who has asked us if we want to go to San Carlos? Who has the right to tell us what to do?"

Chihuahua stood. "I won't go to San Carlos. My people won't go there."

"Nachite's and Loco's people are happy there," the agent said.

"Those people all grow sick and weak," Victorio said. "I've listened to the words of the White Eyes for the last time. I'll never go onto the caged earth again."

"I'm afraid you have no choice." The agent made a motion with his hand, indicating the agency police, who had circled the leaders while they talked. "I have orders to take you to San Carlos, and I'll carry out those orders."

Prodded by gun barrels, the warriors were gathered and herded into the agency corral. Ulzana felt a rage build within himself, but there was no opportunity to fight or run. The police surrounded the corral with a circle of rifles. He was caught with the others like a dumb beast. He stood in the dung-filled corral, surrounded by the pungent odor, suffering the indignity in silence.

The agency blacksmith worked the great, leather bellows and fanned the flames in his forge. One by one the men of the *Cho-ken-en* were shackled and chained together. Their women and children stood silently in the yard, watching. Tears streamed down Kah's cheeks as he watched his father fettered and herded into a wagon.

Ulzana stared at the chains on his ankles, not believing what he saw and felt. Geronimo and Juh had been at war. It was an honorable war, because of the broken promises. But perhaps the Americans were justified in putting chains on them. However, the others had kept the peace. What of Victorio, and Nana, and Chihuahua, and himself? What crimes had they committed to be treated like animals? Why were they chained? In his heart he could not find an answer.

5

THE AGENCY at San Carlos consisted of drab adobe buildings scattered here and there on the gravelly flat above the confluence of the two rivers. Dejected lines of scattered cottonwoods, shrunken, nearly leafless, marked the course of the streams. Almost continuously, dry, hot, dust- and gravel-laden winds swept the plain, denuding it of every vestige of vegetation. Flys, gnats, and unnameable bugs swarmed everywhere.

The sun beat on the earth, driving the coolness from the land, and the air turned thick and syrupy with the heat. The rays cut through the cottonwood's sparse branches and left a spotted carpet of sun and shade on the ground. Ulzana's eyelids grew heavy and it became increasingly difficult to keep his eyes open. His head sagged and his chin nodded toward his chest. His eyes closed, his head dropped, and he slept.

A sound came into his dreams, and he looked up to see Alchise squatting beside him. The two men did not speak. There was nothing to talk about here at San Carlos. The men could not hunt; there was no game to be found.

A soldier hurried across the sun-baked yard and entered the agency office. The Americans were always in a hurry, preoccupied with a concern for the fleeting moments. Ulzana found the white man's concept of time virtually impossible to comprehend. Each day of the week had been given a name, and it was required that certain things be done on certain days. The day called Monday was set aside for issuing beef. If the women went to the agency on any other day, there was nothing for them. The day called Sunday was designed for speaking to the gods, so that they could be forgotten or ignored on every other day.

Alchise nodded toward the door where the hurrying soldier had disappeared. "He goes to tell the agent that Victorio has left San Carlos."

Ulzana sat up quickly, forgetting his fatigue. "What? Victorio has left? When?"

"Last night," Alchise said. "He took forty of his warriors and headed for the mountains in Mexico. He won't be coming back."

Deep in his heart Ulzana felt an envy of Victorio. He would be in the cool mountains again, free to be a man. Brushing a gnat from his arm, he wondered if the ways of war were not better than dying here in this alien land. Perhaps Victorio was right. If he died in the mountains, at least he would rest under the skies of his nativity, under the shadow of the peaks he had loved so well.

6

THE AGENT tried to teach the *Cho-ken-en* how to use their hunting ponies to plow the arid land. But it was difficult to learn this method of working. The ponies fought against the unaccustomed harness. The men found no pleasure in dodging sharp hoofs and tearing their skin on the wooden handles. There were many bruises and scrapes, and even a few broken bones, before any degree of proficiency was obtained.

Ulzana stomped into the wickiup. "I won't do it," he raged. "Today was the last time."

Sy-e-konne handed him a gourd of cool water without speaking.

"I'm too old to learn this," Ulzana said, holding out his raw, blistered hands. "Look at that. Is this any way for a man to live?"

"I'll put some grease on them," Sy-e-konne offered.

"It isn't only my hands. Everything about this way is bad. The harness cuts my pony. You should see the sores on his chest and haunches. Then the flies get into the wounds and in this heat, they fester before you can do anything about it. Beneactiney's already lost two good horses."

"Rest now. You'll feel better in the morning."

"I won't feel better. The earth is full of stones that break the plow. Nothing will grow here anyway. There's no water. I'm a warrior, not a farmer. The caged earth is a bad place. Perhaps we should run away and join Victorio?"

"Is it better to crawl into the earth like a snake? If we try hard enough we can make this life work."

"If we try hard enough! That's all I ever hear. I say we've already tried too hard. Who decided their way is better?"

"They're stronger. It's the way of things to follow the strongest."

"Enough! I don't want to hear any more about stronger or weaker. I'm through learning their ways. Our people have always lived in villages with our lodges side by side. We've always hunted and fought together. If we farm, we must work alone and see our neighbors only once in a while. It's unsociable and lonely. People weren't meant to live that way."

Sy-e-konne sighed. "I know it isn't easy."

"Everything we do is wrong. The agent tells us to cut wood in the summer when it's hot, to use in the winter when it's cold. We're supposed to cut grass before the frost, and dry corn and beans and save sugar and flour. When we don't the agent says we're lazy and stupid." Ulzana had grown up in a society that used and enjoyed whatever food and fuel and pasture was at hand, and then moved on to where there was more. It was the natural way to live. "I tell you I'm too old to learn these strange ways."

"Please, for Kah and me. Try a little longer."

Ulzana was too tired and discouraged to argue. "All right, I'll try for a while longer. But I won't live as a farmer forever."

Sy-e-konne laid a gentle hand on his shoulder. "Just try it for a little bit longer."

Ulzana stopped at the end of a furrow and, with the back of his hand, wiped the sweat from his brow. His red headband was soaked through, no longer stopping the rivulets of perspiration that stung his eyes. His back ached from the strain of bending, and muscles he had never used before screamed out in resentment of the labor.

Flexing his shoulders against the stiffness, he examined his pony's sores where the harness had already rubbed away the flesh. First he applied a layer of animal fat and then attempted to cushion the raw spots with folded pieces of cloth. Turning, he watched Beneactiney lifting and moving the larger boulders.

Ulzana was about to start another furrow when he heard soft steps behind him. Sy-e-konne set down the leather bucket and waited while Ulzana took the gourd dipper and drank. The cool moisture opened his throat, closed by the swirling, stifling clouds of dust that his crude plowing had raised. He took another drink and swished the water in his mouth before swallowing.

"How is it going?" Sy-e-konne asked.

Her voice was no longer musical. The heat and dust and insects and lack of food were making her old. Her eyes were inflamed from the wind and sand, drawn in from constant squinting into the steady glare of white-hot sun. Her skin was sunburned and rough, creased by a thousand wrinkles of worry and weariness. The once-soft black hair was bleached and brittle from the weather and, instead of falling in supple locks, was swept back and tied behind her head like an old woman's. Her hands were raw and red, with each joint standing out sharply.

"This land wasn't meant for growing things," Ulzana answered, picking at a broken blister on the palm of his hand. He saw the look of despair in Sy-e-konne's eyes and tried to smile. "But I can farm as well as I can hunt. If anything will live here, I'll make it grow."

Ulzana stood a moment watching her carry water to Beneactiney. There was a listlessness to her step and a sagging to her shoulders. The terrible emptiness of this vast desert, where they were forced to live, was too much for her. This land was too hard. The hot sun dried and baked everything. It wrinkled and burned, turning the soil to dust, which grated on the skin like sandpaper.

He had also noticed the harshness of the land reflected in Kah's eyes. There was no longer a hint of childish fun and laughter in them. It was a sad thing, a thing that gnawed at Ulzana's heart.

He attempted to combat the despair. He laughed and smiled, trying to show his wife and son that there could be joy in this place. But even as he tried, he knew he was failing. His laughter had no mirth and his smile had no depth.

The corn that Ulzana and Beneactiney planted did not prosper. Tilling the soil was alien to them, but they listened to the agent and tried to learn the ways of a farmer. They dug furrows for the seed and fought the weeds that threatened to choke the new plants. But the agent came from a land where rain fed the vegetation all summer and a man had little else to do but throw seeds on the rich soil and watch them grow into abundant crops. In this land there was never enough water. The corn burned and withered as soon as the tender shoots pushed up out of the earth. Those plants that survived the heat and drought were consumed by grasshoppers and locusts that swarmed in and ate everything.

Ulzana and Beneactiney fought for their crop as hard as they had ever fought for anything. They carried water from the creek in leather buckets and poured it on the young, green sprouts until their backs were stooped from the weight and their arms ached from the lifting. But they could not bring it fast enough. The water that did not evaporate into the dry air quickly sank into the porous earth below where the searching roots could find it.

The stalks grew, but they were stunted and weak. When

the small, shriveled ears of corn appeared, their slight weight bent the weakened stalks which should have stood straight and tall. The leaves withered and turned brown in the heat. When the corn was harvested, the kernels were small and bitter, barely covering the cobs. The entire spring and summer, the tears and prayers, the aching muscles, the lost vitality — all were wasted.

Ulzana felt the nagging pangs of hunger in his belly, but the ache in his heart pained him more. He could endure famine because he was a man and had learned to bear discomfort. But Sy-e-konne and Kah depended on him for food and blankets and security, and he could not provide them. It was a hard thing for Ulzana to watch their suffering. When he faced the starvation of his family and could do nothing to help them, something inside of him died that would never heal.

"That isn't enough food for us," Ulzana complained, examining the small piece of meat and hide that Sy-e-konne had gotten at the agency.

"It's all they gave me," she answered, her voice betraying her own disappointment. "Some of the others got even less."

"When I was a boy I saw the Americans give gifts," Ulzana said. "Cochise was right. First they take what they want and give the rest to us. We can't live on this."

When the fleshless old cattle were killed and divided among the hungry mouths, everything had to be eaten: the horns, the hoofs, and even the hide. The bones were broken and the marrow was sucked out.

When there was no food in his kettle, Ulzana frequently broke the rules and left the reservation to hunt in the hills for fresh meat. But there was little game to be found. Once he brought back a gaunt doe, too weak to find its way into the distant mountains, but usually there was nothing. He considered it a successful hunt if he brought back a rabbit or an occasional bird. But these small animals did not go far among all the empty bellies.

The time of Ghost Face approached and the *Cho-ken-en* were hungry. But they remained on the reservation. They would try the ways of peace as long as there was strength in their bodies.

7

ULZANA SQUATTED in the doorway of his wickiup, in a futile effort to find a breath of cool, fresh air. Nothing stirred. He could hear Sy-e-konne behind him in the darkness of the squalid lodge, trying to sleep in the stifling heat. Kah, now five years old, slept fitfully beside his mother.

The moon was just a thin yellow sliver above the distant mountain rims, and the desert around him was thick with shadow. He thought he saw a movement in the gloom near Chihuahua's lodge. The shadow stirred again, and this time he recognized the shape of a man.

Ulzana eased himself out of the doorway and silently made his way across the small stretch of desert, moving so slowly that he did not seem to be moving at all. The shadow became distinct, hunched in the darkness, not yet aware of Ulzana. Shiny gold buttons of an Army coat glistened in the night. He was almost ready to plunge his knife into the man when he recognized Alchise.

"What are you doing here?" Ulzana asked, deliberately turning his knife so that the moonlight sparkled off of the blade.

"I didn't want to frighten you with my new coat," Alchise said.

"Did you kill a soldier?"

Alchise laughed. "No. I wear the coat because I'm now a soldier."

"You! A soldier!"

"It's better than watching my family starve. The Americans pay me money to be a scout."

In the darkness Ulzana shook his head. "But it would mean going against our own people."

"We don't have to fight. The soldiers do that. We only have to show them the trail."

"It's a hard thing — going against our friends."

"These are difficult times. We have to do many hard things."

Ulzana thought of Kah's lean belly. "How do I become a scout?" he asked.

"Go to the agency. They'll give you a blue coat and put your name on the paper."

Ulzana sighed. He did not want to help the Army, but he had to do something. Perhaps Alchise was right. Maybe a man could do this and still retain his honor. With this thought Ulzana made his decision. "I'll go to see the agent tomorrow."

8

THE SUN SLIPPED into the pocket of sky behind the sharp western peaks and melted. Molten fingers of red and orange probed the sky, touching, then staining the cotton clouds with fiery hues. The night's deep blue-black swept from the east and scrubbed the sky, washing the colors back toward the pocket until only a red rim remained over the jagged peaks. Finally that too was cleansed away and the sky was clear black, salted with stars.

Cook fires blazed in the pitch black of the desert, making little rooms of light where the soldiers huddled, secure within the walls of darkness.

While the troopers ate their ration of salt pork and bacon, Ulzana and Alchise crouched in the shadows away from the fires and ate their own supply of jerky.

Victorio had come north of the border, raiding into Arizona and New Mexico. Ulzana and Alchise had been assigned to a patrol from Fort Apache that was scouting down the San Pedro Valley, south of Tucson.

From the camp fires the voices of the soldiers drifted on the night air. Ulzana listened, trying to comprehend this language. A harsh voice, one that Ulzana recognized, spoke. It was Private Sytkowski. Since the first day that Ulzana had been a scout, Sytkowski had made it apparent that he thought the Apaches were animals, beneath the dignity of men.

"As far as I'm concerned, all the trouble out here is caused by them damned 'Paches," Sytkowski said, his voice edged with contempt. "The only good 'Pache is a dead one, and the only use to make of 'em is fertilizer."

"Come on, Sytkowski," Kautz said. "You know that ain't true. There's good 'Paches and bad ones, just like us."

"I still say that the quicker them murderin' Injuns are killed off, the quicker I'll get a good night's sleep."

"How come you're so bitter against 'em?"

"Just wait until you've seen what those savages do to white women. When you've seen 'em staked out in the sun, the flies thick on their bloated bodies, or the little kids with their heads smashed in, or some poor guy lashed over a fire until his brains are roasted, you'll know what I mean." There was a long silence because no one knew how to answer Sytkowski's rage and hatred.

"They're fightin' for their lands," Private Rutherford said. "It's a war."

"You can take this war and stuff it. The Mexes had the right idea. A bounty on scalps. Kill 'em all. Every man, woman, and child, just like you'd kill so many rattlesnakes."

"I don't hold with killin' women and kids," Kautz argued.

"The squaws are the worst ones," Sytkowski said. "They just love to torture prisoners. And what do we do about it? Nothin'. We pamper the redskin bastards."

A footstep sounded near Ulzana and he turned away, glad for the interruption. The sound of hatred was making him sick.

Lieutenant William Creighton squatted on the ground beside his scout. "*Jeunie*," he said, using the Apache greeting. Not many Americans took the trouble to learn even a few words.

Creighton was a new soldier, still soft and untested, but Ulzana liked him. He had courage and was not afraid to ask questions and accept the advice of his scouts.

"Do you know Victorio?" Creighton asked in English. It was not an officer speaking with a soldier, but two men talking as equals.

"Yes," Ulzana answered, the unfamiliar language rolling roughly off his tongue.

"What sort of man is he?"

Ulzana shrugged. "He is a man like other men. Braver than some. Smarter than some."

"Do you think we'll be able to catch him?"

"The soldiers are too slow," Ulzana said, shaking his head. "Victorio goes faster on foot than we do with the horses."

"Will he come back to San Carlos?"

"No. For him the caged earth is — is — I do not know the words. He is like the eagle. He dies in a cage."

There was a long pause. "What do you think he'll do now?" Creighton asked.

"It is hard to read another man's thoughts." Ulzana turned over in his mind what he would do if he were Victorio and the soldiers were following him. "He will keep scouts out watching the soldiers. When they stop he will stop. He will run when they run. If there are too many soldiers, or if they come too close, he will fight. But mostly he will run."

"He'll have to stop running some time. No one can run forever."

"The Apache is used to running." There was a slight hint of bitterness in Ulzana's voice.

"Well, what would you do to catch him?" Creighton asked, ignoring the scout's tone.

Ulzana was silent a moment, and noticed with respect that the young officer waited patiently for an answer. Most of the Americans were in too much of a hurry, and had to speak before they could think. "The fires are no good," he said at last. "In the night Victorio can see them for miles."

"I'll have them put out."

"It is too late for that. His scouts have already seen."

"What do you suggest?"

"Victorio thinks the soldiers are sleeping. If we sleep now, for half of the night, and then march, we will gain much time. As long as Victorio thinks that the soldiers are here, he will stop to rest."

Creighton stood. "Sergeant Hoffman," he called.

A figure detached itself from the group around one of the fires and trotted over. "Yes, sir," Sergeant Hoffman said.

"Bed the men down," Creighton ordered. "In two hours we'll resume the march. Detail four men to stay behind as fire tenders. They are to keep the fires burning for twenty minutes after we leave, and then rejoin the patrol. Have the rest of the men secure their spurs and any other equipment that might rattle."

Sergeant Hoffman moved off, and Ulzana smiled in the darkness. This man, Creighton, would be a big chief some day.

9

IT WAS BETWEEN one and two o'clock when a rough hand on his shoulder shook Lieutenant Creighton. He came awake and bolt upright instantly. Ulzana was beside him.

"It's time."

Creighton rubbed the sleep from his eyes. The cold dampness made him shiver. "Don't you ever sleep?" he asked.

"When it is necessary," Ulzana answered.

Creighton was still too new to this land to completely appreciate the strangeness of the Apaches. They never seemed to sleep, yet they never appeared to be tired. He shrugged. "Wake up Sergeant Hoffman."

A shadow crossed in front of him. "I'm ready, sir," Hoffman whispered.

"Good. Wake the troops and prepare to move out. No unnecessary talking or noise."

"Yes, sir."

In ten minutes the patrol was moving northwesterly up the ghostly valley, leading their mounts. Alchise and Ulzana disappeared into the night as they pushed ahead and to the flanks, scouting the terrain, and checking for signs. Ulzana stayed closer to the patrol, disappearing and reappearing, like a bird dog on a good scent, constantly keeping Creighton apprised of the situation and on the correct trail.

The moon was obscured by high clouds, and the desert was black. Creighton tried to pick his way carefully, but he could not see the sharp leaves of the yucca plant, or the thorns, or the needles of the prickly pear and barrel cacti that stabbed at his legs and stuck through his cavalry trousers. Knifelike rocks cut into his boots and attempted to twist unsuspecting ankles. A trooper, also blinded by the darkness, stumbled in a hole or crevice, and a soft curse rent the air.

"Sergeant Hoffman," Creighton whispered.

"Yes, sir."

"Get the name of the man who just cursed. Pass the word that anyone else who makes a sound will spend the next thirty days in the guard house."

"Yes, sir."

"And have the men mount up. We'll ride for an hour."

This is a hell of a country, Creighton thought as he allowed his mount to pick a path, leaving him free to think. In the vastness, the barrenness of this territory, there was something that made a man turn into himself. As he traveled the dark night, Creighton reminisced about the things that had brought him to this desert.

Even when he had been a little boy, he had dreamed of being a soldier. His first memories were of the War of Rebellion, and his father, Hiram B. Creighton, a major in the Sixth Pennsylvania Cavalry. During the winter of 1863, when the Army of the Potomac was in winter quarters around Washington, Major Creighton had been able to come home on leave. He could remember the smells of tobacco and sweat and liniment and mildew that lingered around Major Creighton when the war stories unfolded like a rippling battle flag. Squadrons of cavalry charged together on magnificent horses. Sabers flashed. Cannons roared. Then being a soldier was not enough. William had to be a cavalryman.

When the news came, in early May, 1865, that Hiram

Creighton had been killed in a foreign place called the Wilderness, William's resolve for a military career was not diminished.

He realized early that if a man were going to be a soldier, it was not enough to merely enlist. He should be an officer. A career officer should go to the academy at West Point. Thus, the idea became an obsession. He badgered his congressman, almost becoming a fixture in the dusty old office. His persistence resulted in an official letter of acceptance to the military academy.

The initial year at the academy was extremely difficult for a boy away from his family for the first time. But an elegant pride in the tight, short-jacketed gray uniform with the rows of shiny buttons sustained him. Although he was not a good scholar, he applied himself diligently and managed to remain in the top half of his class.

It was during the summer between his second and third years at the academy that he first noticed Emma Anderson. He had known her all of his life, but had never paid any attention to the skinny, freckle-faced girl. However, Emma had suddenly grown up. When he was introduced to her at a dance, he was certain that he had never seen anyone prettier. Other young men had also appreciated her beauty. There was always a long line of admirers, and Emma gave no hint that she favored anyone.

When his summer leave was ended, he wrote a long letter every week and once a month he received a reply. There was no talk of love, but between the bland sentences, there was a hint of growing affection.

By the time he graduated and received his commission as second lieutenant of cavalry, he knew that he was in love.

As he rode through the darkness, swaying to the rhythm of his horse, he remembered the last time he had seen Emma. It was the night before he had left for his first duty post, Fort Apache, Arizona Territory.

They had sat together on the porch of her father's house,

letting the warm summer air serenade them with the music of the crickets. Creighton had felt brave and handsome in his stiff new uniform. He could not imagine what his new assignment would be like, but he felt pride in being sent to the Apache country of Arizona.

"It might be dangerous with those savages," Emma had said. "I'm afraid for you, Bill."

"There's nothing to be afraid of. I can take care of myself." But Creighton had felt a tightening of his throat when he saw the genuine concern in Emma's eyes.

"Do be careful," she had said, her voice soft and musical.

"I will." He felt a dryness in his throat. "Emma, will you wait for me?"

"Oh, yes."

They had kissed then, and Creighton could still feel the warmth and softness of her lips, and the beating of his own heart in his desire for her.

But Fort Apache and Arizona Territory had proven to be unglamorous. It was hot and boring and dirty. He was glad that Emma was not here to suffer. He had watched the women wither in this territory. Even the Indian women grew old and haggard before their time. What the earth and sun failed to destroy, the Apaches did. Always they hung over the land like the shadow of a vulture. The women grew old and weak bearing children and burying their men.

The darkness was beginning to break when Alchise and Ulzana returned from their scout. They spoke in whispered tones. Creighton had never become accustomed to the sound of their language. The speech was guttural, indistinct, hissing, beginning in the mouth and dying away down the throat.

"What is it?" he asked, stopping the patrol.

"Victorio has been this way. Three, maybe four hours ago."

"Good. Then we should catch up with him."

Ulzana nodded. There was a look of something held back.

"What else?"

"A small rancho. Victorio was there. The Americans are dead."

"How far?"

Ulzana shrugged. "One hour if we ride."

"Then we'll ride."

10

THE SUN was already bringing a heat to the desert when the patrol came in sight of the ranch. From Sharp's Mountain the land leveled for two miles, stretching flat and unbroken to Brawley Creek. Across the creek the prairie rolled and buckled again for a mile to where the Baboquivari Mountains, veiled in a bluish mist, jutted from the earth. Green cactus and sage dotted the landscape and along the brown ribbon of the creek, cottonwoods and willows grew in profusion. The ranch was nestled in a grove of those trees, the adobe buildings standing darkly in the early morning sunlight. The smoke lay close to the land, a gray cloud rising from the burnt embers and climbing to the treetops before flattening out in a layer of cold air.

The house stood intact, the adobe refusing to burn, a few thin wisps of smoke curling from its gaping windows. But the tool shed was destroyed, with only the fire-blackened door and its charred supports still standing. Wavering heat lines rose from the ashes and supported the choking columns of smoke.

The sweet, sickening odor of burnt flesh hung in the air. The rancher was where Victorio had left him, a pitchfork rammed through his chest, his naked body hanging on what remained of the charred shed door. His flesh was burnt black, and blue-green flies covered the corpse, feasting on the carrion. Private Kautz tried to brush them away, but they were too glutted to fly. He pulled the pitchfork from the body and let it collapse to the ground. The flies swarmed a moment and then resettled. Kautz took a blanket from his bedroll and covered the corpse. Then he turned aside to be sick.

The woman was still alive — barely. She was tied, spread-eagled on the ground, her naked body filled with arrows. Her eyelids had been torn away, leaving her blood-filled eyes staring at the pitiless sun, while ants and flies swarmed in the thickening blood. Her voice was a harsh whisper. Creighton had to lean down with his ear against her cracked lips to hear.

"Kill me," she pleaded. "Please kill me."

Creighton looked away while Sergeant Hoffman, taken with compassion, cut the thongs that bound her arms and carefully placed his huge service pistol in her tiny hand. There was a loud explosion in the silence of the morning. Hoffman picked up his revolver from where it had whipped to in recoil from the single shot. Creighton knew that he would not mention this in his official report.

"Hoffman," Creighton said in a harsh whisper. He could taste the bitter bile rising in his throat. He had to swallow continually to keep his breakfast down against the corruption in his nostrils. It would not do to be sick in front of his men. "You and Claiborne make this woman decent for burial. I want her to have something on. Get the unmarried men out of the area. Get them busy on the graves. I want these people buried as soon as possible."

He walked away from the bodies then and stepped into the cabin. The first people dead by violence were a sick thing in his mind. Creighton knew the picture of them would be in his thoughts for many days and nights, until others would fade their image into the shadows of his mind. But he also knew that he would never completely forget the sight or the smell.

The air in the cabin was thick with smoke, making

Creighton's eyes water. The heavy kitchen stove had been overturned and black smoke poured from the broken pipe. It had been a clean kitchen. The packed dirt floor, moistened to keep the dust down, showed the marks of a daily sweeping from a brush broom. The few pieces of scarred furniture, carried like dreams from somewhere back East, were broken and strewn on the floor. A Bible lay on the floor beside a smashed table.

He picked up the Bible and opened the tattered, well-worn cover. A light feminine hand had written on the inside page. *Presented to John Rielly and his wife, Mary Mulhern Rielly, on their wedding day, August 10, 1876.*

Creighton felt an unreasoning dislike for John Rielly. The man had paid the price of his folly. But why would any man bring a woman out here to suffer and die as Mary Mulhern Rielly had done? Once that hideously disfigured woman had laughed and loved and lived. Creighton slammed the Bible shut. This was a Godforsaken land where life was as cheap as sand and often of no more importance.

He stepped outside into the sunlight and saw Ulzana coming toward him. With a shock Creighton realized that his corporal of scouts was an Apache, a vicious, savage Chiricahua. His people — maybe even his friends — had done this. He remembered having seen a gold cross and chain around the Apache's neck, and for an instant he wondered if it were a relic from some murdered settler. He looked into Ulzana's eyes and saw nothing. His eyes, his face were inscrutable. *He doesn't feel a thing,* Creighton thought. *He's butchered Americans himself and now he doesn't feel anything.*

"There was a child," Ulzana reported.

"What?" Creighton knew that his stomach could not stand the sight of a butchered child. But there was no one else. He came out of his stupor and forced himself to be-

come an officer taking the report of one of his men —
nothing more.

"There was a child," Ulzana repeated. "A boy. Maybe
three — maybe four years old."

"Where is he now?"

"Victorio took him."

"Why?"

"Take American, Mexican boys and girls. Raise like
Apache. When they grow up, they will be Apaches."

"Not this one. We'll get him back."

The bodies, wrapped in issue blankets, were buried on
the banks of the creek. Private Rutherford lashed sticks together to form crude crosses and stuck them into the
ground at the head of the fresh graves. The men stood
around the mounds, their heads down, their hats removed.
Creighton opened the Bible to the psalms. Words formed
and he spoke softly, the prayer rising in the still air.

*"The Lord is my shepherd; I shall not want. He maketh
me to lie down in green pastures; He leadeth me beside the
still waters . . ."*

Creighton gave the order and the patrol moved out.
Under the brilliant sun, there was no need for silence, yet
there was little conversation. Creighton could sense a general irritability among the members of the patrol. A
stubbed toe would bring a snarl of profanity, entirely out of
proportion to the pain felt. The usual careless cheeriness
of soldiers in the field was gone. The troopers' senses were
blunted by the memory of the atrocities they had seen.
With no Apaches to fight, they took their grievances out on
the closest objects that irritated them.

The sun crawled across the ashen sky while the lumbering horses and plodding men slowly devoured the long
miles. Creighton felt the pain of his cracked lips. His dry
tongue wiped across them, coming away with the salty taste

of blood. Again he wondered why he was enduring this in an alien land. The blinding glare, the terrific heat, the clouds of alkaline dust that rose from every footstep to fill eyes, nose, throat, and lungs with a torturous film. And the thirst — a thirst that walked with the patrol like a consuming flame, paralyzing tongues and throats, eradicating voices and shriveling lips to leather.

It was noon, the sun straight up in the sky, and the patrol was in the steepening foothills of the Santa Ritas when Creighton called a halt to rest and eat. The soldiers sank to the earth, worn to the bone, too tired to relish the greasy bacon and drying salt pork. Despite the stifling heat, and sore feet, and clothes stiff from dried sweat, and the roughness of the crotch, they lay in what shade they could find and slept.

Creighton was only vaguely aware that his scouts, Ulzana and Alchise, did not rest. They scampered through the range of foothills, searching for signs. In less than an hour, Ulzana was back at the bivouac with his report.

"Victorio is ahead," he said.

Creighton was drugged by the heat and lack of sleep. For a moment the news made no impression on him. Then the light came into his eyes and he spoke. "How far?"

Ulzana eyed the weary soldiers and tried to calculate the distance they still had in their bodies. "Maybe one hour."

"Good work," Creighton said, clapping Ulzana on the shoulder. "Sergeant Hoffman."

"Yes, sir."

"Pick the man with the best horse and send him back to tell Colonel Evans that we've found the hostiles. We'll attempt to engage the enemy until he comes up with reinforcements. Then get the patrol ready to move out."

"Yes, sir."

The soldiers rose from their drugged sleep, unrefreshed, soaked with lethargy. They trudged up the slopes as if in a trance. But with each step they came closer to battle and a chance to avenge the people they had buried in the early morning. Slowly they came awake, alert, ready to fight.

But there was no battle. Victorio's own scouts saw the soldiers, and the quarry fled. The Army mounts and the bone-tired troopers were not able to pursue. Tasting the bitter gall of failure, they turned and dragged themselves back toward Fort Apache.

11

THERE WAS no fanfare when the detachment returned to Fort Apache. The tired, frustrated men wheeled their mounts into line and awaited their sergeant's pleasure.

"You men see to your animals before you crap out. Just to make sure your efforts are appreciated, there'll be a stable inspection in one hour. Dismissed."

Amid the usual complaints and mumbled protests, the troopers moved toward the long, low stable buildings.

The scouts, not so particular about their ponies, turned them into the large, open corral.

"Give them some oats," Creighton said to Ulzana. "They've earned them."

Ulzana shrugged indifferently and walked toward the stables. It seemed foolish to feed the horses special grain merely because they had been worked hard.

The stable was one of the few places on the post that Ulzana liked. Here, the pungent, acidy odor of horses and manure overshadowed the stale, flat stench of people living too long in one place. He moved silently toward the oat bin on the far end of the long building, but his presence was noticed by a group of soldiers.

"Hey, here's our brave 'Pache scout," Private Sytkowski jeered. "Come to steal some oats?"

"Creighton say me come," Ulzana answered.

"Tell me somethin', 'Pache. How many scalps have you collected?"

"'Paches don't take scalps," Private Rutherford said. "You oughta know that, Sytkowski. They just butcher people."

"Why don't you guys leave him alone?" Kautz said. "He ain't causin' any trouble."

Sytkowski put down his currycomb and walked slowly toward Ulzana. "What do you mean he ain't causin' any trouble. Didn't he warn off Victorio?"

"No help Victorio," Ulzana replied, feeling anger beginning to pound in his blood.

"Oh, come on, Injun, admit it. You're both Cherrycowa, ain't you? You 'Pache sonofabitches always stick together."

"Leave him alone, Sytkowski," Kautz said again. Most of the troopers had stopped working and were watching the show. "Hoffman will be here in a minute and you'll have all of our asses in a sling."

"I ain't gonna hurt him." One of the horses emptied his bowels into the stable walkway. Sytkowski pointed to the fresh manure. "Hey, 'Pache. Clean up that crap."

Ulzana ignored the order, dipping a bucket into the oats.

"I said to clean it up," Sytkowski shouted, pushing Ulzana away from the bin, knocking the bucket from his hands.

"Leave him alone," Kautz warned again.

Ulzana picked up the bucket and once more dipped it into the oats. His stomach was twisted with rage, but he kept a tight rein on his emotions. There was no profit in fighting this soldier.

"He's gonna clean up that shit," Sytkowski insisted, having committed himself too far to retreat gracefully.

He reached out toward Ulzana. With deceptive speed, Ulzana grabbed his arm and pulled. Sytkowski's forward momentum carried him past the Apache. His feet tangled and he sprawled onto the floor. Ulzana turned back to the oat bin.

Sytkowski scrambled to his feet, grabbing a pitchfork. "You redskin bastard. I'll teach you to push a white man." He lunged forward. With one practiced movement Ulzana stepped aside and drew his knife. The fork brushed past, one tine grazing his chest and ripping the flesh. With a half pivot, Ulzana brought the knife up, and with the full weight of his body behind the blow, drove it to the hilt into the trooper's stomach.

Sytkowski moaned and fell to the floor. "I'm killed."

Before Ulzana could turn and flee, something hard crashed down on his head and he knew no more.

He came awake slowly, crawling out of the black pit of oblivion, not completely aware of where he was. For a long time he lay limply, feeling only the cool, straw-covered earth beneath his body, letting his mind come alert. Slowly he recalled the taunting jeers, the pitchfork, and the knife thrust.

His eyes opened to see nothing but deep shadows. There was no sound of movement around him. After a long wait, he sat up. His head nearly burst from the pain and for a moment he thought he would be sick. When the waves of nausea passed, he looked around. The only illumination was a faint border of light seeping from under the heavy wooden door. He was locked in a small adobe cell, smelling thickly of urine and sweat and mold. But he was alive, and for a moment that puzzled him. He had fully expected to be killed by the soldiers.

A panicky feeling of the narrow space and the foul air was weighing down on Ulzana, who had previously known only the open world. Time stood still for him. For a while he paced restlessly around the small cell, but that only increased the sensation of closeness. When he tried to sleep, his rest was interrupted by terrible dreams of being buried alive.

When he woke from one such dream, muffled voices came to him from the outside. There were scraping noises at the door as the heavy lock was unfastened. He considered making a bolt for freedom when the door opened, and gathered himself for the effort. But when the door swung back, the blast of bright sunlight was like a physical blow. A tall figure loomed in the opening before Ulzana could recover.

"Are you all right?" Creighton asked.

Ulzana did not answer.

"Did the surgeon fix your wound?"

Again Ulzana made no reply.

"Do you realize how much trouble you have caused?" Creighton asked. "It's no small matter to wound a soldier."

"He not dead?" Ulzana asked, disappointed.

"No. Another inch to the right and that would have finished it. But the surgeon was able to stop the bleeding."

"I tried to kill him. He deserved to die."

"Stabbing a soldier was not right. If he caused trouble, you should have told me. I would have made sure he did not do it again."

"He tried to kill me."

In the darkness Creighton nodded. "The other soldiers told the story. But what you've done is wrong."

"For the white man it is wrong. For the Chiricahua it is not wrong."

"Well, we have to do something about it. It wouldn't be right to let scouts go around stabbing soldiers."

"You will shoot me?" Ulzana asked, not realizing that only Creighton's arguments had saved him from exactly that fate.

"No. We do not shoot men for defending themselves. You are free to go, but we must take away the blue coat. You can never again be a scout."

Ulzana gave back the blue coat and returned to his rancheria. The ways of the Americans puzzled him. But he did not waste any efforts in attempting to solve that which had no explanation. In his heart Ulzana was happy to be released from the Army. He would no longer have to associate with crazy Americans.

12

WITH THE MONEY he had been paid for his services, Ulzana bought food and blankets for Sy-e-konne and Kah. Then for the rest of the summer he did nothing. It was too late to attempt planting. His time was spent in idle games, and in listening to stories of the war.

Victorio's successes were a great temptation to the hungry, restless *Cho-ken-en.* He had made peace with the Mexican peasants who lived in the small towns south of the border, allowing them to live on the land if they would give him food and shelter and weapons. Thus, with his base of operations secure, he raided against the Mexican soldiers and into Arizona and New Mexico. However, during the time of Earth Is Reddish-Brown, the late fall, the news reached San Carlos that Victorio was dead.

The *Chi-hen-ne* leader took his people into the Tres Castillos Mountains to rest. The stronghold was in the place where the mountains formed a deep basin which could only be entered through a box canyon. It was a good location because only a few warriors could hold the entrance against an army. However, this time the Mexicans had entered the basin first, and were waiting. As soon as Victorio's people had passed through the canyon, the rocks echoed with the guns of the enemy. There was no escape. Victorio and most of his band perished. The few survivors scattered, leaderless, in the mountains.

Word also came concerning Pi-hon-se, who had joined
Victorio in Mexico. After Victorio's death, Pi-hon-se returned to San Carlos. There were rumors that he had been
with Victorio at the end, and had escaped under suspicious
circumstances. No one was alive to present the facts, but
once a man has been a coward, the stigma remains with
him. Because of the past, and the new stories, the wickiups
of the *Cho-ken-en* were closed to him. With his own clan
against him, he turned to the Sierra Blanca People and married a girl from the camp of Sanchez. Pi-hon-se was no
longer a *Cho-ken-en*.

With the spring, the season of Little Eagles, Ulzana tried
to plant again, using the lessons he had learned the preceed-
ing year. Beneactiney and Alchise worked with him, goug-
ing deeper into the earth with their plows so that the seeds
could take advantage of the moisture that might remain in
the soil. Perhaps this time they would have better luck.

Then came the news that all of the fighting *Shis-Inday*
were not dead. Six months after Victorio died, old Nana
gathered together fifteen warriors and began an excursion
north of the border. Nana was an old man, past seventy. It
was said that he was too crippled with aches and pains to
take over where Victorio had left off. But Nana was determined to prove that he was not too old to be a warrior. It
was July, the season of Large Leaves, when he crossed the
border and sped through Arizona and New Mexico, killing
ranchers, herders, miners, anyone who fell into his hands.
For almost two months Nana outwitted the soldiers before
slipping back into Mexico.

For the People at San Carlos, it was a ray of hope in an
otherwise drab existence. Nana had proven that small
bands could evade the soldiers and raid successfully, retreating behind the sanctuary of the border when they were
pressed too hard.

Ulzana watched his corn wither and die under the relentless, parching sun and felt the call of freedom that Nana had raised. Perhaps the *Shis-Inday* could survive away from the caged earth.

13

ONLY LOCO spoke against leaving. "I don't think it's a good idea to go from the reservation," he said. "As soon as we cross the line that marks the caged earth, the soldiers will follow and kill our people."

Geronimo spat on the ground. "Is this life any better than death? Here we depend on the charity of the Americans. We forget our dignity and beg for food. Then the agent cheats us. In Mexico at least we can be men again."

"Sometimes in order to have peace a man must suffer," Loco said.

Chihuahua sprang to his feet, impatiently interrupting. "We agreed to a peace with the Americans and Mexicans. Nothing was ever said about our conduct among ourselves. Now the Americans say that we can't beat our wives or drink *tiswin*. We aren't children. Even the soldiers at the post drink wine and whiskey. The way we treat our women is our own business. When a woman won't listen to her husband, he has a right to punish her."

When Chihuahua sat down, Mangas stood. "My children cry during the night because they are hungry. A man can't be a man if his children are starving. When we go to the agent and ask for more food, he gives us the book of songs. We've tried to grow our own food. The first year our corn and melons died, and the agent didn't bother us. This year we've learned more, and our crops were much better. Then the agent sent his police into the fields and had them ride down our crops. He said that we couldn't grow food, that we had to eat only what the agent gave us."

"Now the Americans take away the reservation," Geronimo said. "First, because copper was found to the east, they took those lands. Now coal is discovered at the head of Deer Creek and the Americans want our southern lands. The agent says we must sign a paper giving them up or the soldiers will kill us."

Ulzana stood. "When we made peace we never agreed to this land as a reservation. We were brought here against our will."

"I say that we don't wait any longer," Chihuahua said. "Cochise would not have waited so long. Soon we'll be too weak to fight. I'll take those of my people who wish to go and leave this reservation."

Loco hung his head. "I don't know what to do. I only want to live in peace."

"You know the things we've said are true," Geronimo argued. "Here at San Carlos death is the only peace we'll have."

"Yes, my people also starve." Loco stood a moment, knowing deep in his heart that leaving San Carlos would not solve the problems of his people. The day of the *Shis-Inday* was gone. "When you leave, I'll go with you," he said softly.

14

THE THIN WIRE of the telegraph line passed through the branches of the scrubby mesquite. It was there that Ulzana cut it and tied the ends together with a strip of rawhide so that the break would not be found too quickly. If the talking wire could not speak, it would take longer for the soldiers to learn that the *Shis-Inday* had left San Carlos.

For the first day the warriors stayed with the old people, the women, and the children. They pushed relentlessly, trying to put as much distance behind them as they could before the talking wires spoke again. Everyone traveled without complaint. The bitter times, the empty bellies of San Carlos were already becoming a memory.

The fugitives did not stop for the night. They pushed on for the safety of the border, resting only a few hours to water the stock and eat. With the dawn, the small raiding parties spread out from the main band. Much food and many blankets would be needed for seven hundred fugitives.

By the night of the second day, the fugitives were high in the mountains of New Mexico, equipped with all of the essential supplies. They stopped to rest, eating some of the captured food. After the long stay at San Carlos, they were weak and hungry. Two more days of travel would find them safely across the border.

Because it had been an exceptionally dry spring, most of the streamlets and desert water tanks were dry. A single warrior, or a small party could subsist on the tiny pools of water available even in the most extended drought, but the large band of fleeing people had to follow the water courses. They realized that the Army, with their Indian scouts, would be able to anticipate their march by the amount of water in the rivers. It was Loco who suggested that the warriors fight a rear guard action.

Thus, the women, children, and old people, with a small escort of warriors, turned southwest, away from the nearest soldiers. Chihuahua and Loco, with seventy-five of their best warriors, stayed behind. In the Hatchet Mountains, where the Americans would cross the broad trail of the *Shis-Inday,* the warriors set their ambush.

Horse Shoe Canyon was a perfect spot for holding the soldiers. To the west were lofty cliffs, impossible for soldiers to climb under fire. In the middle of the gorge stood a huge mass of rocks, forming a small peak, joined to the western wall by an escarpment about thirty feet high, creating a causeway over to the central rocks.

Positioned high in the canyon, Ulzana was able to watch the drama unfold.

A scouting party of two soldiers and a dozen Yuma Indians approached the canyon foothills, riding directly into the ambush, when they halted at the foot of the canyon. A thin wisp of smoke curling above the rocks at the head of the gorge had alerted the Yumas. After a brief discussion with the soldiers, the scouts advanced very cautiously along the broad trail.

Because of some movement, or possibly just a general sense of danger, the patrol halted again. After another conference with the soldiers, one of the Yumas rode forward and raised his head above the nearby boulders. He found himself staring into the faces of fifteen of Loco's warriors, who had been hidden behind the rocks waiting to close the trap when the patrol had passed. The ambush was sprung.

A single rifle shot broke the silence. The Yuma who had seen the warriors sat his horse for a moment, gradually falling forward as the life eased out of him. For what seemed hours, everything was still. No one moved or breathed until the scout pitched to the ground. Then the *Cho-ken-en* in the rocks opened fire, knocking three more Yumas from their horses. The lieutenant waved his arms and shouted for the rest of the patrol to retreat.

Extending out from the main ridge was a high, rocky spur, terminating in a small promontory, where the lieutenant withdrew with his men. They began piling rocks in front of their positions as a barricade while one of the Yumas galloped away toward the advancing column of soldiers.

Naked warriors leaped up, showing their posteriors to the enemy in obscene mockery. They made foul gestures, accompanied by shouts of contempt, in an effort to entice the scouting party to come forward.

"Now is the time to crush them," Chihuahua argued. "Before they have time to get settled."

"No," Loco decided. "This is my fight and I'll say when to attack. We would lose too many warriors trying to kill a few scouts. Our purpose will be accomplished just as well if we hold the Americans where they are."

Ulzana did not understand Loco's plan. "It won't take long for the soldiers to rescue them."

"It doesn't make any difference. Even when the other troops arrive, they won't be able to advance while we remain in the high places. As long as we hold the soldiers here, the women and children will have time to cross the border."

For over an hour the *Shis-Inday* waited. Then the supporting column of soldiers arrived, their horses white with lather, stumbling from the sixteen-mile run they had just made. Five troops of calvary, over three hundred soldiers, gathered in the valley at the foot of the canyon, outnumbering the *Cho-ken-en* by more than four to one.

There was a rippling crash of gunfire and the warriors at the foot of the canyon withdrew, with the soldiers following in three prongs. Two troops of dismounted cavalry came from the west, two more troops along the eastern flank, and one troop up the middle of the gorge in a skirmish line.

Ulzana fired his new rifle, delighting in the kick against his shoulder. With each cracking shot, with each whining ricochet, he experienced a release from the frustrations of the past year. It was a good feeling to be striking back.

The soldiers advanced from rock to rock, constantly maintaining a spitting, snarling rifle duel. One by one the forward positions were enveloped as the outflanked warriors retreated deeper into the canyon, giving up ground as slowly as possible.

In the calm, hot air, the gray smoke of burnt powder settled and hung over everything like a fog. The constant noise of gunfire was as a raging inferno. A denser, choking fog began to fill the gorge. A muzzle flash somewhere in the canyon had started the brush burning. With the dying sun showing dull through the smoke, the warriors withdrew. It was every man for himself as bullets snarled and whined through the gorge. Behind the cover of dense clouds of hot, heavy smoke, Ulzana scrambled across the causeway and onto the western wall.

The sounds of gunfire slackened and died, leaving only the softer crackle of the fire. Ignoring the bone weariness and the blood flowing from his wounds, Ulzana mounted his horse. He followed Chihuahua and Loco west toward the *Cho-ken-en* home mountains. Thirteen dead warriors remained behind among the smoky cliffs and rocks of the canyon.

Even in the pain and fatigue, Ulzana felt an elation in the

accomplishment. With the Army entangled in the rocks of Horse Shoe Canyon, their horses exhausted, and nursing their wounds, the old people, the women, and the children would be able to cross the border safely, at least a day ahead of any pursuit.

15

ULZANA RODE loosely, slumping forward on his pony's neck.
It had been a long, hard ride from San Carlos, and the fight
in Horse Shoe Canyon had sapped his strength. Now, safely
across the border, he could relax, letting his taut muscles
begin to unwind. He was tired and the places where bullets
had creased his flesh were beginning to throb. He knew
that the wounds were not serious, but he was anxious to
reach the women and children so that Sy-e-konne could
bathe them in cool water and apply grease to speed the
healing and prevent infection.

His head jerked up and he strained to hear. Faintly, carried on a sudden puff of wind, he could hear a distant popping noise, the low, crackling rumble of gunfire. He turned
toward Beneactiney and saw that he also heard. Ulzana felt
a sinking in his heart. Without a thought for his aching
body, he dug his heels into the pony's ribs and galloped toward the sound.

His thoughts raced ahead, trying to comprehend. It
seemed like a trick. He knew that the Americans were behind him, stopped by the invisible line of the border, and
Mexican soldiers rarely fought the *Cho-ken-en*. How could
it be? After the fight at Horse Shoe Canyon, after the warriors had bought time with their blood, why were the
women and children not safe?

In his memory he could see again the burning camp when the soldiers had killed Sons-ee-ah-ray. He imagined the wailing of the baby, still in its cradle, and the gunshot that had silenced it. He rode heedlessly, a feeling of dread for Sy-e-konne and Kah clutching at his guts.

His staggering horse at the limit of its endurance, Ulzana crested a shallow ridge. In an instant his experienced eye saw the terrible story. An accident, the merest chance of fate, had caused the tragedy. The women and children, with their small escort of warriors, had followed a narrow trail into a mountain canyon where a troop of Mexican cavalry had stumbled onto them. Slowly drifting puffs of smoke indicated the Mexican positions in the rocks on the high ground. Several women and children lay in the center of the trail where the first volley had caught them unaware. Scattered bodies on the hillsides showed where the *Cho-ken-en* had tried to flee. The sides of the canyon seemed to be covered with Mexicans chasing down women and children who had managed to escape the initial onslaught.

There was no time to think. Leaving their horses, the warriors screamed their rage and charged into battle. There was no plan, only a rush to halt the Mexican advance and extricate as many of the People as they could.

The Mexicans turned to meet the newly arrived warriors. Bullets sang in Ulzana's ears like angry bees, their breath hot against his cheeks. Tiny puffs of dirt kicked up the earth around him. He zig-zagged and dodged, trying to present as small a target as possible. The soldiers fell back momentarily, and Ulzana paused behind a rock to reload his rifle.

There was a grunt behind him and Ulzana turned to see a warrior stumble and fall, an ugly red stain on his chest, a puzzled expression on his face. Then Ulzana was running again.

Suddenly, amid all of the confusion, he saw Sy-e-konne

on the eastern wall of the canyon, trying to carry Kah up the steep grade. Even as he began running toward them, he saw three Mexicans just above his wife on the slope. Unaware of the danger, Sy-e-konne was headed directly toward them.

Ulzana fired on the run, his bullet chipping the rocks beside one of the soldiers, attracting their attention. In a dozen leaping strides he was past Sy-e-konne and among the enemies. Firing from the hip, he spun one of the soldiers backward. He turned toward the other two and heard the sharp click of the hammer falling on an empty chamber. He swung the useless gun, smashing the stock over the head of a Mexican. An explosion at his ear nearly deafened him. The last soldier dropped his pistol and crumpled. Beneactiney stood over him with a smoking rifle in his hands.

"That way," Ulzana shouted, pointing down the canyon. He threw aside his shattered rifle and picked up one of the Mexican weapons. Beneactiney was at his side, and they fired into the hillsides around them, slowly retreating after Sy-e-konne and Kah.

Steadily the warriors withdrew from the canyon, gathering as many of the scattered women and children as they could. The Mexicans, satisfied with their victory, and having no desire to chase the warriors into the hills, where they would have the advantage, remained behind.

In a few moments it all over. Ulzana stopped on the top of the slope, safely out of range of the soldiers' rifles. In the canyon, bodies and equipment were scattered everywhere. During these brief moments of battle, the *Shis-Inday* had been shattered. Eleven warriors and ninety-nine women and children had been killed or captured.

But for now Ulzana was concerned only with his own family. Kah was moaning softly, his leg dangling limply, with blood streaming freely from a wound just below the knee. Ulzana gently touched the leg and Kah gave a sharp little cry of pain.

"Try to be brave," Ulzana said, his fingers probing. "The bone is broken, but the bullet went all the way through."

Beneactiney knelt beside him. "I'll hold him."

With a sharp jerk Ulzana yanked the leg, feeling the bone straighten. With sticks and pieces of torn shirt, he made a crude splint. He left the wound open. The flow of blood had nearly stopped, and the air and drainage would rid the leg of poisons. He sprinkled hoddentin liberally into the wound.

"Come," he said softly. With Sy-e-konne holding her weeping son, they turned and left the canyon of death. His family was alive and well, but Ulzana felt the grief of his people. Both his mother-in-law and his father-in-law had died. The flight from the bitter captivity of San Carlos had been a disaster. It would be many years before the wounded hearts would heal.

16

THE FUGITIVES STOPPED to nurse their wounds deep in the Mexican Sierra at the junction of the two well-watered canyons. Cooling breezes wafted down from the heights, refreshing them. Pines, oaks, and cedars grew in profusion in the fertile soil of the steep slopes. Sy-e-konne grew heavy with child again. The abundance of the mountains, the change from the quickly fading memory of the barrenness at San Carlos brought more fruit to the union of man and woman.

Fed rich meat and strong broths, Kah healed rapidly. His wound became a white scar on his tan body. The bone mended straight and strength came back to the muscles. Only a slight limp, when he was tired, remained to remind them of the near tragedy.

Ulzana watched Kah's young body filling out. The flesh of the deer became muscle and Kah laughed again, joining his friends running and playing and wrestling. During the short days and long nights, Ulzana taught Kah how to make a strong bow and stalk the small creatures, just as he had been taught so long ago by San-dai-say. Free in the mountains, he could teach his son the ways of the land.

The wounds to the flesh were healed more quickly than the injuries to their hearts.

At night Ulzana would lie under his blankets and think.

He was happy, but not with the same happiness he remembered as a boy in his home mountains. Too much had happened to his people since those days for him to be completely free from grief. He listened to the wind wailing through the dense pine forest and wondered if the winter storms cried for the summer's dead, lamenting what had been and would never be again.

There was dissension among the People. Loco had lost his wife and daughter in the canyon of death. His heart was sick and he no longer had the will to fight. If his path had not been blocked by soldiers, he would gladly have returned to San Carlos. Geronimo, always arrogant and boastful, had tried to induce Chihuahua's fighting men to join him. Finally he argued with Chihuahua, took his people, and with Nachite, moved farther south into the mountains.

The *Shis-Inday* had fled San Carlos to be together, but the fates had decreed differently. Each camp went its separate way.

17

"It's a thing that must be done," Ulzana said, strapping his two ammunition belts into place.

"I know," Sy-e-konne murmured. "It's just that the raid will be dangerous. The baby will need you." She glanced down toward her swollen belly.

"Don't worry. I've always been lucky. This time won't be any different."

"Be careful," Sy-e-konne whispered. She stepped forward and they embraced. "I'll pray for your safe return."

For an eerie moment Ulzana felt he had seen this scene before, when his father had left, never returning. He gently pushed Sy-e-konne away. "Don't worry. I'll be all right."

He stepped into the sunlight. Kah was standing in front of the wickiup, holding his horse. Ulzana reached out and mussed the boy's hair. "Take good care of your mother."

"I will," Kah answered.

Turning to the east, Ulzana threw a pinch of hoddentin toward the sun. "With the favor of the sun, I am going out to fight. I pray for the sun to help me."

Chihuahua came from his dwelling and mounted his horse. Followed loosely by Ulzana, Chatto, Beneactiney, Alchise, and twenty other warriors, he rode out of the valley.

The small band crossed the border under the cover of

darkness and stopped in the Mule Mountains of Arizona.

"We'll go separately from here," Chihuahua said. "Chatto, take eight men and go east to the Mimbres Mountains. Ulzana, take some men and go north as far as Apache Pass. I'll take the rest and go west to the Santa Cruz River. Five days from now, we'll meet again in this place."

The sun was barely edging above the mountains when Ulzana discovered the charcoal camp. The three workers were busy building their morning fires and did not notice the *Cho-ken-en* creeping up. Ulzana's shot dropped one American, but the others quickly ducked inside their tent. The warriors fired into the tent, ripping the canvas to shreds. When there were no answering shots, Ulzana and Beneactiney broke from cover and dashed forward.

The two White Eyes rose from the ruins of their tent and fired. Ulzana fell and rolled behind the scant protection of a large wooden box. Beneactiney was not so quick. Both shots hit him. He was dead before he struck the ground.

Ulzana fired rapidly, staggering one of the Americans, and a fusillade from the warriors in the brush cut down the other.

While the charcoal camp was ransacked for ammunition, Alchise and Ulzana scooped out a shallow grave and buried Beneactiney. There was no time for mourning, but in their hearts they felt the loss. It was almost as if the closeness they had felt was too strong to be canceled out so quickly.

The burden of Beneactiney's death went with Ulzana through the slashing raids of the next days. He felt responsible. There had been nothing wrong with the attack on the charcoal camp. It had been the fortunes of war, but that did not keep him from blaming himself.

On the morning of the sixth day Ulzana rejoined Chihuahua in the Mule Mountains. Overall the raid had been a great success. The three parties of raiders had killed twenty-six Americans and had captured thousands of rounds of ammunition. The *Cho-ken-en* had lost only Beneactiney.

Alchise rode in silence until the raiding party was safely across the border. Then he stopped his horse on the crest of a ridge and looked back toward the north. Ulzana reined in beside him and saw tears in his friend's eyes.

"What's wrong?" Ulzana asked.

"I'm tired," Alchise answered. "My family died in the canyon of death. There's nothing left for me in these mountains."

Chihuahua rode up and put his hand on Alchise's shoulder. "It isn't wise to let these things bother you. They get inside and hurt more."

Alchise nodded. "I've suffered when you suffered. I've been hungry when you were without food. Beneactiney is dead. I've lost my best friend. I can't go on. I'm going to leave you and return to my home country."

"Beneactiney was my friend also," Ulzana said. "He saved my life in the canyon of death. He worked beside me in the corn field at San Carlos. Come back with me. My family will be your family."

"No. I'm too weary. I have to go north."

"A man must do what his heart tells him is right," Chihuahua said. "You've been a good friend. If you wish to return to San Carlos, that's what you have to do. We won't try to stop you."

Alchise removed one of the ammunition belts crossed over his shoulders, and handed it to Ulzana. "I won't need this at San Carlos, and it might be of use to you." He turned his pony and gave a short salute with his free hand. "Good-bye."

Ulzana watched him ride down the slope, making his solitary way back toward the border. On this raid he had lost his two best friends.

Ulzana turned his mare loose to graze and walked slowly toward his wickiup, his heart bearing a heavy pain. There was no pleasure for him in war.

He looked up to see Sy-e-konne coming to greet him. First he noticed that her belly was no longer swollen, and then he saw the blanket-wrapped bundle.

"Say hello to your daughter," Sy-e-konne said, smiling.

Ulzana took the baby from her arms and looked into the wrinkled face. "It's a beautiful baby," he said, poking his gnarled finger at it.

Sy-e-konne lowered her eyes. "I'm sorry that it isn't another son."

"A man needs daughters, too." He was pleased to have a girl child. She would grow and marry, and her husband would come to live with him and Sy-e-konne. There would be someone to provide for them in their old age, just as he had provided for Bes-he and Zha-ah-zhe. "We'll call her It-ay-day, our daughter."

He handed the infant to her mother, and together they walked up the trail to the wickiup. It was necessary to make arrangements for a shaman to perform the cradle ceremony.

18

It was a beautiful day, the warm sun glancing on the wings of the bright blue birds that flashed, singing among the trees. Flowers dotted the valley meadows, growing thicker as the days warmed. Sy-e-konne finished changing the absorbent padding in It-ay-day's cradle and secured the three-month-old baby inside.

It-ay-day was her pride and joy. A man-child did not really belong to his mother. As soon as the breast was denied him, he turned away and sought comfort and training from his father. With It-ay-day it would be different. Sy-e-konne could imagine the years of her daughter's growing when they would remain close. Even when It-ay-day was grown and married, they would stay together as friends and helpmates.

She looked across the lazy camp to where Kah played. She felt a strong love for her son, but it was tempered by the knowledge that his time with her was short.

A sound came to Sy-e-konne. It was not really different from the spring sounds of the mountains, yet there was something about it that told her all was not as it should be. For a moment she did nothing, just continued to amuse It-ay-day. But she listened. Then the sound came again, the scraping of rocks knocked against each other on the slopes far above her.

Not moving, not appearing to have noticed, her eyes searched the hillside. A brown body flitted from behind a large rock and disappeared into a bush. She thought it strange that the warriors, returning from a raid against the Mexicans, should sneak up on camp. Then she saw a flash of blue, not bright and shining in the sun like the birds, but dull, flat, like cloth.

"Kah," she called. "Come here."

The boy obeyed immediately, giving up his arrow game. "Yes, Mother," he said, trotting to her side. "What do you want?"

"Stay close to me."

The boy sensed something wrong. "Why? What is it?"

"Don't ask questions. Just do as I say."

She was already edging away from the camp with Kah following, and It-ay-day in the cradle slung over her shoulder, when the first shot was fired. There was a sound like a rock slapping mud, so close after the gunshot it sounded like a continuation of the first. She began to run. Around her the camp erupted in screams and shouts as bullets sprayed through the open areas. She scrambled through the brush and made her way down a stream bed, ignoring the branches that grabbed at her and the rocks that tried to entangle her feet.

When the crackling of the burning wickiups reached her ears, she stopped and lowered the baby from her shoulder. A thin trickle of blood traced a course down It-ay-day's face from the small hole just above the right eye. Sy-e-konne's heart stopped and the grief welled up inside her. Tears streamed down her face and she staggered as her knees buckled, but she made no sound.

Sy-e-konne needed no one to explain what this death meant. She was like an animal shot and dying. The land had taught her about hardships and pain and grief. She had learned to be strong; she had learned to accept death —

sudden and violent — as a part of life, as common as the deadly creatures that lurked in every shadow, and as certain as the mountains that marked the boundaries of her world. But this was a thing apart. Her baby's death was a cruelty she could not accept.

For an eternity she stared at the unmoving body, remembering It-ay-day as she had been. She did not want to accept that her baby was gone. It was too great a tragedy for Sy-e-konne to bear.

Finally, with her naked hands she scratched a shallow grave in the gravely soil and placed the baby inside. She needed something to hate, something real to vent her feelings on. The war became her cross, the root of her grief. It was too hard, too cruel. The war took, ever reaching and clutching and it gave nothing back. Sy-e-konne felt a wild hatred. Her tears stopped and she found the strength to support herself. Her hatred gave her the courage to take Kah's hand and lead him to safety.

19

ALCHISE TROTTED through the canyon, his eyes constantly sweeping the terrain around him, his feet falling among the rocks without making a sound. He slowed to a walk when he sensed eyes upon him. The sharp click of a gun hammer being cocked stopped him.

"Don't shoot," he said, holding his rifle out at arm's length. "I've come to talk."

Ulzana and Chihuahua stepped from among the rocks at the side of the gorge, their rifles held hip high, the muzzles pointing at Alchise.

"You don't need guns," Alchise said. "I've come as a friend to talk with you."

"The last time we spoke there was friendship between us," Ulzana said, holding his rifle steady. "Then you said that you had had enough of war. You were going to return to your people."

Chihuahua spat on the ground. "Your people are the soldiers. You bring them into our camps."

"There's still friendship between us," Alchise said. He slowly lowered his rifle and laid it on the ground in front of them. He reached under his belt and carefully drew out a sack of tobacco and some thin brown papers. He handed these to Ulzana.

Ulzana took the makings and sat on a rock, laying his rifle

across his knees, the barrel still pointing at Alchise's chest. He rolled a clumsy cigarette and passed the tobacco to Chihuahua. The three men smoked in silence until Alchise felt the pause had been long enough.

"I heard that you have a daughter. How is she?" he finally asked.

"Dead." The single word had a flat, final sound.

"You should know this better than us," Chihuahua said. "You killed her when you brought the soldiers into our secret camps."

Alchise was visibly shaken. He had not known of It-ay-day's death. "I'm sorry," he said. "But what I've done was for the good of you and your people."

"Is it good for us to bury our children?" Ulzana asked, anger hot in his eyes.

"I'm sorry for that. I didn't want anyone to die. We've been like brothers since we were babies."

"You're no longer our friend," Chihuahua said, almost shouting. "Tonight there will be mourning in our camps. Is that what you call friendship? Is that how brothers treat brothers?"

"I'm sorry for that."

"How is it that the Americans are here in Mexico?" Chihuahua asked. "They never before crossed the border."

"They signed a paper with the Mexicans allowing them to come here."

Ulzana could not easily put aside the years of companionship. He could see the pain in Alchise's eyes from the deaths of the *Cho-ken-en*. "Why did you come into these mountains with the American soldiers?"

Alchise squatted on his haunches. "I went north after leaving you, and found things changed at San Carlos," he said. "A new man leads the soldiers. He is Nantan Lupan, Chief Gray Wolf. He wants to help our people. I brought him here to speak with you."

"At least his guns speak truer than the white flag," Chihuahua said, a bitterness in his voice that startled Alchise. "You've done us no favor."

"Do you enjoy the ways of war? It has brought nothing but dissension among your people. Loco is always weeping for his dead. Geronimo has moved his band away because he can't live in your camp."

"Do you think it's easier to live at peace without our families?" Chihuahua thrust at Alchise with his rifle barrel. "What about my family? Where are my wife and children now?"

"They haven't been hurt. Nantan Lupan holds them in your old camp."

Ulzana lowered his rifle. "It's hard to hold a gun on an old friend."

Alchise smiled. "Come in and talk with Nantan Lupan. He's a fair man."

"He'll put chains on us and take us away to prison," Chihuahua said. "That's no way to live. I'd rather die here."

"No. If you come in now and return to San Carlos with him, he'll forget all that has happened. He doesn't want to punish anyone."

"How can we be sure of that? The Americans speak two ways."

"I'm the proof. I was with you on the raid across the border. The soldiers know this, but they didn't send me to prison. No chains were put on my legs."

For a long time Chihuahua sat in silence. Then he lowered his rifle. "All right. I'll go in and speak with Nantan Lupan."

20

CHIHUAHUA PUT his heels to the flanks of his pony and rode down the deep canyon where the Americans had made a camp, filling the valley with their small white tents. The sun was already leaving the sentinel peaks when he dismounted and approached the tent of the White Eye's nantan. The human wall of scouts and soldiers separated, allowing him to pass.

The tent flaps opened and General James Harrison, called Nantan Lupan, stepped out.

Chihuahua had seen him only one other time. When Cochise had been alive, during the time of the reservation in the home mountains, Nantan Lupan had visited the People. He was older now, with more gray showing in his hair and beard, but his eyes had the same hard glint. It was Nantan Lupan who had fought the Sierra Blanca People and defeated them. At the time the *Cho-ken-en* had moved to San Carlos, Nantan Lupan had been away, fighting the Sioux and Cheyenne in the north.

"My village has been destroyed," Chihuahua said, the sadness evident in his face. "My wife and all of my property is in your hands. I will surrender to you."

"I do not want to take you and your people prisoners," Nantan Lupan said firmly. "You have committed many crimes, killed many people. I would rather fight it out here and now until you are beaten into the ground and cannot cause any more trouble."

Chihuahua was staggered by these words, but he quickly regained his composure. "You speak of crimes we have committed, but you do not tell of the things that have been done to us. Perhaps we should punish the Americans."

"I have spoken with Alchise and the others. They have told me of the trouble with the agent, and the stealing of land. These things have been corrected."

"Then you know why the Chiricahua left. There was no other way."

"Some of the Apaches did not leave. Alchise came back when he realized that he had done wrong."

Chihuahua slowly nodded. His spirit was broken and he did not have the strength to argue. "I have made a mistake. My people have already been punished. We have lost many in this war. We are now ready to return to San Carlos, and you say that we cannot. That we must fight it out to the death. What would you have me do?"

Nantan Lupan allowed compassion to show in his eyes. "If you will promise to live in peace and never again leave the reservation, I will allow you to return."

"I promise."

"What about the rest of your people?" Harrison asked.

"They are hiding in the hills. I have sent runners to gather them together and tell them to come in here to this place to surrender."

"What of Geronimo and the other chiefs?"

"I cannot speak for them. We are no longer living in the same camps. I will surrender with my people regardless of what the others do."

"Then I will take you and your people back to San Carlos."

"I ask only one favor," Chihuahua said. "My people are scattered everywhere. The young will suffer and die from

the cold and fear. I ask that you allow us to go into the hills
to find them and bring them in."

Harrison considered for a moment, his eyes studying Chihuahua's face. "I trust you. Go out and bring in your people."

Without another word, his shoulders sagging under the
weight of defeat, Chihuahua turned and left.

Nantan Lupan waited in the canyon for several days
while Chihuahua collected his dispersed people. One by
one, the other leaders came in to surrender. Geronimo,
Loco, Mangas, Nachite, Bonito, and even old Nana put down
the lance. Only Juh, whose home was in these mountains,
refused to come in. He took his band of *Ned-ni* deeper
into the Mexican Sierras.

The long line of soldiers and *Shis-Inday* made their way
out of the Sierra Madres and headed slowly north toward
Arizona and San Carlos.

The People moved cautiously across the border. The
Army was with them, but still they were apprehensive. The
hatred of the miners and settlers ran deep. If they saw the
band of *Cho-ken-en*, they might fire on them, and the *Shis-
Inday* would be forced to defend themselves. But the Army
formed a cordon around them, keeping the other white men
away, and there was no trouble.

After three weeks of hard travel, the column reached the
headlands above San Carlos. The *Cho-ken-en* looked down
on the arid, barren flats and shuddered. There had been no
change in the year and a half they were gone. It was still a
barren, lifeless place, with a thin haze of dust and smoke
hanging over the desolate agency buildings. Here there
would be the same suffering, the same sickness, the same
starvation.

Not a single bird sang in greeting. The naked, dirty children of the reservation *Cho-ken-en* did not laugh. There

was no joy in the faces of the tired women who looked up without interest as the renegades returned. Here there was only hopelessness, desperation, and a sense of death.

But the People had seen enough of war. No matter what the Americans did now, they knew that this place would be their home forever. Here they would live again and try to forget the death and fear of war. From this day they would live in peace with the White Eyes.

PART FOUR
the parting

To die and part is a less evil;
But to part and live,
There, there is the torment.

—LANSDOWNE

1

THE CORPORAL rapped briskly. At the muffled acknowledgment from within, he stepped inside, his muted voice carrying back into the waiting room. "Lieutenant Creighton sends his compliments, sir, and asks permission to speak with you."

The reply was too soft to be intelligible.

The door swung open and the corporal held it for Creighton. "The general will see you now, sir."

"Thank you." Tucking his hat under his left arm, Creighton stepped up to the desk and saluted smartly.

Without looking up, General James H. Harrison returned the salute. "Have a seat, Creighton. I'll be with you in a minute."

"Yes, sir." Creighton sat stiffly on the edge of a wooden chair, nervously fingering the visor of his cap, his glance sweeping the room. All of the furnishings were plain, almost Spartan in design. An American flag on its staff in the corner, and a somber painting of Abraham Lincoln were the only objects to relieve the monotony of the colorless room.

After several moments, General Harrison scribbled his signature on a document and leaned back in the swivel rocker. "This damn paperwork will be the death of me yet. Don't ever let them make you a general officer, Creighton. You'll spend the rest of your life making out reports for some pompous ass in Washington."

Creighton smiled as was expected of him. "Yes, sir."

Harrison opened a box on his desk and took out a long, fat cigar. "Care for one?"

"No, thank you, sir."

"Don't smoke, eh? Good for you. It's a vile habit. I make it a personal rule to keep my consumption down to four a day." He lit the cigar and took a deep puff. "My first one today. Well, lieutenant, why did you want to see me?"

"It's about the Chiricahua, sir."

"A remarkable people. I understand that you've been making an effort to learn their language. A capital idea. Now that we have them on the reservation, the government should use the opportunity to study their life-way. But of course they won't. I'm not so sure that we couldn't learn a thing or two from them. They don't look like much. No feathers or fancy beadwork like the Plains Indians, but by God, they're fighters. If they had a couple thousand men they'd whip our pants off." He stroked his beard thoughtfully. "But I'm sure you didn't come here to discuss their customs or fighting ability."

"No, sir. I'm afraid it's more serious than that. Since I've been rather closely associated with the Apaches, I've been in a position to hear the rumors circulating in their camps. Some of the young men are talking openly about leaving the reservation. And in a way I can't blame them. These flat lands at San Carlos are unhealthy. The Chiricahua don't have any immunity against the diseases here."

"I know. My spies have been bringing in very discouraging reports." Harrison smiled when he saw the lieutenant's raised eyebrows. "You didn't know about my spy system, did you? And I can see from your expression that you disapprove. Well, if it makes you feel any better, I don't care much for the idea myself, but I consider it a necessary evil. These Indians don't trust us, not that I blame them, but it's important for me to know what's happening in their camps.

An opportunity to nip trouble in the bud, so to speak. The young men have always been discontented — some of them would be unhappy in Eden. It isn't just the reservation here at San Carlos. They want their freedom. How would you like to be shut up on what they call the caged earth?"

"I wouldn't like it, sir, but that's not the point. I wanted to ask if you have ever considered moving their reservation?"

"And where, my young lieutenant, would you suggest that I move them — back to the Chiricahua range?"

"No, sir. But there's open land in the White Mountains near Fort Apache. The Turkey Creek area has water, trees, and abundant game. It would be more like the ranges they're accustomed to."

"Placate the savage by giving him a reservation as close as possible to what he wants, eh?" Harrison smiled at the lieutenant's changed expression. "Don't get excited. I happen to agree with you. Turkey Creek would be an ideal location. But my hands are tied. One of the disadvantages of being a soldier is that once the fighting is over, no one listens to you. The Indian Bureau has decided that the Chiricahua should live at San Carlos regardless of what might be to the best interests of them or the territory. Have you ever tried to argue with bureaucrats?"

"No, sir. But if something isn't done soon, we may have another war on our hands."

"Half of the politicians hope there will be a war. It gives them an opportunity to make fortunes out of government contracts. They aren't particularly interested in the number of lives a conflict would cost."

"I'm sorry, sir, but I don't understand the politics of these things. I just know that if we moved the Chiricahua to the White Mountains, their leaders would be better able to control the young hotheads."

General Harrison slammed his fist on the desk. "Damn it,

you're right. What good does it do to have these stars on my shoulders if I don't shake things up once in a while? By the time the bureaucrats can decide what to do about it, the first year's crop will be ready to harvest."

Creighton stood up. "Thank you, sir."

"Not so fast, Lieutenant. If we do relocate the Indians, some smart young officer will have to go with them and act as their agent. Someone who'll have the backbone to stand up to the civilians when they start howling. You're due for a leave, aren't you?"

"Yes, sir."

"You're going back East to be married, as I understand it."

"Yes, sir."

General Harrison drew his short legs from under the desk, stood up, and walked to the window, where he stood a moment looking out. "Creighton, if I move the Chiricahua to Turkey Creek, would you consider postponing your leave until they're settled?"

"I don't know, sir. The thought never occurred to me."

"Damn it, I know it's a hard thing to ask you, but you're the best man for the job. You like these Indians and they need someone they can trust. If that girl is going to be an Army wife, she should be willing to wait."

"May I have some time to think about it, sir?"

"Certainly. Sleep on it. Let me know your decision to-morrow."

Creighton skirted the bare parade ground, nearly deserted in the afternoon heat. His angry steps were directed toward the long row of dismal cubicles known as the bachelor officers' quarters.

He's got no right to ask me to do this, Creighton thought. I've got some right to my own life.

In his cool, dry quarters, Creighton removed his tunic and stretched out on the cot, letting his mind work over the problem that confronted him. On one side was the question of duty and the loyalty he owed to the service. On the other was the question of his personal happiness. After all these years he had no right to expect Emma to wait any longer.

Still struggling with the dilemma, no closer to a solution, he rose and moved to the shelf that served as a desk. Perhaps putting his thoughts into a letter would help. But for a long time he stared at a blank page, not able to formulate any relevant words.

How can I explain to Emma that these people deserve a chance, he thought. With this reflection concerning the needs of an alien people, he came to understand that he had already made his decision. He would stay.

2

IN THE EARLY SPRING Ulzana sat his horse, surveying the cattle. There were no thoughts of returning to the old ways. His heart told him that the day had come when he must provide for his family using the methods of the Americans.

The Indian Bureau had insisted that the *Cho-ken-en* live by agriculture. However, Ulzana and most of the other men did not enjoy tilling the earth. He had grown up learning the ways of animals and he was a kindred spirit with them. Obtaining the necessary livestock had not been easy. The Indian Bureau, comfortable in their Washington offices, had refused to consider any alternative to farming.

"We are not farmers," Chihuahua had explained to Nantan Creighton. "We have never been farmers."

"Let us have cattle," Ulzana urged. "Then we can raise our own meat. Animals we understand. No man can love a weed."

"I understand your problem, and I'd like to help, but it just isn't that simple. The chiefs in Washington must approve such a venture, and they have already denied our requests."

"Talk to Nantan Lupan for us. The men in Washington did not want us to come to Turkey Creek, but when he moved us, they allowed it. If Nantan Lupan wants us to have cattle, he can cause it to happen."

Creighton sighed. He knew that General Harrison was already in trouble with the bureaucrats, but there was no way to explain the situation to the Apaches who believed that Harrison could accomplish anything.

"I'll see what I can do," he finally agreed. "But don't count too heavily on it. Even General Harrison has limited powers."

Chihuahua smiled. "All we ask is that you tell Nantan Lupan."

It took several weeks of hard arguing, but at last General Harrison and the Chiricahua prevailed. Permission came for the Indians to start their cattle herd. There was an immediate reaction from a vocal segment of the local white population. Marginal ranchers feared that competition from the Chiricahua would hurt them financially. Only by the most diplomatic negotiations was Harrison able to prevent serious complications.

Some of the scrawny heifers were furnished by the government, and some were purchased by trading ponies for cows. Creighton made arrangements with an American rancher in the valley to supply a bull for stud services. The grama grass in the White Mountains was good fodder, and the fleshless cattle became sleek and fat. Six of the cows grew heavy with calf, a dividend on their investment.

Now, as he sat his pony, watching the longhorns graze in the narrow valley, he speculated on the way of the world. There was a great drama here in these mountains and valleys. It was a fierce struggle against the blind and pitiless power of this rolling desert. Perhaps in the end there would be only defeat and loss, and a hopeless gathering of worn-out things, a growing older with no dreams ahead. But if he won, if he could make a new life, learn new methods to teach Kah, then there was hope for his people.

He no longer owned the heritage of his people to give to his son. But men being what they were, he could forge a

new birthright from the shattered dreams of his own youth.
It was this heritage, this desire to give his son the knowledge that he would need to survive in a world thrust upon
his people that gave Ulzana the courage he required for the
struggle. If he could endure, if Kah could learn, then the
Shis-Inday could survive.

Unfortunately the boy was not so eager to take advantage
of the opportunities to learn.

"I don't want to go to the new school," the ten-year-old
boy protested. "It isn't a good place."

"It's the only thing to do. This new life will be easier for
you when you learn to speak the white man's language and
read the words he puts on paper."

"If the old ways are good enough for you, they're good
enough for me," Kah argued. "You can teach me everything
I need to know."

"That's foolish talk. The old ways are dead. I don't know
the new customs, and I'm too old to adjust. But if you grow
up with the new ways, it'll be all right."

Sy-e-konne spoke softly. "We've always been a proud
people. Our ways and ideas are good. Do you want Kah to
forget all that?"

"Don't you understand that what I want isn't important?
A new wind is sweeping the land. Old trees like us will be
blown away. The young trees must learn to bend with the
wind if they are to survive."

"I won't go!" Kah declared.

"You *will* go. It's a thing that has to be done. You'll go to
the school and do your best to learn everything you can.
When you come home you'll tell us so that we can know
how to live and what to do. You'll be our teacher."

Ulzana tried to explain these matters to Sy-e-konne, but
she did not understand. Nor was she sure that she wanted
to understand. It was easier to trust in the man she loved.
If giving Kah to the school would assure his welfare, then
she would accept Ulzana's decision.

3

Not all of the People worked hard to make the ways of the Americans their own. Geronimo, Mangas, Nachite, and their followers remained unhappy on the caged earth, making only halfhearted attempts at farming or cattle raising. They refused to give up the old customs, and constantly yearned for the freedom of the mountains. It was because of this that they came to see Chihuahua.

They sat in an open spot — Chihuahua, Geronimo, Mangas, Nachite, Nana. As they spoke of generalities, Chihuahua noticed that his visitors' eyes were red and hollow, sure signs they had been drinking.

"My wife made *tiswin*," Mangas said, finally speaking of the thing that had brought them here. "We drank last night and talked of the old days. We had too much, and there was a fight."

"There'll be trouble over that," Chihuahua said. He did not have to ask if anyone had been injured. These men would not have cause to mention the fight if no one had been killed.

Geronimo looked directly into Chihuahua's eyes. "That's why we've come to you."

"What has this to do with me?" Chihuahua asked. He did not like Geronimo. There was something in his deep-set eyes and the cruel slit of his mouth that repelled him. "I wasn't with you."

"The *Shis-Inday* are one people," Geronimo said. "If we're going to survive, we have to stay together. Come with us to speak with Nantan Creighton. If all the leaders speak, it'll show that we stand together."

"Whose idea was this?" Chihuahua asked, suspicious of Geronimo.

"We all decided to speak with you," Geronimo said.

Chihuahua shook his head. "I don't know. What you've done is forbidden. It'll cause trouble."

"We're not children," Mangas said angrily. "Nantan Lupan was wrong to forbid this. We should be able to drink *tiswin* if we want. The soldiers are allowed to drink whiskey."

"But we don't want any trouble," Nachite said quickly. It was difficult to believe that he was the son of Cochise. There was none of his father's firmness in him.

"If we don't stay together, then the People have nothing," Chihuahua answered. A voice inside told him that he should not do this thing, but he was a *Cho-ken-en*. "I'll go with you to see Nantan Creighton."

It was not yet sunrise, although the forewarning light had already spread across the land, when Lieutenant Creighton stepped from his tent to meet the assembled chiefs.

All of the leading men and about thirty of their followers were gathered in the open space beside the stream. Not a single woman or child was in sight. Two warriors, armed with rifles, were clearly visible on the small hill which commanded a view of the approaches from Fort Apache. The chiefs were unarmed except for their ever-present knives. It did not require an expert on Indian affairs to know that something serious was in the air.

Creighton smiled. "What brings you here before the sun?"

"We wish to talk," Loco said.

"Come into my tent where it's warm."

The chiefs silently entered the tent and squatted in a half-circle on the floor.

"We all drank *tiswin* last night," Mangas stated flatly. "All of us here in the tent and outside. And many more."

"The rule against *tiswin* is no good," Geronimo added. "We made no agreement about this in Mexico. We are men and should be able to do what we want."

"General Harrison had good reasons for making the rule." Creighton knew that he was in a difficult situation. This was not the first complaint he had heard about the prohibition, but it was the first time that all of the Apaches had spoken together against it. "A drunken Apache does not know what he is doing. He might kill someone and cause a war on the reservation. Not more than a month ago, a drunken Chiricahua stabbed his wife."

Creighton was pleased with the reaction his statement caused. The Indians had hushed up this incident, doctoring the woman themselves. He could see in their faces that they did not think he had known of it.

"What are you going to do about the *tiswin?*" Geronimo asked severely. "Are you going to put us all in jail? You have no prison large enough even if you could arrest us all."

"This is too serious a matter for me to decide," Creighton finally conceded. "I follow the orders of General Harrison. He gave these regulations for your own good. I will have to speak with him and let him decide."

"Nantan Lupan is far away. It will take a long time to hear his words," Geronimo said.

"I will send him a message on the talking wire. It won't take long." He hesitated a moment. "Will you accept General Harrison's judgment?"

Although it was obvious that the others were not happy with any sort of judgment, Chihuahua saw it as a way out of the trouble. "Yes," he said. "Whatever Nantan Lupan decides will be done. We will wait for his answer."

4

"Have you heard from Nantan Lupan?" Chihuahua asked. Two days had passed since the talk with Creighton and there had been no answer.

Geronimo ignored the question. He was so nervous that he was barely coherent. "You must take your people and run to Mexico," he urged.

Chihuahua felt the old fear tighten his stomach. "Why?" he asked. "My people have done no wrong."

"The soldiers will be coming for you soon. If you don't run, they'll kill you," Geronimo said.

"Why?" Chihuahua repeated. "Has Nantan Lupan ordered this?"

"Yes. He's sending soldiers to seize you, me, Mangas — all of us." Obviously Geronimo was badly frightened.

"No!" Chihuahua shouted. He had had enough of running and hiding. He shook his head firmly. "I won't go. Nantan Lupan is a fair man. He'll listen to the truth. My people didn't drink *tiswin*. I'll stay and talk."

"It's too late for words," Geronimo insisted. "He won't listen over the blood of white men."

"There hasn't been any blood."

"Nantan Creighton is dead."

"Creighton dead? How?" Then Chihuahua understood. "You murdered him!" His hand went to his knife and Geronimo backed away. "I should kill you. Creighton was our friend."

"There was nothing else I could do. Chatto and Nantan Creighton were coming for me. I had to kill him."

"You've betrayed your people," he said. In his heart Chihuahua knew that he would have to run again. When he had talked to Nantan Creighton, the words that never lied had been put on the paper. Nantan Lupan would see the paper and believe that he had assisted the murderers.

Geronimo turned to leave. "Do what you want," he said. "I've warned you."

Chihuahua halted his band in the hills south of San Carlos and looked back toward the reservation. The gains his people had made in the last two years were gone. The crops, just beginning to mature, and the cattle, ready to calf, were lost to them.

Ulzana halted beside him. For a short time neither spoke.

"My brother," Chihuahua said. "My heart is weary. I thought the ways of war were done. I hate to run and hide again."

"It's Geronimo's fault," Ulzana said bitterly. "If he hadn't killed Creighton and Chatto, we wouldn't have to run."

Atelueitze looked up, his face full of surprise. "Nantan Creighton isn't dead."

Chihuahua turned on his son, anger quickly replacing the sorrow in his voice. "This is no time to be joking."

Atelueitze was startled by the force of his father's anger. "I'm not joking. I saw Nantan Creighton only a short time before you sent word that we were leaving. He was at Fort Apache."

The silence was pregnant with hatred. No man loves to be fooled by another, but when that lie puts his family in danger, it is even worse.

"Geronimo will die for this," Chihuahua vowed.

"Wait!" Os-kis-say, his wife, shouted. "It's just like a man to forget his duty in the heat of anger. You must think of your people. The soldiers will come after us soon. What will we do while you chase Geronimo?"

"Ulzana is capable of leading."

"No," Ulzana said. "Os-kis-say is right. What has been done is over. We haven't done anything wrong. We can return to the reservation."

"By now the soldiers know we've gone," Chihuahua said. "They'll be after us. If they see us, they'll fight."

"If we hide in the mountains for a few days, the soldiers will follow Geronimo's trail south and we can go back on the reservation," Ulzana argued.

Chihuahua knew that Os-kis-say and Ulzana were right. No blood had been spilled. If they were able to return to Turkey Creek, then Geronimo's lies would not matter. "We'll go north," he said, turning his horse. "Ulzana, you stay here and watch the soldiers."

He led his twenty warriors and sixty women and children back toward Fort Apache and the reservation, circling wide to avoid Army patrols.

Ulzana lay flat on the rock shelf watching the back trail. A wide view of desert lay before him, empty except for the troop of cavalry moving south. The soldiers had stopped in the distant valley where the trail of Geronimo's band continued south, and the trail of Chihuahua's people turned north. Ulzana could not put his finger on the exact moment of realization, but even before the troops resumed their march, he knew they would follow the northern trail, leaving the southern trail to the patrols Nantan Lupan would have placed at every water hole along the border.

He scrambled down from the rocky shelf and began jogging through the system of canyons. He did not relish telling his brother they would not be able to wait in the mountains and quietly return to the reservation. Only a miracle would save his people now, and Ulzana had long ago lost his faith in miracles.

His eyes moved up to the clear, almost white sky. What had the *Cho-ken-en* done that their gods had deserted them? Where once the People had been favored above all others, they were now completely forsaken. Perhaps the answer was in the changing order of things. Perhaps the gods were no longer the same. Maybe, with their superior strength and great power, the Americans had caused the gods to assume new identities. Perhaps now White Painted Woman was the person the Americans called Virgin Mary. Perhaps Child of the Water was now the one called Christ.

The questions were too complicated for Ulzana. He was of the land. The deeper things of the spirit were alien to his mind. He knew only that the *Cho-ken-en* must once more run and hide and fight and wait in fear.

5

LIFE IS A WHEEL, Ulzana thought. A man stands still, facing toward the future, and if he lives long enough, the wheel makes a revolution and repeats itself. How many times had he run, watching the horizon for the drifting dust of pursuing soldiers? How many times had he raided ranches, securing supplies for a people running from death into fear? How many times had his heart skipped a beat at the sound of a distant gunshot or the nearby snap of a twig? It seemed that his entire life was composed of running, then stopping for a year or two, then running again.

But everything was not the same. The revolving wheel was always a little more worn. Fewer and fewer of the People had the courage or strength to run. Last time, when Loco had fled with them, there had been seven hundred. Now there were only eighty.

For nearly a month Chihuahua's band twisted and doubled back through the rugged ranges of New Mexico and Arizona, searching for an open place on the border where they could cross into Old Mexico. But the international boundary was sealed by a curtain of soldiers.

"We can't run much longer," Chihuahua said. He stood on the promontory looking toward the Mexican mountains visible only a few miles to the south. "Our strength is nearly gone. The soldiers are coming closer."

"Then let me make a path for you," Ulzana suggested. "If

I ambush one of the patrols, the others will come to help, and you can slip past them into Mexico."

Chihuahua shook his head. "You would be killed. I need you with me."

"It is better for a few to die, than for all to perish."

For an extremely long time Chihuahua stared into space. "Do what must be done," he finally said in a harsh whisper.

With the cordon of patrols closing in on them, five warriors left the main band: Ulzana, Atelueitze, Don-she-dan, Es-kel-tay, and Notar. They rode north and east, directly into the closing ring of troops. No matter what the risk, they were to create a diversion so that the others could escape into Mexico.

It was a perfect spot for an ambush. The country was open, rolling in gentle swells away from the hills. To an inexperienced eye it would have appeared that even a jack rabbit could not have hidden in the low sage. But the land was crisscrossed with gullies and dry washes that were invisible until a rider stumbled onto them.

The five warriors waited in the depressions. There was no plan beyond the first shot. Fire. Then hold the soldiers here. Draw the patrols from the border. Then run, every man for himself.

The squad of buffalo soldiers rode lazily, confident in their numbers, secure on the open plain. Birds sang, lizards darted from their path, and to the shaded eyes of the patrol, the land was as empty as their canteens.

As silently as a passing cloud, Ulzana moved into position. He fired, and the earth around the enemy erupted in a quick volley. Stunned by the sudden onslaught, the soldiers froze until another volley cut into them. Horses screamed and pitched and died. Soldiers dove behind dead horses and into hidden gullies and emptied their rifles at an enemy they could not see. Dust clouds swept from the border and Chihuahua led his band through the opening.

Ulzana ran hunched over down a wash until the sound of

gunfire was only a faint popping noise behind him. From down the wash behind him came the dull clatter of metal on rock. Ulzana crouched under the bank, in the natural fortifications of some boulders. The sound of feet moving quickly on gravel came to him, closer this time, and he knew that someone was in the wash with him. He gripped his knife and waited.

Atelueitze trotted around the bend and stopped short when Ulzana stepped out.

"We did it," the boy whispered. A huge smile split his face.

Ulzana laughed softly.

Together they jogged into the gathering darkness of the June night.

6

EVEN THE LIFE in Mexico had changed, Chihuahua reflected as he walked beside the gurgling stream, the fragrance of the cook fires pleasant in his nose. The responsibility and the trust that had been laid upon him were a bitter, lonely burden. He felt the great isolation to which all men are heir, but which is infinitely greater for those who must lead and make decisions.

His people credited him with intelligence, but he was acutely aware of his limitations. If he had possessed the wisdom of Mangas Colorado, or even of Cochise, then, perhaps, he would have felt equal to the task of guiding his people.

As the sky darkened Chihuahua glanced up and saw the first star step into the ocean of blackness. Momentarily he was filled to bursting with the serene beauty of the night. The sky was clear and deep, so vast that he felt he could be lost among the countless stars and float free as a bird. Then reality laid its icy hand upon his soul. Somewhere up there were the sleeping gods of the *Shis-Inday*. He wished that they would speak to him, give him some sign to ease the burden he found increasingly difficult to bear.

His mind was so filled with his thoughts that he was not aware of the approaching shadow until a twig snapped at his side. He turned, his hand automatically going to his knife.

"I didn't mean to startle you," Ulzana apologized.

Chihuahua smiled. "My thoughts were speaking too loudly for my ears to hear." He was glad that Ulzana had come to him.

The brothers walked in silence for a time, their minds preparing words to speak of things they did not dare communicate to others, even their wives. It was Chihuahua, the older, the leader, who spoke first.

"I've been searching for wisdom, but nothing comes to me. My people turn to me for answers, but I have none. Do you remember when you were a little boy and had received your first bow? I watched you stalking a bird, but your feet snapped a twig and the bird flew away. That's the way it is with me now. I seek the freedom bird, but my mind is as clumsy as your feet were. Whenever I approach close enough to capture it, the bird flees."

Ulzana nodded. "I was inexperienced. Hunting was a new thing to me. Experience teaches a man to accomplish things which at first seem impossible."

"I don't know. Perhaps there is no longer time to gain experience. Perhaps freedom for the *Shis-Inday* is only in the grave."

"I'll never believe that," Ulzana said.

"The years have mellowed you, my brother. There was a time when your impatience was great — when your heart was filled with hatred."

Ulzana nodded. "A man learns. Now I know that the only hope is to learn to live with the Americans. We have to make a lasting peace."

"Don't you think I'd have tried anything if there were any hope? Nantan Lupan won't give us peace after we've broken our promises to him."

"Maybe it isn't too late," Ulzana argued.

Chihuahua stopped walking. "Tempers are too hot."

"Nantan Lupan is a good man. If we could talk with him

and explain what happened, he would allow us to return to Turkey Creek and live as we did before Geronimo's lie."

Chihuahua sighed and resumed walking. "The time for talking has passed. The soldiers are in the mountains to kill us. When it was impossible to return to Fort Apache, I believed that I could hide in these mountains and allow time to cool the heat of battle. Now there will be no cooling."

"Nantan Lupan would listen to us at Fort Apache. I could go north to speak with him and arrange a truce for all of us."

Chihuahua's first impulse was to reject the idea. Any excursion north of the border would verge on suicide. There was very little chance that Ulzana would ever reach Fort Apache alive. The thought of losing his only brother, his friend, almost stopped Chihuahua. But a leader had to think of his people first.

"It would be a dangerous journey," he said at last.

"If we stay here in the mountains, the scouts will eventually find us and we'll all be killed."

"Once before I sent you to seek peace. Do you remember the time of Eskiminzin? Then you were not so eager to go on a reservation."

"Ideas must change with the times."

Both men walked in silence. Chihuahua knew he could not order his brother in this matter. Ulzana was a man, master of his own actions. However, he realized that Ulzana would stay if he asked him to remain.

"You're right," he decided. "We have to try. If you want to do this thing, take as many warriors as you'll need and go. My prayers will go with you."

7

It had taken Ulzana only a few moments to complete his preparations for the journey. He made an effort to eat, knowing that it might be a long time before he could fill his stomach again. But he was too nervous. He could only pick at the boiled venison.

From the time that he told Sy-e-konne about the mission, she had not spoken a word, seemingly occupied with her household duties. Beneath the calm exterior, fear and resentment had smoldered until she could no longer contain her emotions.

"Chihuahua can't force you to go north," she said, throwing a basket against the wall. "You can stay here and no man would dare question your courage."

"It was my idea," Ulzana said. "Chihuahua didn't order me to go."

"Then why? Are you tired of living?"

"If you don't understand why I have to go, I can't explain it to you."

"Well, I don't understand! If you go north you'll be killed. There isn't any honor in dying for nothing."

"You're speaking with the heart of a woman," Ulzana said, angrily throwing a branch into the fire, scattering sparks around the cooking pit.

"I speak with the heart of a woman because I am a woman."

"I don't want to argue about it."

Before Sy-e-konne could respond, a voice came from the darkness in front of the wickiup.

"I'm coming in."

After a respectful pause Atelueitze ducked though the low opening. The urgency of his own mission made him oblivious to the tension in the air.

"Uncle, let me go on this journey with you," the boy pleaded, his eager eyes sparkling in the firelight.

Ulzana slowly shook his head. "No. I'm taking only ten men and I've already chosen them."

"One man, more or less, won't make any difference here," Atelueitze insisted. "I can help you."

"All the warriors want to go," Ulzana explained. "If I let you come, others will also want to join. Besides, you're too young."

Atelueitze snorted his impatience. "I wasn't too young to be with you when we ambushed the patrol at the border crossing."

"This time it's different" Ulzana said.

"I've already spoken to my father," Atelueitze said. "He told me that this is your mission and the decision is yours."

Ulzana smiled weakly. "Sometimes I wish I still felt the enthusiasms of youth. How easy it is to risk death when you believe you're too young to die." He placed another limb on the fire. "Go back and speak with your father. If you still want to go in the morning, you may come."

Atelueitze's face broke into a broad grin. "I'll be ready before first light."

As soon as Atelueitze left, Sy-e-konne spoke. "Are you proud of yourself? You've condemned that boy to his death."

"Silence!" Ulzana shouted. "I won't hear any more of your talk about this." After a long pause he spoke again. "Where's Kah?"

Sy-e-konne did not look up from her sewing. "It's his turn to watch the horses. He'll be back at moonrise."

"I'm going out," Ulzana said, rising from the fire.

It was a dark, cloudless night, with only the stars casting their pale light across the land. The cool mountain air was fragrant with the scent of pine. Ulzana paused in front of the lodge, allowing his eyes to adjust to the night.

When the dark shadows began to assume familiar shapes he walked up the slope behind the camp and urinated against the side of an arroyo. Even in the starlight he could see the steam rising from his body water. The mountain frosts were not far in the future.

In spite of the coolness beginning to penetrate his light cotton shirt, he stood on a slight promontory watching the thin sliver of the early November moon begin crawling above the mountains.

The moon was the width of two fingers above the peaks when he saw his son's dusky form approaching from the direction of the horse herd.

"Kah," Ulzana called in a whisper.

The boy froze in his tracks, his figure crouched and ready to spring. "Who is it?"

"It's me."

The boy relaxed and stood to his full height at the sound of the familiar voice.

"Walk with me," Ulzana said. He remembered the long-past time when his father had left on his final raid. It had been night then also, and he could remember Nah-kah-yen only as a shadow. For a fleeting instant he wanted to reach out and touch the boy, but he knew that Kah would not understand the gesture. His son was too old to be fondled.

When man and boy entered the wickiup, Sy-e-konne began to put away her sewing. "There is venison in the kettle," she said to her son.

While Kah squatted beside the fire and dipped his fingers

into the pot, Ulzana walked to the back of the lodge and took down one of his rifles.

"This is for you," he said, handing the weapon to the boy.

"For me?" Kah asked, his voice high with excitement.

"While I'm gone you'll have to help protect the camp."

Sy-e-konne looked up, the distress obvious on her face. "The boy is too young to have a rifle. You didn't have a gun at his age."

"Times have changed. The young must grow old more quickly today."

"If you weren't going away, the warriors could protect the camp. There wouldn't be any need to give guns to boys."

"The enemy doesn't ask a boy's age before they kill him. Perhaps in a different way we will be protecting our camp by going away." Ulzana flopped down on his blankets. "There won't be any more arguments. I'm doing what must be done."

The fire died to a bed of embers and Kah's breathing settled into the deep rhythm of sleep, yet Ulzana could not rest. Whether it was fear or anxiety that kept him awake he could not say.

When the autumn cold began to penetrate the walls of the lodge, Sy-e-konne stirred at his side. "Are you sleeping?" she whispered.

"No."

"I'm sorry for the things I said," she whispered, moving closer and laying her tear-stained cheek against his shoulder. "Every time you go away, I'm afraid you won't come back to me."

When sleep finally came, husband and wife were wrapped together in the warmth of their embrace.

8

ATELUEITZE WAS already awake, but did not stir until Ulzana laid a hand on his shoulder. The sun was high, and in
spite of the snow in the high mountains, it was exceptionally
warm in the rocky foothills. He had not slept well in the
heavy heat, and although he was physically awake, his
thoughts were muddled.

"When the sun is halfway down the sky, wake Don-she-
dan," Ulzana said.

Grunting his acknowledgment, Atelueitze picked up his
rifle and scrambled to the top of the southern ridge. From
the commanding ridgeline the sentinel could distinctly see
across the wide valley to where smoke rose from cooking
fires on the San Carlos reservation. "It's been a long journey," Atelueitze said half-aloud. "But now it's over."

During the hard days of the journey Atelueitze had used
every opportunity to study Ulzana, trying to emulate him.
Even now he could close his eyes and picture his uncle's
face. The strain of this venture wore heavily on Ulzana. It
was obvious that his eyes had seen too much war and hard-
ship, and had grown stern from viewing such scenes. They
were cold and steady, and when he laughed, they did not
grow warm and soft.

After crossing the border, the ten warriors had quickly
traveled high into the most difficult parts of the rugged
peaks. By dawn their trail had been discovered, and the

talking wires sent the hue and cry throughout the territory. All around them dust clouds on the horizon had shown where hundreds of troops and civilian posses had taken the field to cut them off and exterminate them.

For three weeks Ulzana had led his band north through the mountains and across the open plains, traveling mostly at night, and resting during the days. Twice they had almost stumbled into Army patrols, being saved only by Ulzana's constant vigilance.

But now the mission was nearly completed. Last night, after crossing the Gila River, they had made this camp, only four miles from their destination, Fort Apache.

Atelueitze scanned the valley, his eyes sweeping beyond and through the grass and thick undergrowth. Satisfied that nothing unnatural marred the scene, he sat back in the sun and fought against the drowsiness that overwhelmed him.

A sound entered his consciousness and he tried to come alert. He heard the soft twang of a bowstring and the airy exhaust of an arrow at the same instant that he felt the stabbing pain in his back, just below the left shoulder. Before he could react, a strong brown arm reached around his body and pulled him backward. Atelueitze tried to yell, but the sound was cut off by a hot, sharp knife slicing across his throat. A hand pulled his head back until he could see only the blue sky and a single white cloud standing motionless on the edge of the universe. Warm fluid pumped over his chest and vaguely Atelueitze was aware that it was his own blood. The world grew dim and his head filled with a loud buzzing. There was no pain, only a wonderful lightness. He tried to cry out, but the effort forced the blood up and he choked on the crimson flow from his throat. The hands released him and he began a long fall toward the ground. He was light, light as a feather. He was floating in a dream, watching the unreal earth come up toward him.

Something disturbed his sleep. Ulzana awoke quickly all over, but lay completely still until it came back to him where he was. His mind instantly concentrated on the world around him. He could hear the horses grazing on the grama grass, natural and undisturbed. There was no other sound. The tiny animals that usually scurried in the brush were quiet in the late afternoon heat.

A noise, like someone shaking a blanket, broke the stillness and startled the horses. Ulzana sorted through the memories of a hundred sounds, and in an instant he recognized it as the flapping of large wings. He threw off his blanket and jumped to his feet, his body crouched and tense, his rifle ready in his hands.

On the ridgeline where Atelueitze should have been, a huge buzzard squatted. The vulture took slow flight in an angry flapping of wings as Ulzana dashed up the slope. Behind him he could hear the sounds of the other warriors coming awake and beginning to follow him up the hill.

Atelueitze's headless body lay chest down, the shaft of an arrow protruding from his back, just below the left shoulder blade.

Ulzana stood motionless, shocked, as Qual-si-dice and Es-kel-tay quickly scanned the ground for signs. He could not take his eyes from the headless corpse of his nephew.

Es-kel-tay broke off the arrow and brought the feathered shaft to Ulzana. He pointed to the special markings — the jagged slashes of lightning, the yellow moons. "Sierra Blanca," he said.

But Ulzana's eyes read even more. There was a peculiarity in the way the feathers were attached and the manner in which the markings were arranged. In the distant past he had seen this before. Then knowledge came to him and he spoke the name. "Pi-hon-se."

The rage, the frustration welled up inside Ulzana and almost choked him. There was no sense to this death. They were coming in to surrender. They had risked the soldiers for three weeks, avoiding fights. And now, now that they were so close to the end, this had to happen. This was not war. This was murder.

"Sierra Blanca blood must pay for this blood," he vowed.

"What can we do?" Don-she-dan argued. "There are only ten of us. The Sierra Blanca are many and they have the soldiers to protect them."

Ulzana turned on him in anger. "Since when do the *Cho-ken-en* measure their courage in numbers? Courage grows in the heart." He struck his breast savagely. "Atelueitze was my blood relative. I *will* avenge his death. You don't have to come."

"Where you lead, I'll follow," Es-kel-tay said. "He was my friend and companion."

"We'll all go," Don-she-dan murmured.

The sun was dropping behind the Mogollons when they finished burying Atelueitze. Then the ten warriors mounted their ponies and followed Pi-hon-se's trail down out of the foothills toward San Carlos.

9

The Sierra Blanca camp was quiet under the darkness of early evening. Cook fires sent probing fingers of light under blanket-draped doorways. Soft voices, a hum of indistinct sound mixed with the light and floated on the calm air.

The *Cho-ken-en* rode slowly into the camp, stopping their horses in the center of the village, surrounded by their hereditary enemies. Their rifles lay carefully across the necks of their ponies, ready for instant use.

"Pi-hon-se!" Ulzana shouted, silencing the murmur of voices from the wickiups. "Pi-hon-se! Sneaking coyote! Woman of the Sierra Blanca! If you're not afraid of the *Cho-ken-en*, come out!"

For what seemed an eternity, there was no response. Ulzana was about to call again when a blanket-draped entrance suddenly exploded with light. Pi-hon-se stepped from the lodge, framed by the firelight behind him.

"I'm not afraid of any man," he said defiantly, a rifle cradled in the crook of his arm. He squinted at the horsemen as his eyes adjusted to the night. "Ulzana? It's been many years since we've spoken to each other."

"I haven't come to speak of old times," Ulzana sneered.

"Why, then? There's no friendship between us."

There was a soft rustling in the deep shadows as Sierra Blanca warriors slipped from their wickiups and circled the

Cho-ken-en horsemen. Ulzana felt, rather than saw, his men
shift positions to meet the new challenge.

"I've come for a blood payment," Ulzana said.

"What concern is that of mine?"

Ulzana felt the anger building up within. In the old days
he would simply have ridden in and killed all who opposed
him. But actions, like men, change. Tonight he would have
his revenge, but if possible, only the man responsible for
Atelueitze's murder would die.

"We followed a pony here from our camp," he finally said.
"A Sierra Blanca killed one of our warriors and took his
head."

"I know nothing of this death. But in war killing is not
murder." Pi-hon-se spoke with a careless defiance. "The
Americans pay twenty-five gold dollars for the head of
every hostile we bring in."

Ulzana spat on the ground. "You lie in the manner of the
coward you are. Do you think I have grown too old to recognize your arrow?"

Moonlight flashed on the gun barrel as Pi-hon-se brought
his rifle up. Without shifting position, Ulzana fired. The
bullet threw Pi-hon-se backward against the wickiup, his
rifle discharging harmlessly into the air. Flashes of light
and sharp reports split the night as the other Sierra Blanca
fired from behind the cover of their lodges. Calmly, undisturbed by the fight around him, Ulzana fired two more bullets into Pi-hon-se's twitching body.

Satisfied that Pi-hon-se was dead, Ulzana dug heels into
his horse's flanks and the pony bolted forward. A shadow
rose from the earth and grabbed at him. Ulzana chopped
down with his rifle barrel and the Sierra Blanca disappeared
under flashing hoofs. Another figure loomed out of the
darkness and Ulzana fired. The shape melted away. Then
he was clear of the village.

Stopping a mile from the camp, in a shallow wash, he

pursed his lips and from deep in his throat came the warbled cry of the nighthawk. It was answered from far out on the desert. One by one, his men appeared from the shadows until all nine were with him in the arroyo.

"Is anyone hurt?" Ulzana asked.

"The Sierra Blanca can't shoot straight," Soz answered.

"Es-kel-tay is bleeding," Notar said.

"It's nothing," Es-kel-tay said. "A bullet just brushed my arm."

"What now?" Soz whispered.

"We can't go to Fort Apache," Parlo said. "The soldiers will be on the lookout for us. Remember what Pi-hon-se said. Each of our heads is worth twenty-five American dollars."

Ulzana spat on the ground. "I was stupid even to attempt this journey. The Americans don't want peace. They want to kill us all. We'll go back to Mexico."

"It won't be easy," Es-kel-tay said.

"Nothing is easy."

"But the soldiers will be alerted. They'll know where to look for us."

"Then we'll have to be smarter than the soldiers. We won't go back the way they expect. Do you have any other plan? Is there any other course open to us?"

No one spoke.

Ulzana turned to Es-kel-tay. "Will you be able to ride with us?"

"Yes."

Ulzana wheeled his pony and headed north, the others following silently.

Ulzana felt a measure of satisfaction in the revenge he had exacted. Pi-hon-se had paid with his blood for Ate-lueitze's life. Yet there was another empty spot in Ulzana's life. Five boys had sworn brotherhood on that day so many years ago. Chino had died at the stage station. Beneactiney was dead for two years at the charcoal camp. Alchise was a scout with the enemy soldiers. Now Pi-hon-se was dead by Ulzana's hand. The years had not been kind to the sworn brothers.

10

THROUGHOUT THE DAY Ulzana kept his men near the foot of the mountains, where the hard, rocky soil would hold dust clouds to a minimum. With night he moved away from the rocky hills, and into the center of the valley, where it was sandy and the sound of a moving column would be muffled.

The raiders rode without pause, turning and twisting through the mountains, hiding their trail in the rocky places or doubling back to confuse the pursuers. There was no need to explain to these veterans that pursuit by one patrol or another would continue until they were killed or until they reached Mexico. There was no malingering as they followed Ulzana's killing pace.

Even a *Cho-ken-en* could not go on forever without rest. By the second night, only the jolting gait of his horse, sending spasms of pain through Ulzana's body, kept him awake. He knew that his men were as tired. During his time as a scout, he had learned that the soldiers stopped to bury the dead. It was time to use this lesson to his own advantage.

Sweeping down through Aravapai Canyon, the *Cho-ken-en* surprised a lone prospector near Black Rock. The mutilated body was left in the open, where it was sure to be found. At the sub-agency, east of San Carlos, they ambushed another man. This one, badly wounded and certain to die, was left naked, spread-eagled on the sand. Near Bear Springs another American was lanced to death.

Satisfied that the tenacious pursuit would be temporarily halted, Ulzana faded into a hidden place in the Gila Mountains, where he allowed his men to sleep.

The soldiers were delayed, but the talking wires remained busy. They spread word of the raid throughout the territory. Even as Ulzana's men slept, troops came from every direction, taking the field against them.

The *Cho-ken-en's* ponies were on their last legs, too exhausted to even browse on the mountain grasses. Ulzana knew he would have to replenish his stock if he were going to avoid capture.

The sun gained speed as it dropped toward the gaping, saw-toothed mouth of the western mountains. The red ball touched the edge of the peaks and was slowly devoured as the victorious shadows began their race across the desert. From a window of the ranch house a light shone like a caught star, separated from its fellows by the black hulk of the mountains. When the light flickered and disappeared, Ulzana led Don-she-dan and Es-kel-tay across the dark desert.

Inside the strong adobe buildings, cowboys slept lightly, pistols under their hay pillows and Winchesters standing loaded and ready beside their beds. A corral of stout palisades, the heavy gates locked and barred with thick chains, protected the precious remuda.

Using hatchets, carelessly left at the woodpile, muffling the chopping sounds with blankets, he and Es-kel-tay cut through enough palisades to open a narrow gap. Then the three *Cho-ken-en* selected the dozen best mounts and herded them silently out of the valley.

Just before dawn, Ulzana joined the rest of his band where they had remained hidden in the foothills. While the fresh horses were being saddled, Soz pointed behind them. As the sun pushed back the horizons, a heavy cloud of dust was exposed, sweeping along their back trail.

"Soldiers!" Soz warned when Ulzana joined him on the ledge.

Ulzana shook his head. "Too much dust. Soldiers ride in a column of twos. These riders are spread out. They're cowboys after their horses."

"Do we run?"

"No. This time we'll fight."

The small canyon near Ash Fork was a perfect spot for an ambush. Buzzards were already feasting and circling where the worn-out mounts had been slaughtered. The black birds, visible across the miles of desert, were drawing the cowboys into the trap.

Es-kel-tay and three warriors were positioned on the south side of the trail where the canyon narrowed. Ulzana and three others waited among the rocks opposite them.

The cowboys rode too quickly along the trail. Their eyes were clouded with dust, and their senses dulled by anger. The *Cho-ken-en* crossfire cut the disorganized posse to pieces. Two cowboys were dead and the rest were frantically seeking protection behind the rocks when Ulzana signaled and led his band into the desert.

Instead of heading directly for the border on the usual exit route between the Whetstone and Dragoon mountains, as Ulzana guessed the Army would expect, he followed the Gila River into New Mexico.

For five days the raiders rode back and forth, seeking an open corridor toward the southern border. Each day the ring of soldiers grew tighter, drawing inward, ever narrowing the open areas in which the hostiles could run.

Finally, near the American town of Alma, Ulzana caught two lonely prospectors who were heading for that haven of safety. The mutilated bodies were staked out in the road.

Once more Ulzana went to ground and allowed his men to sleep and regain their strength.

11

ULZANA LAY in the shade of a gnarled scrub oak and delighted in the cool, fragrant softness of the grass. The sun was gone and the dark had begun to creep down the mountain slopes, but the sky was clear and light yet. The sun's dying rays reached across the desert, painting the tips of the eastern mountains a soft golden color. A lone cloud burned where the sun had touched it in passing, but the valley where he lay was cool.

It had been over a month since he had left Sy-e-konne and Kah. A month of lonely nights and long, endless days. His heart ached to be reunited with his wife and child.

With his thoughts, his loneliness, Ulzana suddenly felt an uneasiness stirring in the back of his mind. A vague, nameless fear scratched at the pit of his stomach. The bushes stood straight and calm in the quiet air. Heat waves still rose from the desert floor, causing the distant mountains to dance in the shimmering glare. The land was silent. There was no movement, no noise; even the wind held its breath. The uneasiness grew. Then he knew it was the silence that bothered him. With the sun falling, the small animals should have begun their scraping sounds as they searched for food. Only when they hid in fear were the tiny creatures completely quiet.

To his left, higher up the ridge, metal flashed in the failing sunlight. The slanting rays of the sun sometimes tripped on a piece of broken glass or a shiny stone and touched off a blinding white flash, but in this land of sudden death a man learned to read those reflections. This had been dull, like a beam of sunlight glancing off a worn rifle barrel.

It was the flash that saved them. Ulzana fired his rifle into the air and followed the report with a yell.

"Soldiers!"

In two bounds he was on his pony. The brush at the open end of the canyon erupted with blue coats and calico shirts, as a troop of dismounted cavalry and their Navajo scouts burst from cover. In an instant the camp was empty as the warriors grabbed their rifles and disappeared into the chaparral.

Ulzana bent low over his laboring horse's neck, the buckskin's flanks heaving between his knees. He could hear nothing of his pursuers over his own pounding blood. His eyes were fastened on the safety of the ridgeline ahead. Then he heard the hollow sound of a bullet striking solid flesh and felt the buckskin falter. The horse staggered the few remaining feet to the crest of the hill, each step spraying the rocks from a crimson jet. He leapt clear as the buckskin died on its feet and fell.

Before turning to run, he looked back to see the soldiers in his abandoned camp, in possession of all his horses and supplies. Then he left, dodging and running away from the troops.

12

THE CABIN, an unpainted clapboard with a sagging roof, was nestled in the small valley on the shores of a mountain lake. A dozen horses, restless in the late afternoon sun, idly shuffled in the corral, nibbling on the bits of grass that grew around the corral poles. A thin mist of smoke rose from the crumbling chimney. Nothing else stirred.

While the main party approached the corral, Ulzana and Es-kel-tay walked boldly to the front of the shack. Raising his foot, Ulzana lashed out, kicking open the door.

The strong, putrid odor of whiskey and unwashed bodies hit him like a blow. Two men were slouched over a table in the center of the room. An empty jug lay on the floor, and another was on the table. The room was filthy. Bits of clothing and rags littered the floor, along with scraps of food covered by swarms of huge, black flies.

The glaring sun blinded the two men, making Ulzana and Es-kel-tay only shadows that filled the doorway. Their whiskey-fogged minds did not register danger until Ulzana fired from the hip. The clay jug exploded, spraying alcohol over the men and the table. One of the Americans looked blankly at the blood welling from a cut in his hand, puzzled. The next two bullets knocked the men sprawling amid the trash on the floor. Ulzana turned and walked out while Es-kel-tay kicked over the potbellied stove, spewing burning coals onto the floor. Greedy flames were licking at the wooden shack when they left the valley.

With his men mounted on fresh horses, Ulzana resumed his southward march. Moving slowly along the plain of the upper Gila, the raiders stumbled on two men who were panning the gravel in the shallow stream bed.

One of the surprised Americans grabbed his rifle and fired first, his hurried shot staggering Notar's horse. A flurry of return shots cut down the Americans. However, the cracking gunshots had alerted a patrol. From the sounds of their galloping horses crashing through the thick brush, it was obvious that the soldiers would not be long in reaching the river.

Ulzana wheeled his mount and entered the shallow river. He led his men downstream, safely out of sight of the dead Americans.

"Don-she-dan, take the others and go on foot through the stream. Leave your horses with me."

"What are you going to do?"

"I'll lead the soldiers away. If I'm successful, I'll meet you at Sentinel Peak. If that place is dangerous, then at Alamosa Springs. Wait two days. If I'm not back then, go on without me."

As his men waded downstream, Ulzana led the horses up the river bank, carefully to leave an easily found trail, but not one so obvious that the soldiers would become suspicious.

After riding east for perhaps ten miles, he headed into the rugged foothills. At every cross canyon, he released a pony, whipping it with a thorny branch to make it run. He wanted the Americans to believe that the band had separated.

Finally, he abandoned his own mount and continued on foot. He circled around until he was satisfied that the soldiers were on the false trail. Then he headed toward Sentinel Peak.

Finding a patrol of soldiers camped at the base of the rendezvous, he skirted the peak and jogged toward Alamosa Springs. He had to move cautiously because there were patrols everywhere.

On the evening of the second day, he found his band assembled near the spring. Ulzana threw himself down on the ground and slept.

When he awoke, it was dark. He climbed to the top of the high rock where Es-kel-tay lay watching the terrain below them. The territory was literally swarming with troops. Their campfires sparkled in the valleys like a widely scattered city, a handful of fireflies trapped in a dark bowl. It was becoming more and more difficult to move safely across the land. The constant pressure and fear were beginning to destroy his men as surely as enemy bullets.

"We won't ever see the mountains of Mexico," Es-kel-tay said. There was no emotion in his words, just a simple statement of fact. "Eventually the soldiers will corner us and we'll be killed."

Ulzana was tired, not from lack of sleep, but from the mental strain. The effort to remain one step ahead of the relentless pursuit was sapping the strength from his body.

"What do you suggest?" he asked wearily.

Es-ke-tay was silent a moment. "If we travel separately, maybe we can sneak back on the reservation. Once we're among our own people, Nantan Lupan will listen to us."

"It's too late," Ulzana said, shaking his head. "We've killed too many Americans. We'd be murdered for the twenty-five dollars."

"Our friends wouldn't kill us," Es-kel-tay insisted.

"Who can we call friend?"

"At least we could try. This way, there's no hope at all. It's only a matter of time before we're caught."

"There's always hope," Ulzana said, trying to believe he wasn't lying to himself. "But you're right about one thing.

Ten men make too wide a trail. We'll split up. In four days we'll meet again by the spring in the Burro Mountains. From there it's only a short run to the border."

Ulzana looked around at the rest of his band. They were all listening to the discussion. "I can't tell you what to do. I won't quit until I'm back with my family, or I'm dead. Even if the soldiers let us return to Turkey Creek, there's nothing there for me." He picked up his rifle. "I'll be in the Burro Mountains in four days. Those who want to do so can meet me there."

"We'll be there," Es-ke-tay said. He shrugged and smiled. "We've come this far together, we might as well finish it together."

13

WHEN ULZANA REACHED the rendezvous he was physically exhausted. Although he had come cautiously, scouting carefully, his legs ached and his lungs burned. It was a shock for him to realize that age was encroaching on his physical powers. The miles no longer disappeared under the effortless pumping of his legs.

Ulzana swept his arm in a semicircle to the north. "There's almost a solid line of troops, combing the mountains and valleys. A coyote couldn't avoid them."

"You're just saying that to make us feel good," Don-shedan joked.

"However, to the southeast there's only one patrol," Ulzana continued. "It's a large one, but if we divert their attention, we should be able to get past them and swing west."

"Without horses we won't be able to do much," Soz observed.

Ulzana felt the fatigue in his legs, but the *Cho-ken-en* were men of courage and endurance. "We'll stay to the high ground until we have a chance to get horses. In the rocky places, a man on foot can move more quickly than a man on horseback."

Ulzana kept his men concealed in the narrow pass, allowing the lone courier to go through the gorge unmolested.

The larger prize, the troop of cavalry, was still coming up.

The soldiers moved out with the mists of morning cold around them, their butts not yet warmed to the still stiff saddle leather, the rough wool of their uniforms not yet sweat damp. Their breakfasts were still warm in their stomachs, their muscles still limbering to the new day's work.

Then suddenly there was a ring of fire around the soldiers. From behind a boulder, a tuft of buffalo grass, a clump of cactus, curls of smoke drifted, and for each puff of smoke, a soldier fell. There was no visible enemy, no cover from the hail of bullets. The Americans fired wildly at the puffs of smoke sprouting from the hills, but the pass was no place to stop and fight. They could do nothing but retreat out of the death trap.

Ulzana did not wait for them to regroup and come back. He signaled and his warriors melted back into the hills, leaving five dead soldiers and as many wounded in the dust of the pass. There would be no immediate pursuit. The southern corridor was temporarily open.

On the day the Americans called Christmas, Ulzana's band jumped two vaqueros guarding the horse herd on a ranch only five miles from the American town of Carlisle. The butchered bodies were left warming at their campfire while the *Cho-ken-en* cut out fresh mounts.

Ulzana hoped the evidence of the dead vaqueros would lead the Americans to believe that the band intended to cross the border south of Carlisle. Doubling back on his trail, he led the small band directly west, and crossed into Arizona, heading for the rugged Chiricahua Mountains. He had no intention of killing again.

The two prospectors virtually committed suicide. If they had remained hidden, Ulzana would have ridden on, unaware of their presence. Perhaps the white men became irrational with fear. Perhaps they believed that they would be able to kill all of the *Cho-ken-en* and collect the bounty money. Whatever the reason, they fired on the raiders from ambush.

Parlo received a bullet which passed through his lower leg, and hit his mount in the heart, killing it instantly. A bullet grazed Qual-si-dice's head, knocking him to the ground, unconscious. Soz and Notar, scouting the flanks, unseen by the white men, fired into the prospectors from the rear, killing them both.

Ulzana helped carry the wounded into the old strongholds of his people. It was in the canyon of Ulzana's birth that the band rested, doctoring their wounds, and preparing for the last run to the border.

14

LARGE MASSES OF CLOUDS rolled and buckled across the sky, their bottoms heavy with dark moisture. The clouds met, merging into one giant mass that pressed toward the earth from its own weight. First only the mountain peaks, then the entire range was swallowed by the hungry clouds.

There was no wind yet on the desert foothills where Lieutenant William Creighton rode with his patrol when snow began with scattered flakes of large, wet fluff, instantly melting where it settled. Then the winds came, stabbing, slashing down from the heights, cooling the earth. The snowflakes multiplied, overcame the lingering warmth of the land, and began to grow like a white moss on the rocks and the cacti. Soon the swirling mist was a curtain obscuring objects only a few feet distant.

A shadow materialized out of the snow in front of him, and Creighton raised his hand, halting the patrol.

"The snow hides the tracks," Alchise said, pointing toward the peaks invisible now in the southeast. "More snow in mountains."

"Is there a place where we can camp?"

Alchise nodded. "A small canyon. Less than one mile."

It took over an hour to travel that distance. Visibility had become so limited that only the rump of the horse in front was barely discernible through the icy veil.

"Sergeant, make camp here. We'll wait out the storm."
Reluctantly Creighton gave his horse to a trooper and
bent over the fire his men had started in the shelter of a
small arroyo. He knew that further pursuit was futile.

Last night, on their annual fall roundup, the cattlemen of
the San Simon Valley had gathered at the ranch in White
Tail Canyon. Even though they knew hostile Chiricahua
were in the area, they were confident in their numbers.
They had awakened this morning to discover their corral
empty. Now the hostiles were mounted on thirty of the best
horses in the territory. By the time the snow settled, they
would be safely in the warmer climate of Mexico.

As he warmed his hands, Creighton's mind wandered. He
remembered Ulzana from the patrol, a little more than five
years ago, when they had been chasing Victorio. A lot had
happened in those five years. It seemed to Creighton that
he had spent every moment of that time chasing some rene-
gade band of Apaches. But, in the process, he had become
a veteran, accustomed to the land and the people who lived
here. Deep in his heart, he had known from the beginning
that he would not catch Ulzana, that no one would catch
him.

"Cup of coffee, sir?" Sergeant Hoffman asked, squatting
beside him.

"Thanks." Creighton sipped the steaming fluid, feeling
the warmth spread throughout his body. "Do you think
we'll be able to catch the hostiles when this storm lets up?"

"No, sir." Hoffman smiled over his coffee. "I reckon
they're over the border already. It'd be a simple matter to
slip past the patrols in this storm."

"I believe you're right. You know, Hoffman, when I was
at the academy, we studied the campaigns of all the great
military leaders, but I can't remember a single battle to
match this raid of Ulzana's. Unless it would be the Spartans
at Thermopylae."

"Thermopylae, sir? I don't think I've ever heard about that one."

"The Spartans were an Apache type of people in ancient Greece. About two hundred of them held off thousands of Persian soldiers at a pass in the mountains."

"Did they win, sir?"

Creighton shook his head. "No. A traitor led the Persians around behind them and the Spartans were all killed. But they put up a hell of a fight."

Hoffman sipped his coffee. "There were only ten 'Paches on this raid, sir. And it looks to me like they won."

Creighton did some mental calculations. "Yes," he finally said. "Ten hostiles and over three thousand troops in pursuit for seven weeks. And we didn't even get a glimpse of the Apaches."

Hoffman remained silent, reflective.

"It's eerie the way they just disappear," Creighton continued. "One minute you figure you've got them trapped, and the next minute they're gone just as if the earth had swallowed them. I thought for sure we had them this time, when Captain Finley found their slaughtered horses. Maybe we would have, too, if it weren't for this storm and the fresh mounts they stole last night."

"It's a big territory," Hoffman said. "It's pretty hard to find ten men, especially when they know the country better than we do."

"Maybe that's the problem," Creighton agreed. Ulzana had covered over twelve hundred miles, stealing at least two hundred and sixty horses and mules. Twice he had skirmished with the soldiers, and both times had escaped unhurt. Counting the twelve White Mountain Indians at Fort Apache, the raiders had killed at least thirty-eight people in Arizona and New Mexico. Creighton wouldn't even guess how many more bodies might never be found in hidden canyons where lonely prospectors had been caught and killed.

"Just think of the wasted time and effort," Creighton reflected aloud. "This just isn't our kind of war. We were trained for mass cavalry assaults and frontal attacks." He brushed the snow from his face. "I guess the only way we'll ever get the hostiles is to go into Mexico and dig them out of their home camps. If we can."

Hoffman put down his cup of coffee. "Do you think they'll put this raid down in the books you studied, sir?"

Creighton almost laughed. "No. I don't think so. They don't think we can learn anything from a bunch of ignorant savages."

"I don't know about that, sir, but I sure would like to have a troop of Chiricahua fightin' for me instead of against me."

Creighton drank the last of his coffee and threw the bitter dregs into the snow. "I think you're right about that, Sergeant. I sure do believe you're right."

15

William A. Creighton, First Lieutenant, USA, began keeping a journal when he first arrived at Fort Apache, finding it a convenient way to remember the details of daily life he included in his letters to Emma. It had never been intended for any other purpose. Yet, in later years, it became his link with the past. His children, and eventually his grandchildren, read it, and saw life as it had been when wild Indians still dominated the desert plains. Each time that Creighton examined it, he was carried back to the sounds and smells of days forever gone, when he had been young and strong. Especially vivid with memories was the campaign of January 1886.

Sunday, January 3. This morning, after a warm breakfast, we left Nacori, Sonora, on foot, carrying twelve days' rations on three of the toughest, meanest mules I've ever seen. Besides myself, our party consists of Captain Finley, Lieutenant John Taylor, Assistant Surgeon Theodore Daniels, and seventy-five Chiricahua serving as scouts.

Nacori is evidence enough that we are in the heart of Apache country. The citizens of the pueblo have erected an adobe wall completely enclosing their settlement, as protection from the savage raiders. Naturally they consider us insane for going into the mountains after the hostiles, pro-

tected only by our Apache scouts, whom the Mexicans do
not trust at all. I'm sure they believe we'll be murdered in
our sleep.

There is a rugged grandeur to this country. The great
mountains dominate everything, rising ten to twelve thousand feet above the desert valleys. Their flanks are slashed
with ravines such as I have never seen before. On the
higher elevations are forests of pine, while on the lower
slopes there are jungles of subtropical growth. I am convinced that we are penetrating areas never before seen by
white men.

In the vast splendor of uncharted canyons and the alien
majesty of upthrust spires, I sometimes feel insignificant.
The seventy-eight men in our expedition are like so many
grains of sand lost in the desert.

Monday, January 4. We have crossed the Haros River
and ascended the high hills beyond, where the scouts discovered a large, well-beaten trail. The entire band of hostiles evidently passed here six days previously, having
moved their camp from the junction of the Haros and Yaqui
rivers. They are headed east toward the extremely rugged
mountains known as *La Espinosa del Diablo*, "the Devil's
Backbone," situated between the Haros and Satachi rivers.

Thursday, January 7. The march has become a nightmare. Our Army boots, with their hard soles and heels,
proved too noisy on the rocky trails. At Chatto's insistence,
the scouts furnished us with moccasins, which enable us to
move more quietly, but our soft American feet are not used
to them, and we are limping badly.

To remain hidden from the prying eyes of the hostiles,
we march mostly at night, which does not help the situation. The scouts lead us over the rocks and down into deep,
dark canyons, along narrow paths that would test the agility

of a mountain goat. We generally halt at midnight, sore and tired, and try to sleep. In the high mountains, the nights are bitterly cold. We each carry a single blanket, which is scant protection against the elements. At times the cold stabs so viciously we can't sleep at all. Surprisingly, the hardships don't appear to affect the Indians.

The scouts prepare all of our coffee and food, cooking it during the daylight hours. They build fires of carefully selected dry wood to avoid any telltale smoke. While we eat and cuss our blisters, our tireless guides range ahead searching for trails.

There are no fancy roll calls, stable inspections, morning reports, or musters out here in the mountains. It's just as well, since we certainly don't appear very military. Tears in our black trousers have been partially repaired with white thread blacked on the coffee pot. Uncut hair is sticking through holes in our campaign hats. If an inspector general could see us now, we'd all be cashiered out of the service.

We lost one of our mules last night. The poor creature slipped on some loose shale, and pitched off the trail into the gorge. It was so dark that we were unable to see the donkey falling, but it screamed all the way down. A mule's scream is by far the most unearthly sound that can be imagined. I'm sure that if the hostiles are anywhere within twenty miles, they must have heard the commotion. The loss in supplies is not too serious, as the animal was carrying some rations and ammunition, of which we have an adequate supply. However, the sound of that scream kept my nerves on edge for several hours.

Saturday, January 9. At sunset tonight Chatto, our first sergeant of scouts, sent back word that a hostile rancheria has been discovered only twelve miles ahead. The Apaches are camped on a well-protected high spot, with a commanding view of the surrounding terrain. Finley has allowed us twenty minutes for resting. No fires are permitted, so we have to eat hard bread and raw bacon. I believe he is planning another night march.

Sunday, January 10. What a night march we had! It was by far the most difficult trek I have ever attempted. All night we toiled through the dark and moonless mountains. Most of the twelve miles led over solid rock and down canyons so dark that they seemed bottomless. Sometimes the descent became so steep that we could not go forward, and had to climb back and find another way. We crossed and re-crossed rivers and canyons, clinging by toes and fingernails, hoping every moment that the hostiles would not discover us.

When I was certain that I could not go another step, we were there. In the false dawn, I could see the dim outline of the rocky fortress occupied by the hostiles. The command quickly dispersed for an attack, attempting as our first objective to surround the enemy camp.

I had nearly reached the farther side of the position when I heard the braying of a mule. Like the geese of ancient Rome, that abominable mule saved the hostiles.

The first, faint light of morning was breaking when the firing began. The darkness was lit by yellow flashes of rifle fire, the reports echoing and re-echoing from the cliffs.

I could see dim forms scurrying down the mountain, disappearing into the darkness below. A hostile, attempting to escape on a horse, loomed in front of me. I fired two quick shots from my pistol and the horse went down. The Apache bounded away among the peaks, obviously unhurt.

The rest of the hostiles scattered like quail through the canyons. Our scouts were too tired to pursue them. The only known casualty suffered by the Apaches was the horse I had killed.

But we had captured their entire pony herd and all of

their camp effects. There is not much. Apparently the Apaches are suffering greatly from the constant pursuit. The captured food consists only of some mescal, some pony meat, a small part of a deer, and a little dried meat of unknown origin.

Monday, January 11. With the first true light of dawn, an old squaw came into camp begging food for her children. Our supplies are dangerously low, but Finley generously gave her coffee and flour. Then the squaw told us that the chiefs had sent her to ask for a parley. Needless to say, we are all delighted. With the Chiricahua alerted to our presence in these mountains, it would be unlikely that we should have another opportunity to surprise them.

Finley sent the squaw back to her people with the message that we would talk with the leaders tomorrow, at the river, a mile below our camp. Lady Fortune, who has so far avoided us, is at last about to smile.

Tuesday, January 12. Finley allowed us to build fires in the camp so recently occupied by the hostiles. However, even with the fires, it was bitterly cold in the high mountains. The chill and hunger kept me awake most of the night in spite of my fatigue. Our scouts were equally exhausted, and consequently were not as vigilant as is their usual custom.

I must have finally dozed, because I was aroused at daylight by cries from the scouts. A heavy fog hung over the mountains, limiting visibility and making the morning light very faint. My first thought was that Major West and his scouts had discovered our position and mistaken us for hostiles. I dashed forward, agonized by the thought that we were being attacked by our friends.

As I moved ahead, I could see dusky forms moving in the distance. The crash of rifles and the flames from the muzzles lit up the scene. The firing continued for fifteen minutes before it became known that the attacking force was a troop of Mexican irregulars. Three of our scouts had been wounded, one seriously, in the exchange of fire.

Since I speak some Spanish, I advanced with Captain Finley fifty or seventy-five yards. Calling to the Mexicans, I explained as best I could who we were and that we had driven the hostiles from this position yesterday morning.

The Mexican major, a lieutenant, and two soldiers came forward to speak with us. The major explained that they had mistaken the scouts for hostiles. This may be true, but it is common knowledge that the irregulars receive no pay from either the state or national government. Their only remuneration comes from captured booty and from scalp bounties — two hundred pesos for a warrior's scalp, one hundred pesos for that of a woman or child. The hair of an Army scout is indistinguishable from that of a hostile.

As we parlayed with the Mexicans, our scouts lay with their heads peering over the rocks. The click of their breechblocks sounded clear in the morning air as they loaded their rifles. Captain Finley turned and spoke to me in a harsh whisper. "For God's sake, don't let them fire."

At the same moment, the major turned to his troops and called, *"No tiren!"*

I had just started back to warn our scouts not to fire, when one shot rang out distinct and alone. The echoes in the fog were such that I could not tell where it had come from, but it sounded like a death knell. It was followed by volleys from both sides.

I immediately went to Captain Finley, who had fallen forward on his face. A ragged hole showed in his head and his brains were running down his face, staining the rocks. He was unconscious, but still breathing shallowly.

The major fell where he had been standing. The Mexican lieutenant and the two soldiers turned to run, but were killed by a fusillade of bullets.

I dragged Finley back to our lines, but Surgeon Daniels

informed me that it was only a matter of time before he
would die. Being the next senior officer present, I assumed
command.

The fire fight with the Mexicans continued for two hours
before they retreated, taking up a strong position in a line of
hills.

My command is dangerously low on food and ammunition. Confronted by a superior force of Mexicans, surrounded by hostile Chiricahua, two hundred miles below
the international boundary, I have concluded that the wisest and safest course is a strategic withdrawal.

Saturday, January 16. We were again contacted by the
hostiles. Geronimo, Nachite, old Nana, Chihuahua, and
fourteen warriors approached our camp.

Knowing that we are in retreat, the hostiles were extremely belligerent. Geronimo asked why I had come down
here. I told him that we are here to capture or destroy him
and his band. Geronimo then said that when we reached
his camp, he had felt that there was no longer a place where
white men would not pursue him. I assured the hostiles
that if they did not surrender, neither the Americans nor
the Mexicans would allow them rest.

After a brief consultation among themselves, the Apaches
agreed to meet with General Harrison twenty miles south of
the border at *Cañón de los Embudos,* "the Canyon of the
Funnels," in two months' time. This was provided that regular troops should not be present. Being in no position to
bargain, I agreed to those terms. To show their good faith,
old Nana, one warrior, two women (one of whom is Geronimo's wife), and nine children have agreed to accompany me
north.

Monday, January 18. Captain Finley died today, never
having regained consciousness. His body, wrapped in blan-

kets, was buried near Nacori, Sonora. Stone slabs were placed over the grave to protect it from prowling creatures, and to mark its location so the body may be recovered and receive the honors due a fine and most courageous officer.

16

"WILL THERE TRULY be peace this time?" Sy-e-konne asked. It was cold, but she left the fire, wrapped a blanket around herself, and went to sit in the open flap of the wickiup.

"I don't know," Ulzana said, somewhat harshly. "I can't read the future. It'll depend on Nantan Lupan." In his heart he believed that perhaps, this time, the White Eyes and the *Cho-ken-en* could reach an understanding.

Sy-e-konne turned away from the doorway. There were tears in her eyes. "No matter what Nantan Lupan does, there must be peace," she insisted. "What has this war gained you? Nothing! We don't eat any better now than we did at Turkey Creek. Every day we run, but there's no place to go. I've lost one baby in this war. I won't lose my son."

"Don't worry about me," Kah said, standing to his full height. The firelight gleamed off his body, already heavily muscled. He looked older, much older than his twelve years. "I can take care of myself. I'm almost old enough to be a warrior."

"A warrior! Is that all men can think of? You don't know anything except killing and fighting. You won't be satisfied until we're all dead!"

"Silence!" Impulsively Ulzana reached over the fire and slapped Sy-e-konne hard across the cheek. She reeled back, a stunned look on her face. He was immediately sorry for his fit of temper. It was the first time he had ever struck his wife.

Embarrassed, he looked at his son, and saw in the boy a reflection of himself, as brave and eager as he had been at twelve. The world had changed radically in the intervening years. As the silence grew, he wanted to speak, to say something that would reassure his wife and inspire his son, but no words of his had any meaning. "We'll talk with Nantan Lupan," he finally said.

"That's not an answer," Sy-e-konne answered softly, only vaguely understanding the devils that tormented her husband.

"It's the beginning of an answer," he said. "The answer is somewhere along the way. I'll work for peace. Chihuahua will work for peace. Men don't know what's in another's heart until they speak together. We'll talk with Nantan Lupan. It'll be a start."

He left Sy-e-konne and Kah and walked alone into the January night. He stared up at the winter moon, floating like a huge disk on the frost-covered surface of a great lake. It was a hearth glow in the sky, distant and icy, glittering on the hills and frozen valleys. It looked brittle as glass, sharp as the talons of a hungering hawk. It was a beautiful moon, but filled also with a sadness. He was loath to stop staring at it. But it was like the shining hope of peace before his hungering soul. Distant, unattainable, yet that which he most desired.

He held his arms upward in an attitude of supplication. "Oh gods of the *Shis-Inday*, if you still have power, listen to me. Smile upon your people and grant us peace without end."

Then his arms fell and he stood with bowed head, suddenly overcome with physical and mental exhaustion.

17

THE MARCH SUN was past the high point of its journey across the sky when the *Shis-Inday* approached the American camp. The Americans had chosen a strong position on a low mesa overlooking the water, with plenty of fine grass and fuel at hand. The ravine was beautiful. White-trunked, tall, slender sycamores, dark gnarly ash, rough-barked cottonwoods, and pliant willows shaded the rippling waters of a small stream. The volcanic rock was covered with a soft carpet of fallen leaves.

Since Ulzana was not a chief, he would not speak to the Americans. He selected a position on the ridge behind Nantan Lupan where he could watch and listen.

The sun was shining into the canyon, making shady areas on the ground. The small sounds of the men moving and sitting in the dead leaves and the murmur of their voices seemed muffled. The warm sun laid a nostalgic hand on Ulzana's back. It had been a day such as this that he had gone on his first raid as a warrior and Chino had died in his arms. How long ago had that been? He could not even clearly remember Chino's face. That day belonged to a different time, to a different man.

Geronimo, Nachite, and Chihuahua walked among the Americans and sat down. There was a tension in the air that could be seen in the eyes of everyone.

Nantan Lupan spoke first.

"What do you have to say?" Harrison asked, addressing Geronimo. "I have come all the way down from Fort Bowie to listen."

Geronimo remained seated, apparently nervous. Great beads of perspiration rolled down his temples and over his hands. In one hand he held a buckskin thong, which he fingered nervously.

"First I want to talk of the causes which led me to leave the reservation. I was living peaceably with my family, having plenty to eat, sleeping well, taking care of my people, and perfectly contented. I had not killed a horse or man. The people in charge of us knew this to be so, and yet they said I was a bad man, the worst man there. I did not leave on my own accord. Blame those men who started this talk about me.

"Some time before I left, the wife of Mangas spoke to me, saying, 'They are going to arrest you and Mangas,' but I paid no attention to her, knowing that I had done no wrong. Then I heard that the Americans were going to hang me, so I left. Find out who began the bad talk about me. With them is the fault."

He paused, nervously fingering the buckskin thong, and looked around, trying to calculate the effect of his words. General Harrison's face showed no emotion.

"Several times I have asked for peace, but trouble came from the agents," Geronimo continued. "Whenever I have broken out, it has always been because of bad talk. Very often there are stories put in the newspapers that I am to be hanged. When a man tries to do right, such stories should not be put in the newspapers."

Geronimo fingered the buckskin thong and wiped the perspiration from his face. "What is the matter that you do not speak to me? I want you to look and smile at me."

Harrison raised his head and looked at Geronimo. He did not smile. "Finish your talk first."

Geronimo smiled. "I keep in my memory what you told

me, although a long time has passed. From here on I want to live in peace. When we go on the reservation you put agents over us who do bad things. I do not believe you would tell them to do bad things to us. In the future I do not want any man near us who will talk bad about us and tell lies. I want to have a good man put over us. We are all children of one God. God is listening to me. If I were thinking bad, or if I had done bad, I would never have come here to talk with you. I have told you all that happened." Once more Geronimo wiped the perspiration from his face. "Now I want peace in good faith. If I have forgotten something I will tell you of it some other time. I have finished for today."

There was a long silence. Finally General Harrison took a sip of water and spoke softly.

"It seems strange that forty men should be afraid of two. If it is a fact that you left the reservation because of bad talk, why did you sneak all over the country killing innocent people?"

Geronimo squirmed. "We did not know what we had done to Nantan Creighton and Chatto."

"But what has that to do with killing innocent people?" Harrison asked angrily. "There is not a week that you don't hear foolish stories in your own camp, but you are no child. You don't have to believe them. You promised me in the Sierra Madre that our peace would last, but you lied about it. All the Americans said that you were lying when I brought you to the reservation. I have had a constant fight with my own people to protect you from them. The white people say that I am responsible for every one who has been killed. When a man lies to me once, I want some better proof than his own word before I can believe him again."

"That is why I want to know who it was that ordered my arrest."

"That's all bosh. There were no orders for anyone to arrest you."

"Perhaps those who were going to arrest me were under somebody else's orders," Geronimo suggested, hanging his head like a little boy confronting an angry parent.

"You sent some of your people to kill Chatto and Lieutenant Creighton," Harrison asserted. "Then you started the story that they had been killed, and thus got a great many of your people to go out."

"That is not true."

"Everything you did on the reservation is known. There is no use to try and talk nonsense. You must make up your mind whether you will stay out on the warpath or surrender unconditionally. If you stay out, I'll keep after you and kill every last one, if it takes fifty years."

Geronimo lowered his eyes. "I am a man of my word. I am telling the truth about why I left the reservation."

"You told me the same thing in the Sierra Madre, and you lied then."

"Then how do you want me to talk to you?" Geronimo threw up his hands in a gesture of frustration. "I have but one mouth. I cannot talk with my ears."

"Your mouth talks too many ways."

"If you think I am not telling the truth, then you did not come here in good faith."

"I came with the same faith as when I went down to the Sierra Madre. You told me the same things there that you are telling me now. What evidence do I have of your sincerity? How do I know whether or not you are lying to me?"

"I was living at peace with my family on the reservation. Why were those stories started about me?"

"How would I know? Are not stories started in your own camp every day?"

"There is no other captain as great as you. I thought you ought to know about those stories, and who started them."

"Who were the Indians that those stories were started about?"

"They wanted to seize me and Mangas."

"Then why did Chihuahua and Nachite go out?"

"Because they were afraid the same thing would happen to them."

"Who made them afraid?"

"All the Indians here saw the troops and scouts getting ready to go out to arrest me. That is the reason they went out."

"But what did you tell those Indians?"

"The only thing I told them was that I heard I was going to be seized and killed."

"But why did you send up some of your people to kill Lieutenant Creighton and Chatto?"

"I did not tell them to do anything of the kind. If I had said anything like that these Indians would say so."

"That's just what they do say. You reported that they were killed and that is why so many went out with you."

"Whenever I wanted to talk to Nantan Creighton, I spoke by day or night. I never went to him in a hidden manner. Maybe some of these men know about it. Perhaps you had better ask them."

"I have said all I have to say," Harrison said firmly. "You had better think it over tonight and let me know in the morning."

Geronimo stood, obviously relieved at being dismissed. "All right, we will talk tomorrow. I may want to ask you some questions, just as you have asked me some."

18

ULZANA WAS PLEASED with the strategic location of the *Cho-ken-en* camp. It was situated in a lava bed on top of a small, conical hill, surrounded by steep ravines. The lava block breastworks and the commanding terrain would prevent a thousand soldiers from surrounding and taking this position. A mere handful of warriors could hold an army at bay while the women and children escaped through the dozens of ravines and canyons which would shelter them from pursuit until they reached the higher mountains.

From his hidden post, Ulzana had watched Alchise making his cautious approach from the moment he had left the American camp. He followed his movements through the sight of his Winchester carbine as Alchise scrambled over the three deep gulches that separated the *Cho-ken-en* from the White Eyes.

As Alchise clambered up the last slope, Ulzana stood and stepped in front of him. "Why have you come to our camp?" he asked, slowly thumbing back the rifle's hammer.

Alchise stopped and spread his arms to show that he did not have any weapons. "Nantan Lupan asked me to talk with you," he said. "He doesn't trust Geronimo, but he knows you were tricked into leaving the reservation, and that you would like to surrender."

"I speak for no one except my own family," Ulzana said,

turning away. "But come. You can speak with my brother. He's our leader."

The two men walked through the camp, the army scout silently evaluating everything he saw. Some little boys, one with the blue-gray eyes of an American, romped freely and carelessly together. Women worked over the fires, cooking. Some of the warriors sat in the sun playing monte. It did not appear to be the camp of fugitives.

They halted in front of Chihuahua's wickiup.

Streaks of gray showed in Chihuahua's thick, black hair as he raised his head. Lines of concern spread out from the corners of his eyes. "Sit," he said softly. "You come with the soldiers against your friends, but you are welcome at my lodge. I'm too old to have enemies."

"Nantan Lupan sends tobacco," Alchise said, holding out a sack and papers.

There was silence as each man rolled and lit a cigarette. Ulzana held his cigarette between his thumb and index finger, taking short puffs and exhaling immediately. In between he stared meditatively at the glowing tip. When he felt the silence had been extended enough, he spoke.

"It's been a long time since we've talked."

"It's good to have words with an old friend," Alchise answered.

Chihuahua nodded, but did not speak.

"There's no profit in fighting the Americans," Alchise said. "They are as numerous as the grains of sand."

Chihuahua looked across the valley to the lofty peaks. "The Mexicans are also as plentiful as the grains of sand. This has never frightened us. We don't count the enemies we must fight."

"The Americans are different," Alchise argued.

"What terms does Nantan Lupan offer?" Chihuahua asked.

"The Americans offer you the gift of life."

Chihuahua made a motion with his hand as if to brush away a foolish remark. "The Americans are closer to death than we are. If I raised my hand, their bones would already be white under the sun." He paused a moment to let his words have their desired effect. "If my people surrender, it will be because we wish to live with our families again, not because of idle threats."

"What terms do the Americans offer?" Ulzana repeated.

"If you surrender, you'll be held in prison at a distance from the reservation."

"For how long?" Chihuahua asked.

Alchise shrugged. "Two — maybe three years. I don't know. Until you have learned the ways of peace. The only choice Nantan Lupan offers is for you to return to the mountains and fight it out."

"I've already decided to surrender," Chihuahua said. "You may tell him that I think all of the *Cho-ken-en* will quit fighting, but regardless of what the others do, I'll bring my band into his camp at noon."

"What of Mangas and his people?"

"I don't know," Chihuahua answered. "He left us and went into the mountains with thirteen of his followers. We have not kept in contact with him, and I have not seen him for many months. If Nantan Lupan wishes it, I could send runners to him, and see if he will come in."

Alchise stood. "I will tell this to Nantan Lupan."

19

At noon the *Cho-ken-en* returned to the American camp. Ulzana sat in the same spot on the ridge, listening and watching. He saw his brother take a seat on the ground with the leaders, noticing a slowness in Chihuahua's movements that was unusual.

As soon as everyone was seated, Chihuahua spoke to Nantan Lupan.

"I am very glad to see you and have this talk with you. It is as you say, we are always in danger out here. I surrender myself to you because I believe in you and you do not deceive me. I am satisfied with all that you do. You must be the one who makes the green pastures, who sends the rain, who commands the winds. You must be the one who sends the fresh fruits that appear on the trees every year. There are many men in the world who are big chiefs and command many people, but you, I think, are the greatest of them all. I want you to be a father to me and treat me as your son. I want you to have pity on me. There is no doubt that what you do is right, because all you do is just the same as if God did it. So I believe. Do with me as you please. If you do not let me go back to the reservation, I would like you to send my family wherever you send me."

"But will they want to go with you?" Harrison asked.

"If they want to come, let them. If they want to stay, let

them. I ask you to find out if they are willing to go or not."

Nachite rose and went to Harrison.

"What Chihuahua says I say. I surrender just the same as he did. I give my word, I give my body. When I was free I gave orders, but now I throw myself at your feet. You now order and I obey."

He shook the general's hand. A smile spread across his face. "Now that I have surrendered I am glad. I will not have to hide behind rocks and mountains. I will go across the open plain. I will sleep well, and be satisfied, and so will my people. I will go wherever you may see fit to send us. I hope you will be kind to us, as you have always been a good friend and tried to do what was right for us. I do not know where you are going to send us, but I am afraid that I will not see my friends again."

"Don't worry about that," Harrison said, so softly that Ulzana could barely hear him.

"That is all we have to say," Chihuahua said. "We have spoken with all our hearts. When shall we start from here?"

"I am going back to Fort Bowie tomorrow," Harrison answered. "I have much work to do there. Alchise and the scouts will stay with you and take you over to Bowie. I think you should start in the morning since there are no rations here. Every day I will have a courier from Lieutenant Creighton tell me where you are and how you are doing."

Chihuahua smiled for the first time. "Our stock is very poor," he said. "I was afraid that we would have to travel fast."

"Not at all. You will come along in good time."

Geronimo stood. "Two or three words are enough. We are all comrades, all one family, all one band. What the others say, I say also. I give myself up to you. Do with me as you please. Once I moved about like the wind, but now I surrender to you." He also shook hands. "I do not want anyone to say any wrong thing about me. I was very far from here. Almost nobody could go to that place. But I sent you word that I wanted to come in, and here I am. I have no lies in my heart. I hope the day may come when my word shall be as strong with you as yours is with me."

"You must not pay any attention to the talk you hear. There are some people who can no more control their talk than the wind can."

Geronimo nodded. "I want to let Alchise speak a few words."

Alchise stood. "They have all surrendered. There is nothing more to be done. I will speak only a few words." He pointed at Creighton, who was writing in his journal. "I am mad with Nantan Creighton because he is writing down what I say. I am not a captain, but a small man, and what I say does not count."

"It is best to put everything on paper," General Harrison said, smiling for the first time. "When you are dead your children and your children's children can know what you have said. It is not this kind of paper that lies; it is the newspapers."

Alchise seemed satisfied. "I am talking for these Chiricahua. I do not want you to have any bad feelings toward them. They are all good friends and I am glad they have surrendered, because they are all the same people — all one family with me. You are our chief, the only one we have. No matter where you send these Chiricahua we hope to hear that you have treated them kindly. Now we want to travel along the open road and drink the waters of the Americans, and not hide in the mountains. I tell you that these Chiricahua really mean to do what is right and live in peace."

Ulzana smiled as the conference broke up. There would be peace at last. The *Cho-ken-en* would be sent to an alien place for a time, but the running, the hiding, and the fear were all finished.

20

BETWEEN FOUR and five o'clock in the morning, Lieutenant Creighton was aroused by a rough hand on his shoulder. He came awake quickly, sitting up and rubbing the sleep from his eyes. Faintly visible in the predawn blackness was the shadowy form of Alchise.

"What is it?"

Alchise gestured toward the hostile camp. "They are drunk."

"Drunk! Who's drunk?" Before the scout could speak, Creighton knew the answer. "How the hell can they be drunk?"

In the darkness Alchise shrugged. "American whiskey."

Creighton felt a sickness deep in his stomach. He could sense the hard campaign, the dangers of the past few months begin slipping away in futility. All because some stupid civilian had sold a few bottles of cheap whiskey.

The air was still cold. Creighton shivered as he threw off his blanket and fumbled for his boots. Automatically he turned each upside down and thumped it hard to shake out any scorpions or vinegarroons that might have crawled in during the night.

"Send someone to wake General Harrison," Creighton said as his thinking became organized.

"I will go," Alchise said.

"No. I'll need you. Send someone else. Have them tell the general that I've gone to the hostile camp to check on the situation."

The sun was not yet visible over the eastern mountains but its light was already spreading across the land when Creighton and Alchise reached Canyon Bonito, where Geronimo's band was camping. A thick pall of smoke lay over the land. The grass and woods were smoldering, burning slowly in the dew-covered morning, obviously the result of a neglected campfire. Through the smoke he could see Nachite lying on the ground where he had fallen from his horse, too drunk to regain his footing. Geronimo and several of his warriors were still sitting their mounts, as drunk as so many lords.

Creighton did not advance any farther. There was little hope of reasoning with a drunken Apache. He turned, and returned at a trot to report to General Harrison.

Harrison was up and dressed, waiting for his mule to be saddled and brought to him. Creighton saluted.

"What's the situation?" Harrison asked, evidently in poor humor.

Creighton understood the agony his general must be experiencing. No man had done more to subdue the Chiricahua than Harrison. But the newspapers and the politicians criticized his methods unmercifully, complaining that the Chiricahua should be exterminated, not coddled. Now it was possible that all the good Harrison had accomplished in behalf of the Indians would be wasted.

"Geronimo, Nachite, and several of their warriors are dead drunk. The trouble seems to be limited to their camps. Chihuahua's band appears quiet." Creighton spoke harshly, contemptuously. "Alchise told me that a man named Travis sold them the whiskey. He has set up a tent at Contrabandista Springs on the San Bernadino Springs Ranch."

Harrison nodded. "I know. I'm on my way to put this Travis out of business right now."

"Sir, Alchise suggested that we send a detail of scouts to deal with this man. Unofficially I agree."

"By God, I'd like to do just that. The Apaches know how to handle that kind of man." There was a weariness in his voice. "But I can't. I can't even do anything officially. San Bernadino Springs is in Mexico, and I don't have any jurisdiction here. But, by all that's holy, I'm going to put the fear of God in that man." Again he paused. When he spoke, it was softly, meant for no one in particular because it was a question without an answer. "What makes men do things like this? Are a few dollars worth the blood that will be spilled?"

Creighton turned to Alchise. "Bring my horse."

"No," Harrison said. "You stay here and keep an eye on things. Try to find out what you can. Maybe Alchise can reason with Geronimo when he sobers up." The general swung into the saddle. "And Creighton, stay out of sight. Under no circumstances are you to personally enter the hostile camp. If they so much as see a blue coat, they'll probably stampede back to the hills."

"Yes, sir," Creighton said, saluting.

Harrison responded. "Sit tight and pray. This whole mess is going to be decided by a higher authority than just us."

When General Harrison was gone, Creighton turned to his chief scout. "What do you think Geronimo will do?"

Alchise simply shrugged his shoulders.

Throughout the day Alchise moved between the camps bringing in bits and pieces of information. Rumors were spreading unchecked through the Chiricahua camps. They generally hinted that all the Indians would be punished for the drunken spree, and that Geronimo and Nachite would be hung.

As each story was reported, Creighton sent Alchise back among the hostiles to assure them that if they did not cause trouble now, all would be forgotten. There was nothing else he could do.

During the late afternoon, a heavy rain began to fall throughout the mountains. The sky darkened, and night came prematurely. Creighton sat in his tent, listening to the rain beat against the canvas, sounding like tears from heaven. He heard steps splashing through the puddles outside, and the flap opened. Alchise stepped inside.

"Geronimo has left," he said.

Creighton felt his stomach tighten. The thing he had dreaded most had occurred. "How many went with him?"

"Nachite — twenty warriors — thirteen women — six children."

"What about the others?"

"Chihuahua and his people will stay. They surrendered to Nantan Lupan and will honor their word."

Creighton hung his head. After all the heartache and sacrifice, the bloody war was not yet over.

21

THE RAIN MADE a steady tattoo on the hides covering the wickiup. Usually Chihuahua delighted in the rain. It washed the air, bringing a sweetness to the smell of it. In the splattering raindrops were the fields of flowers and the green grass that would sprout miraculously from the barren desert. Usually, the regular rhythm lulled him, bringing a peace to his soul. But tonight the rain added to his depression.

With a stick he idly stirred the small fire, sending a shower of sparks up with the smoke. He felt a need to speak, to hear someone tell him his decision was the correct one.

"Have I done the right thing?" he asked.

Os-kis-say moved behind him and began to rub the thick muscles at the base of her husband's neck. Her eyes showed the pain in her heart for the agony he suffered.

"I'm only a woman," she said softly. "I don't know about such things."

Chihuahua closed his eyes, feeling the muscles relax as Os-kis-say worked at them with her stubby fingers. "We've been together a long time," he said. "How many years has it been? Thirty?" He paused, not expecting an answer, and receiving none. "You've suffered when I've suffered. We've known joy together. You know our people as well as I do."

"I've always listened to you. What you do for your people has always been wise."

"I hope so. I hope we are on the side of the gods."

For a long time they were silent. Os-kis-say's fingers worked in rhythm with the pounding rain.

"What will Nantan Lupan do about Geronimo?" she asked, breaking the stillness.

"If Geronimo comes back, Nantan Lupan has promised to forget." The fire cracked and popped. "If he doesn't return, the soldiers will hunt him down like an animal."

"What about our people?"

"Nothing has changed. We'll leave for Fort Bowie tomorrow as we planned."

Os-kis-say laid her tired head against Chihuahua's back and breathed the man's fragrance of his body. It was a scent that had become a part of her world.

"You've made a good decision. The ways of war are no longer for our people."

"Trust must begin somewhere," he said.

Chihuahua lay back on the bed of pine boughs. Os-kis-say snuggled to his side. In the cool dampness of the sheltering lodge, her breathing became deep and regular as she slept. He lay a long time watching the patterns of light and shadow cast on the wickiup by the dying fire. His mind was still filled with doubts. Sleep would not come to release him.

The People were ready before the sun. They touched fire to their wickiups and slowly moved toward the north.

Chihuahua sat his horse on the first high ridge and looked back. Columns of smoke rose thick and black from their last free camp. Then he turned to look at his people. They rode and walked in silence. There was no laughter, no mirth. Only the children, too young to understand, were the same.

They did not know that they were the children of a defeated people, going north to be sent away from the deserts and mountains they loved.

22

WHEN THE *Cho-ken-en* crossed the border and began the long march up the San Simon Valley, Ulzana left the column and went by himself up into the home mountains. Some inner sense, some voice directed him to his birthplace.

He searched out the special canyon with the clear stream tracing a bubbly course down its center, and the small grove of pine trees near its head. Everything was the same, yet different. In the forty years of his life, the stream had bubbled down the canyon, sweeping over rocks that never appeared to have noticed. There was peace here, and silence. Even the song of the pinyon jay, flitting among the pine branches, seemed a part of the solitude.

He left his pony at the foot of the canyon and walked to the cluster of pines.

The carpet of old needles was still soft where he sat. Casually he picked up a pine needle and tossed it into the stream where the current seized it and carried it swiftly along. It was caught in the eddy of a large rock, floating slowly in small circles. Then the current took it again and it was swept from sight. Ulzana stared a long time at the spot where he lost sight of the needle in the swirling water.

Life was a river, and he had been a pine needle, carried by a current he could not fight. So many things had hap-

pened in the forty years since his spirit had entered life at
this spot. So many other pine needles had been swept away
by the current and lost in the eddies of the stream.

Where had life gone wrong? Individually the Americans
were no match for the People. But they were too many,
and because of this they could impress their will on their
enemies. The *Cho-ken-en* had lost the war, and they would
be punished for following the ancient customs. These were
not the ways of the White Eyes, and therefore, they were
crimes. For him, right or wrong was no longer clear. Who
was able to say anymore which was the correct way?

He lay back and closed his eyes. From the past, from
thirty-five years of war, came the faces and the voices and
the special things about people he would never see again.
He fingered the tiny gold cross Baychen had given him and
which he had worn all these years. He felt the cooling
hands of Sons-ee-ah-ray when he was burning with the
fever. In his mind he touched again the rabbit ear cap
given him by the shadowy figure of Nah-kah-yen, his father.
He heard Chino, dying in his arms, saying that he would be
brave. There was his stepfather, San-dai-say, who had
taught him so much, and his grandfather, Hosanto, who had
prayed over him, both dead in Apache Pass. Beneactiney
and Atelueitze, friends who had died in battle. His
thoughts even touched on Pi-hon-se, his boyhood friend,
who had died by Ulzana's own hand. And there was little
It-ay-day, who had lived such a short time. So many of his
people had been lost in the void.

Perhaps the dead were the lucky ones. They would not
suffer the indignity which had come to the *Cho-ken-en*.
They would not finish out their lives burdened with customs
that were worse than chains. To die young, or during another time, had been their blessing.

He had never seen the sky so red and golden before.
Above the hill, right over him lay a great cloud shaped like

a bird's wing, glowing within like the heart of a campfire, shining clear as amber. Little golden wisps, like feathers, tore themselves from it and floated out into the sky.

Deep, deep inside was a pain, almost like a sadness, but it was love. He had a love so strong that it was almost a ripping inside because he could not take this mountain or this canyon in his arms and embrace them. How can a man say good-bye to his arm or hand or leg? This land was a part of him as surely as any part of his body.

He got up then and left the canyon. He did not look back. So much had happened. So many pine needles had been swept down the stream. It was no longer the same. There was a sadness there now. He left, knowing in his heart that he would never return to this place again.

23

LIEUTENANT CREIGHTON sat nervously in the hard wooden chair, barely able to breathe the close, stale air in the office. He could feel a drop of perspiration working its way down his back and he had an almost overpowering desire to reach back and rub where it had trickled, but did not move. Instead he watched General Harrison, who was standing in front of the window, his hands clasped behind his back, staring out across Fort Bowie's parade ground. Creighton cleared his throat softly.

General Harrison turned from the window, a stream of sunlight washing over his closely cropped gray hair. He seemed to have aged ten years in the last few weeks. "I'm sorry, Mister Creighton," he said. "Sometimes my mind has a tendency to wander."

"Yes, sir," Creighton answered, feeling foolish and extremely uncomfortable.

"First I have a message for you." He picked up a small pad from his desk. "A young lady — a Miss Emma Anderson — sends her regards and wishes you a speedy return to Fort Apache."

Creighton was thunderstruck. "Emma? Here?"

"At Fort Apache. Apparently she got tired of waiting for you. Young man, I suggest you marry this girl and make an honest woman of her."

"Yes, sir! I intend to do just that."

"I fully realize how anxious you must be to get out of
here and see your Emma, but I would appreciate it if you
would indulge an old man a moment or two longer. I
thought you might be interested in this new development.
After all, you've done as much as anyone to bring in the
Chiricahua."

"Sir?"

"While you were coming in with Chihuahua, I've been in
correspondence with General Sheridan." Harrison paused,
anger suddenly flaring in his eyes. He hammered his fist on
the desk. "Those pompous asses back East — without the
vaguest notion of the way things really are out here — have
stabbed us in the back." He handed a telegram to Creighton. "Read this."

Creighton scanned the message dated March 31, 1886,
signed by General Sheridan. It read:

YOU ARE CONFIDENTIALLY INFORMED THAT YOUR TELEGRAM OF
MARCH 29TH IS RECEIVED. THE PRESIDENT CANNOT ASSENT TO
THE SURRENDER OF THE HOSTILES ON THE TERMS OF THEIR IM-
PRISONMENT EAST FOR TWO YEARS, WITH THE UNDERSTANDING OF
THEIR RETURN TO THE RESERVATION. HE INSTRUCTS YOU TO ENTER
AGAIN INTO NEGOTIATION ON THE TERMS OF THEIR UNCONDI-
TIONAL SURRENDER, ONLY SPARING THEIR LIVES. IN THE MEAN-
TIME, AND ON RECEIPT OF THIS ORDER, YOU ARE DIRECTED TO
TAKE EVERY PRECAUTION AGAINST THE ESCAPE OF THE HOSTILES,
WHICH MUST NOT BE ALLOWED UNDER ANY CIRCUMSTANCES. YOU
MUST MAKE SUCH DISPOSITION OF YOUR TROOPS AS WILL INSURE
AGAINST FURTHER HOSTILITIES, BY COMPLETING THE DESTRUCTION
OF THE HOSTILES, UNLESS THESE TERMS ARE ACCEDED TO.

Creighton felt anger and confusion. "They can't mean
this, sir! There must be some error!"

"There's no error. They mean every stupid word of it."

"But sir, indefinite confinement back East is a death sen-
tence. Psychologically the Apaches would wither and die.

The Chiricahua consider this land the life-source of their people. For two or three years they could endure, but indefinitely cut off from the land, they would be crushed. They'll never accept any terms other than those we agreed to in Mexico."

"Damn it, don't you think I know that? Do you think I didn't protest Sheridan's decision?" In a gesture of weariness, Harrison buried his face in his hands. "I'm sorry, Creighton. I shouldn't be shouting at you. God knows it isn't your fault. It's just that the injustice of this entire myopic policy makes me so angry I have to yell or go crazy. Maybe if Geronimo hadn't run back to the hills, I'd've been able to straighten out this mess."

"But Geronimo's break wasn't your fault, sir."

Harrison nodded. "However, his lack of honor convinces the bureaucrats that none of the Chiricahua can be rehabilitated. When I wired Sheridan about Geronimo's betrayal, he even had the gall to cast aspersions on the loyalty of our scouts." He banged his fist down on the desk again. "By God, I can't understand it. I've never had better, more faithful troops than those Chiricahua. You know as well as I do that if it hadn't been for them, we'd still be stumbling around in those Mexican mountains like a bunch of drunken sailors."

From where he sat, Creighton could see across the room and out the little window. Three quarters of a mile east, on a pretty little bench above the wash, he could see the graveyard, surrounded by a high picket fence. Its white headboards gleamed in the eternal sun. Between the graves, the ground was gay with golden wild poppies and snowy marguerites. Had those men, and the hundreds of others in unmarked graves on the desert, died in vain? He turned to General Harrison.

"What are you going to do, sir?"

"I'm a reasonable man, but I don't understand this," he

said. "I can't bring myself to tell them that the terms on which they surrendered have been disapproved. In my judgment, it would make it impossible for me to negotiate with them, and probably make them scatter to the mountains. There wouldn't be any way for us to prevent it. They trusted me, and now the government wants me to betray them." He handed a sheet of paper to Creighton. "Here's my answer."

Creighton read the neat, precise handwriting.

IT HAS BEEN MY AIM THROUGHOUT PRESENT OPERATIONS TO AFFORD THE GREATEST AMOUNT OF PROTECTION TO LIFE AND PROPERTY INTERESTS, AND TROOPS HAVE BEEN STATIONED ACCORDINGLY. HOWEVER, REGULAR TROOPS CANNOT ADEQUATELY PROTECT PROPERTY BEYOND A RADIUS OF ONE HALF MILE FROM CAMP. THAT THE OPERATIONS OF MY SCOUTS IN MEXICO HAVE NOT PROVED AS SUCCESSFUL AS WAS HOPED, IS DUE TO THE ENORMOUS DIFFICULTIES THEY HAVE BEEN COMPELLED TO ENCOUNTER. THE NATURE OF THE INDIANS THEY HAVE BEEN HUNTING AND THE CHARACTER OF THE COUNTRY IN WHICH THEY HAVE OPERATED IS A HINDRANCE OF WHICH PERSONS NOT THOROUGHLY CONVERSANT WITH THE CHARACTER OF BOTH CAN HAVE NO CONCEPTION. I BELIEVE THAT THE PLAN UPON WHICH I HAVE CONDUCTED OPERATIONS IS THE ONE MOST LIKELY TO PROVE SUCCESSFUL IN THE END. IT MAY BE, HOWEVER, THAT I AM TOO MUCH WEDDED TO MY OWN VIEWS IN THIS MATTER. AS I HAVE SPENT NEARLY EIGHT YEARS OF THE HARDEST WORK IN MY LIFE IN THIS DEPARTMENT, I RESPECTFULLY REQUEST THAT I MAY NOW BE RELIEVED FROM ITS COMMAND.

Creighton put down the paper. When he looked up the sadness and pain were evident in his face.

"Is it wise, sir?" he finally asked. "I'm not questioning the general, but perhaps you should reconsider. After all, the Chiricahua trust you."

"There's no other way," Harrison said. He was back at the window gazing across the parade ground. "I wish there was something else I could do. If I stayed, I would be compromising my honor, and the Chiricahua wouldn't trust me any longer. In Mexico I told them the words we spoke were put on paper so that they couldn't lie. They would last long after we were dead and buried. My words are on that paper also, Mister Creighton."

24

THE TRAIN WAS WAITING at the station in the little town of Bowie. The subdued *Cho-ken-en* stood solemnly in the dusty yard, no one moving or speaking. Even the children had become somber, sensing something wrong.

Ulzana could see in the eyes of the men the question he felt in his own heart. Were they doing the right thing? Would it have been better to go back into the mountains with Geronimo and fight to the death?

Sy-e-konne and Kah stood slightly apart with the other women and children. They would not travel in the same coach with Ulzana, since the Army had decided there would be less likelihood of an escape attempt if the men were separated from their families.

In the eyes of his wife and son were different reactions to what was happening. Sy-e-konne was relieved, almost happy that the time of fighting was behind them. Kah's eyes were aglow with excitement, as he anticipated riding in the train, a fascinating object he had previously seen only from a distance. Neither yet realized the full importance of this forced emigration.

A signal was given. Feet shuffled and the soldiers began moving the *Cho-ken-en* toward the train. For the first time fear became evident. None of the People had ever been on a train. They hesitated, refusing to move. A child began to wail.

"If they won't get on, carry 'em," a sergeant ordered.

A burly soldier grabbed a woman and, against her screams, handed her up to the platform.

Two of the nearest warriors took a threatening step toward the troopers. All the women and children began to raise a loud wailing.

"Wait," Chihuahua commanded, his voice rising above the clamor. "We have agreed to go on the train. We cannot resist now. Do not be afraid. Nantan Lupan would not betray us."

There was a moment's further hesitation, then silently the women and children moved toward one of the railroad cars, the men toward another. Soldiers stood beside the steps, each with a paper in his hand, counting the *Cho-ken-en* as they passed. There were seventy-seven persons in all — fifteen men, thirty-three women, and twenty-nine children. They no longer looked like a proud, strong people. Silently clutching their pitifully small bundles, they were swallowed up by the train.

When it was his turn to enter the coach, Ulzana hesitated. He reached down and scooped up a handful of dust, a bit of the land he was leaving. He held the dirt tightly in his clenched fist as he boarded the train and took a seat beside the only open window.

There was a jerking, a screeching of metal against metal. The whistle screamed its agony shrilly across the vast prairie. Then the coaches began to move. The *Cho-ken-en* yelled and tried to move toward the door, but the exit was blocked by an armed trooper. He motioned them back toward their seats with his rifle barrel.

Ulzana sat stoically and stared out of the window as the train gathered speed. Behind them, in a purple haze, he could see the home mountains, wearing clouds like hats. The sky was the same as he had always seen it. The breeze against his cheek was the same as he had always felt it.

There should have been something special, something more than the ordinary, to set this day apart from all of the others. A man lived and breathed and walked the land and suddenly he was gone, but nothing else changed.

His mind went back and saw things that he had long ago forgotten — campsites visited once and never seen again, the hundreds of little things which together were the sum of his existence. He had lived a good life, a man's life, full of sun and wind, laughter and sorrow, fear and courage. He did not have anything to show for it, only the clothing on his back.

He held the handful of earth out of the train window. Slowly his fingers relaxed their grip and the dirt streamed out and was lost in the wind. He looked at his empty hand, barely seeing the dust-covered palm. He was achingly aware that just as the dirt was now gone, never to be retrieved, so too was life. He was leaving his home, and in that parting was the image of death.

The train shrieked its whistle into the lonely expanse of desert. Suddenly the mountains were gone, hidden behind the trees and hills of the distance.

epilogue

Epilogue

THE FINAL SOLUTION of the Apache problem was as dishonorable as the treatment of Chihuahua's band.

On April 2, 1886, General Nelson A. Miles assumed command of the Department of Arizona, his primary task being to bring Geronimo to bay. He soon determined that his predecessor's method of using Chiricahua scouts to hunt down the hostiles was the only effective means of dealing with them.

In early August, 1886, two Chiricahua Apache scouts, Martiné and Ka-e-ta, were sent into the Mexican mountains on the trail of the remaining hostiles. On August 23, they talked with Geronimo and Nachite, inducing them to come in and speak with General Miles at Skeleton Canyon.

About the time that Martiné and Ka-e-ta began their journey into Mexico, General Miles sent a delegation of the leading Chiricahua still living at Fort Apache to Washington, hoping to impress them with the power of the government. President Cleveland gave each of the Apaches a peace medal and said, "Do not be afraid to come amongst us; I am the great father of you all. Go back to your farms at Camp Apache and settle down quietly. There nobody will harm you. Do just as the commanding officers tell you, and they will write good letters to me about you."

There was no opportunity for these faithful scouts to settle down quietly. The train returning the delegation to Arizona was stopped at Fort Leavenworth, Kansas. They were all arrested on August 20, and sent to Fort Marion, Florida, as prisoners of war, never again seeing their farms.

By far the greatest portion of the Chiricahua had remained true to the government in the outbreak of 1885. The most valuable and trustworthy scouts had been selected from among them. For their allegiance all were rewarded alike — by captivity in a strange land. On a Sunday in late August, 1886, the reservation Chiricahua were ordered to come in to the agency to be counted. There, they were surrounded by troops, herded like cattle into trains, and sent to Florida.

Not aware of these developments, Geronimo, Nachite, sixteen warriors, fourteen women, and six children came to Skeleton Canyon, and on September 4, 1886, surrendered to General Miles. The night before Geronimo reached Fort Bowie, six of the Chiricahua — three men and three women — fled back into Mexico. Geronimo and the remainder of his band were first sent to Texas, and then to Fort Pickens, Florida. No distinction was made between friends and enemies. Martiné and Ka-e-ta, who had risked their lives to bring in the hostiles, were put on the same train as Geronimo's band and shipped into captivity.

On October 14, 1886, Mangas, with three men, three women, two half-grown boys, and four children, was captured by Captain Charles L. Cooper, with twenty enlisted men and two scouts from Fort Apache. This was the only capture of armed Apache men made during the entire campaign. Mangas and his people were sent to join Geronimo at Fort Pickens.

With the inclusion of Mangas's band, the entire Chiricahua nation, a total of four hundred and ninety-eight Indians (ninety-nine men, with three hundred and ninety-nine women and children) had been sentenced to life imprisonment for the crime of fighting too well for their lands.

Although all of the Chiricahua leaders had been sent to Florida, the Apaches were not completely subdued. The six Indians who had left Geronimo's band on the way to Fort Bowie were never recaptured. They joined with other rebels in the mountains and continued to live in freedom. Captain Bourke reports that as late as January 1891, there were occasional raids into Arizona and New Mexico. The International News Service reported that on April 10, 1930, hostile Apaches raided a settlement near Nacori Chico, Sonora, Mexico, and killed three persons. Shortly thereafter, a posse of Mexicans was able to locate the hostile rancheria, and in their attack killed all of the Apaches, except for two children who were adopted into local families. The last pocket of hostile Apaches was thus finally destroyed in 1930.

The Chiricahua suffered greatly in their captivity. Many of their children were taken to the Indian School at Carlisle, Pennsylvania. Many regretted having surrendered. Their treatment convinced them that it would have been better to have remained in the mountains and fought to the end.

Between April 1887 and May 1888, the prisoners from Fort Pickens and Fort Marion were united at Mount Vernon Barracks, Alabama. During the first three years of captivity, one hundred and nineteen of the Chiricahua died of diseases, mostly consumption. Among those who succumbed to the humid climate was Alchise.

General George Crook (General James Harrison in this story) spent the remaining years of his life attempting to obtain honorable treatment for the Apaches, especially for the scouts who had served him so well. In January 1890, he visited the Apaches in Alabama. For the most part, the Chiricahua were confused by their betrayal at the hands of the white men.

Chatto showed his Arthur Medal to Crook and expressed his puzzlement simply. "Why did they give me that, to wear in the guardhouse? I thought something good would come to me when they gave me that, but I have been in confinement ever since I have had it."

General Crook's efforts proved fruitless. He died on March 21, 1890, his demise undoubtedly hastened by his strenuous efforts on behalf of the Chiricahua. The Apaches did not forget their friend. When they learned of his death, they cut their hair and mourned the passing of a man whom they had loved and trusted.

In October 1894, the surviving Chiricahua were relocated at Fort Sill, Oklahoma. Finally, in 1913, after twenty-six years of captivity, the Chiricahua were released as prisoners of war. Those who so desired were allowed to go to the Mescalero Reservation in New Mexico, but none were allowed to return to Arizona.

Two hundred and sixty of the Chiricahua decided to relocate at Mescalero. Of the prominent men who had gone into captivity, only Chatto and Nachite survived to reach the New Mexico reservation.

Ulzana (spelled Jolsanny by his descendants) did not live to see his home mountains again. He died at Fort Sill in 1909.

Chihuahua enlisted as a soldier at Fort Sill, and died there on July 25, 1901, at the age of seventy-nine. It is said that he died of grief following the death of his favorite son, Osceola, five months previously.

Geronimo bought some liquor from a bootlegger, got drunk, fell off his horse in a stupor, and lay in the weeds all night. He was stricken with pneumonia and died, at the age of eighty, in the Fort Sill Indian Hospital, on February 17, 1909.

Loco enlisted as a soldier at Fort Sill, and died of old age on February 2, 1905, a quiet, well-behaved Indian.

Old Nana lived to reach Fort Sill, and died there, unreconstructed, on May 19, 1896, at the age of ninety-six.

Nachite became an upright member of the Dutch Reformed Church and died of influenza at Mescalero in 1921.

Chatto, embittered by his treatment from the government, died at the Mescalero Reservation in March 1934, as the result of an automobile accident. They say that an aura of hate still lingers about his grave.

Now all of the Chiricahua who fought so hard for their lands are dead. But if you walk through the deserts and mountains of Arizona and New Mexico at sunset, you may still hear the sounds of their laughter and their weeping carried on the winds sweeping down from the heights. The mountains remember their dignity.